IRREGULAR LIVES:

THE UNTOLD STORY OF SHERLOCK HOLMES AND THE BAKER STREET IRREGULARS

BY

KIM KRISCO

Paperback ISBN 978-1-78705-032-7
ePub ISBN 978-1-78705-033-4
PDF ISBN 978-1-78705-034-1

Published in the UK by MX Publishing
335 Princess Park Manor, Royal Drive,
London, N11 3GX
www.mxpublishing.co.uk

Edited by Sara Ferguson.
Cover design by Brian Belanger.

THANK YOU . . .

STEVE EMECZ & THE MX TEAM
— FOR YOUR AMAZING ENERGY, AND
  ON GOING GUIDANCE AND
  SUPPORT.

JOE REVILL
— FOR YOUR GENEROSITY OF SPIRIT,
  ADVICE, INSIGHT, AND WRITING
  EXPERTISE.

AND ESPECIALLY . . .

SARA ROSE
— FOR YOUR ENCOURAGEMENT, IDEAS,
  INVALUABLE EDITORIAL EFFORT, AND
  YOUR GIFT FOR BRINGING THE "EYE
  OF THE READER" TO MY STORIES.

CONTENTS

PROLOGUE

SHERLOCK HOLMES JOLTED UPWARD in his timeworn Morris chair, craning his neck toward the window. The morning sea mist danced on the breeze like silk scarves.

Most mornings the barren thoroughfare leading to his modest cottage offered small hope of a diversion, but today was different. A lone cyclist pedaled his way along the Eastbourne to Brighton Road. The visitor was coming to him. This was no extraordinary deduction, for nothing, and no one, lay beyond.

Prior to the war, Sherlock Holmes's retirement had been interrupted by several tantalizing cases, and one alluring woman—*the woman*. But she was gone now, and he was left with a tangle of relief and regret.

A rapping upon his door was the most glorious sound for Sherlock Holmes, for it might herald a new client—a retired sergeant of marines with a message from Scotland Yard, or a barrel-chested German nobleman sporting a black vizard mask. Such doorway visitations were rare now. Holmes was well aware that Mrs. Thornton was at the market and therefore unable to answer the door. He waited to savor his swelling anticipation.

An impatient fourth knock, a single hard smack, told him that he was in jeopardy of missing his, now frustrated, visitor. He braced himself firmly on the arms of his chair, and brought himself to his feet.

"One moment there."

As his hand grabbed the door latch, he was aware of a small, unbidden wish for adventure. He would chastise himself later for allowing this superstition to slither into his well-ordered mind.

As he opened the door, the muted morning light sliced across a seasoned face silhouetting a solitary man. A strong smell of tobacco enveloped the gentleman—a *latakia*, he thought.

The messenger was a heavy-shouldered man with a plain face. He held an envelope. "Holmes? Mr. Sherlock Holmes?"

Holmes nodded. "Yes. What have we now?"

"Good mornin', sir."

The missive was proffered, but Holmes did not take it in hand. "Come in a moment, if you will. I have something for you."

The messenger's brow rose, and he swept his flap-cap from his head as Holmes stepped back to widen the passage. The man hesitated. "Pardon the slub on mi boots, sir."

Sherlock Holmes paused to inspect the man. He was dressed in baggy corduroy trousers braced in a manner that made him appear as if he had grown out of them. The sleeves of his mouse-colored jacket were rolled up his forearms. He had a stump of a nose, and sported a pipe tightly clenched on the left side of his mouth. The smoldering cutty bobbed up and down as he spoke through gritted teeth.

Holmes twisted around toward a tray of coins on the nearby sideboard. "I take it you are new to your job."

"I am, sir."

"But you're from these parts?"

"Aye sir—from Heathfield."

"And you were away at sea?"

"Aye, an ol' Winnick, sir. Sailed near ten . . ." The messenger paused and looked sidelong at Holmes. "I beg pardon, sir. Have we met?"

Holmes, his back still to the man, grabbed a shilling from a tray. "No, sir, we have not."

An uncomfortable silence ensued before the man spoke again. "How'd ye know these things, then?"

Ah, the question Holmes was inviting. A question the good Doctor might have asked, had he been there.

"Your trouser legs, sir, are oily from the bicycle chain. An experienced rider would have worn cycle-clips."

"Aye, I'm new to this work."

"And your expressions . . . 'slub,' for example. It's not surprising that there are more than thirty colloquialisms in East Sussex for mud. And, finally, the faded tattoo on the back of your hand—a grisly concoction of ink and gunpowder, unique to a seafaring man."

Holmes straightened, stretching taller. "Am I correct?"

A grin slowly spread across the man's face. "You are, sir, God bless you."

Holmes held out the shilling. The man opened his hand.

"No, no," Holmes replied, dropping the coin into his hand. "Your visit promises to be the best part of my day."

Holmes watched from the window for some time as the messenger hoisted himself upon the pedals and pumped his bicycle up the road. Not until he vanished in the haze did he

3

turn his gaze upon the envelope. Holmes ran his index finger around the edges, and finally across the raised ink letters on the back flap—R.P.S. His eyes flashed upward.

Then, after an almost imperceptible intake of breath, he murmured: "Royal Photographic Society. H'm."

Curiosity is the wick on the candle that lights the way to adventure. As such, it was Holmes's constant companion. He anxiously tugged at the envelope, popping it open to reveal an engraved invitation:

PHOTOGRAPHER S.P. FIELDS INVITES YOU TO THE DEBUT OF THE COLLECTION: IRREGULAR LIVES.

SATURDAY, MARCH 15, 1919. 35, RUSSELL SQUARE, LONDON.

A small note was enclosed in the envelope as well. He read it:

The lives of the well-off have an arc, with significant achievements posed near the peak. The lives of the deprived hover barely off the ground. Their accomplishment lies at the bitter end— the fact that they survived at all.

Your life, Mr. Holmes, has a broad elevated sweep. And, as you reflect upon your journey, know that, with thanks to you and my mates, a fortunate few were able to find a footing on clean pavement.

Please help me honour and eulogize those that served us both so well.

— S. P. F.

A wave of recollections—of people, places, faces and voices from the past, swept over Holmes's mind like a tidal wave: his many encounters with the band of juveniles that bore his appellation "the Baker-street irregulars."

PART ONE

BLACK AND WHITE IMAGES, COLORFUL MEMORIES.

CHAPTER I

IT WAS THE CUSTOM OF SHERLOCK HOLMES to take the 9.14 from Seaford to London Victoria every Wednesday. His destination was the flat of his finest friend, Dr. John Watson.

Watson had recently been suffering from arrhythmias of the heart. If he had thought about it, Holmes might have judged that this affliction was the result of his friend's over-indulgence in emotions. Watson's lifestyle abetted his conviction that chaos has its genesis in capricious emotions, such as those that had led his friend to the altar. Holmes did not claim that matrimony itself was a chaotic state, but merely that the institution was generally calamitous for men.

Holmes declared that his regular visitations to the sprawling metropolis were intended to replenish his supply of reading material, and to restock his cupboard with a fine burgundy or claret. But this was a poorly hidden ruse.

He rarely stayed the night at the Doctor's rooms on Sheen Lane. However, the invitation had caused him to alter his usual practice. Possibly the good Doctor would wish to attend the photography exhibition. *No*, he thought again. The irregulars were one part of his life that he had not entirely shared with Watson. This invitation was for him alone.

Dr. Watson neatly folded the telegram from Holmes, chortling as he placed it in his waistcoat pocket. It was a quaint touch, he thought, that Holmes sent word via the telegraph rather than calling on the telephone. Sherlock Holmes did not permit a telephone in his living quarters, insisting that the "raucous machine" was installed for the convenience of his housekeeper. As such, the oaken British Ericsson was appropriately ensconced on the back porch of his cottage on the Sussex Downs.

"Norah," Watson called. A dainty blonde—a fetching girl, nearly twenty—stepped into the parlor. Norah carried her own music with her when she moved. Her jolly red hair fell in ringlets about her head, and her pale blue eyes twinkled. Her black house-dress was relieved by a white collar and cuffs trimmed in lace.

"Norah, Mr. Holmes will be arriving tomorrow. The usual preparations, and also see to the guest room. He will be staying the night."

Her hands went sharply to her hips. "You'll be wanting dinner, sir, I suppose? You gave me Saturday evenin' —"

"Mr. Holmes has an engagement—tea when he arrives, and a cold plate for me. You may take the evening off."

"Thank you, sir."

The good Doctor, with his deep appreciation for the lassies, admired Norah in retreat. One might have described her as, not to put too fine a point on it, intensely feminine.

Watson had been snoozing when a motor cab pulled up to the curb outside. He recognized the familiar tread of his friend climbing the stairs to his flat. Norah, being alerted to his schedule, was waiting to receive Sherlock Holmes.

Watson brushed a few ashes from the embroidered collar of his smoking-jacket as Holmes entered the parlor.

"A good trip, I take it, Holmes. Were the crowds bothersome?"

"I had the compartment nearly to myself—just a woman, pensive and mostly silent, I'm pleased to report."

Holmes retrieved a jar of honey from his valise and held it high. "Is it too soon?"

"Oh, thank you, Holmes. I can't get enough of that golden nectar."

This was not the truth. Watson preferred his tea with two lumps, and no milk. Norah would likely reap the harvest from the many busy hives that dotted Holmes's unkempt garden. Holmes's apicultural endeavors, while they continued, had waned among his interests. His book, the *Practical Handbook of Bee Culture,* sat unread upon Watson's bookshelf. Of course, Norah was made aware that, as part of the preparations for Holmes's visits, she was required to dust the massive volume and place it conspicuously on the Doctor's desk.

As the two settled down, tea and shortbread was forthcoming. Norah nodded to the Doctor as she placed the tray before them. "I'll be off then, sir. There is a cold plate in the pantry."

"Right-o, Norah. Enjoy your evening."

Holmes squinted at the housekeeper as she retrieved her hat and coat and walked to the front door. Watson chuckled and tossed a hasty glance at Norah as well. He leaned in closer to Holmes. "Ha-ha. What are you thinking, my friend?"

Holmes wore a look of concern. "Did you notice her scent, Watson?"

"I believe so. A floral of some sort."

"Indeed, a redolent flower. A flower on fire."

"Here, here, Holmes. You're a poet!"

"Hardly, Watson. I believe the lovely Norah has been using opium—mixed with tobacco, I suspect."

"Ha! You look at the flower of womanhood and all you can say is that she smells of burning poppies. Come along now, what brings you here?"

As the door closed behind Norah, Holmes reached into his pocket for his pouch and pipe. He dipped in a second time retrieving the invitation and note, and handed them to Watson.

Watson's face looked puzzled as he read the card and accompanying note.

"I don't recall a S. P. Fields . . . or any Fields, for that matter."

"Probably a *nom de plume*. I suspect that S.P.F. was numbered in the tribe of urchins that we employed in years past. My history with the irregulars runs deeper than you might know. They were at my side when you could not be. When you were with . . . others."

"My wives?"

"Your wives, patients, physicians, mothers-in-law, families . . . whoever occupied your time when we were apart. I have no idea, really."

Holmes would never have said so, but Watson's absences were a source of irritation for him. For Holmes,

Watson's courting and marriages were, not only foolhardy, but also selfish acts.

Watson refilled Holmes's cup. "So, it appears we still have a few secrets from each other. Me and my conjugal lifestyle—you and the irregulars."

"It's not that I intended it to be a secret, you know. I would like to have had you at my side, but there are corners one has had to turn alone."

"I understand, Holmes. We have time to share our secrets . . . if we wish too."

Watson wondered. Not about the secrets so much, but what it is that has us keep secrets. He was aware that behind most secrets lay guilt.

"It's been some time now since we have engaged that urchin army," Watson said. "I believe I told you that I encountered Ugly on the street just before the war. I barely knew him. He really doesn't look so bad with a hat on. And, of course, he's not the bilious youth we once knew . . . in his late thirties I would guess—maybe older."

Holmes shook his head. "I've lost all contact. The war has opened a chasm that has cut off the past."

"But we have the memories—jolly good ones too!"

"Good, Watson? Possibly, but we cannot re-live them, or change them."

"Holmes, this invitation seems to have put you in a melancholy mood. I suggest we change the conversation."

"Very well. How has your health been?"

"Ha, now you will put me in a melancholy mood. But, as you ask, it is worse than I might wish. To be honest, I was relieved when you explained that you wished to go the exhibition alone. Travel, even about town, is tiring for me. My adventures these days are literary in nature. I'm reading a new book of Maugham's, and I'm enjoying this Wodehouse fellow."

"Wodehouse? I suppose we should be grateful you are not reading *Lad: A Dog.*"

"Really, Holmes! And what books will I find on your shelf?"

"I've come across a rather interesting work by Sinclair—Emil Sinclair: *Demian: Die Geschichte von Emil Sinclairs Jugend.*"

"Sounds dreadful."

"It's not a book I should have read in my youth—ruminative, speculative and subjective. However, it suits me now. There is a time for everything, I suppose."

Watson looked sideways at his friend. The man speaking was not the Holmes that he knew. *It was the war,* he supposed. *It has changed everything.*

A long pause ensued, as it often did in their conversations. Their comfort with silence was one of the things that made their long friendship viable. Each was now in his own separate world: the two worlds spinning side-by-side in the same small space.

Holmes was reflecting on *Demian*—and one sentence in particular that echoed in his brain: "Only the ideas that we actually live are of any value."

This same-shared silence caught Watson feeling as though the war had not been won—not really. This was a strange thought for a soldier. And Watson had always thought of himself as a soldier. If anyone understands war, soldiers do. They learn that the whole of the human experience is expressed within battle—anger, despair, and brutality, yet at the same time love, hope, and compassion. Warriors, steeped in this cauldron of emotions, feel alive—*truly* alive. Like the trees and the animals, they experience their true nature. But there is a cost to pay for knowing one's true nature, and war is too high a price.

CHAPTER II

RUSSELL SQUARE HAD BEEN SPARED THE BOMBS and incendiaries dropped from German Zeppelins, but the city streets nearby were dotted with hollow, blackened, shells that served as a reminder of the nearly one million Britons who had fallen in the conflict. The rubble had been removed, but not the memories. Plans were well underway for sundry memorials across the countryside, but the charred brick and broken mortar fashioned an appropriate urn for that momentary sense of victory that had so quickly moldered into ash.

A brass placard confirmed that Holmes had arrived at number 35, Russell Square: *The Royal Society for the Arts, Manufactures, and Commerce*. The multi-paned windows were ablaze with light that splashed out upon the thoroughfare, creating a brilliant web that seemed to ensnare Sherlock Holmes. He retrieved his invitation, and mounted the stairs.

He found the door unattended and entered to find a long table piled with hats and coats. Hushed voices from the rooms on either side beckoned.

When faced with a choice to go right or left, Holmes invariably chose left. He noted, long ago, that most people move to the right, in a counter-clockwise, or easterly, direction. He reasoned that this was due to the predominance of right-handedness in the world at large. This assessment, of course, compelled Holmes to take the alternate route.

The exhibit of photographs was spread along the walls and was lit by an ingenious design, whereby electric lighting shone through panels of frosted-glass suspended from the ceiling. These faux-skylights cast a uniform illumination upon the room, making the black and white images seem to burst from the ivory walls. Small placards were posed beneath each photograph. Each bore a title and one or two lines of text.

Holmes stood at the center of the gallery. The author of these images was not immediately apparent; possibly he was embedded within one of the small groups huddled around various prints. The majority of the photographs were street scenes from the less affluent neighborhoods in London— Spitalfields, Lambeth, and St. Giles. Scattered among the urban landscapes were portraits.

Snippets of conversations floated about the room. Patrons were struggling to describe people and places beyond their experience. For most persons, their experience seldom limited their presumed knowledge. The *voyeurs* in the gallery spoke of the people depicted in the portraits and street scenes with the same fatuous certainty that a preacher describes the glories of heaven and the hideousness of hell.

As Holmes searched for a starting place, one portrait caught his eye—familiar, and yet not. He approached the image and bent lower to read the placard . . .

WIGGINS:
A LAD WHO LEARNED TOO WELL THE LESSONS THAT THE STREET TAUGHT.

The boy in the photograph was twelve years old. He wore a fractional smile that boded guile. He sported a black, broad-brimmed galero, of all things. His dusty coal-colored coat was cut down, and the sleeves loosely re-stitched at the shoulders with white thread. The cuffs were split at the ends and bell-shaped, to cover his hands, which were often filled with other's belongings.

IT WAS FEBRUARY, 1884. The nations of the British Isles were battling it out in the first British Home Football Championship. Oblivious of this epic *mêlée*, Holmes studiously toiled away in his laboratory at St. Bart's Hospital. He stood over his Bunsen burner opening an urgent message from Inspector Tobias Gregson of Scotland Yard. The two had become acquainted over the years. Holmes had distinguished himself in the eyes of the inspector when he went beyond the routine blood and chemical analysis to deduce case-clinching clues from the most insignificant trifles.

Holmes took lunch early so that he could meet with Gregson at the home of Arthur Spain in Canonbury. He arrived at a modest timber-framed dwelling sitting upon a questionable brick foundation. The residence pushed up against the neighboring homes as if to nudge its way into the row. Holmes noticed a constable slouched against the front door, and deduced that this was the proper address. As he was waved inside, he overheard a pugnacious voice emanating from the kitchen at the rear of the home. There he found a thin, pale, unshaven man sitting at the kitchen table with his head in his hands. Standing opposite him was a tall, white-faced, flaxen-haired gentleman with a notebook in hand— Gregson.

"It's good of you to come, sir," the detective said.

Holmes noticed a nervous woman standing off in a doorway to the back porch. Her arms were tightly wrapped around her body.

"Here we have Arthur Spain and his wife Emilia. Arthur here is having difficulty remembering where he left a £136,000 pearl necklace," the detective began.

"Please," the thin man said. "I don't know nothin' about 'em. I don't have no pearls." He slapped his hand on the table for emphasis.

Arthur Spain had a sunken and bloodless complexion that denoted the inveterate gin-drinker. The sleeves of his dirty shirt were rolled above his elbows. Sweat dripped from the end of his nose.

Holmes's eyes flashed to and fro as he took in, not only Arthur Spain, but the surroundings as well. He made special note of Emilia who, when he caught her eyes, turned away. She stepped backward slightly, retreating into the shadows of the back porch.

Gregson turned to Holmes. "Let's go outside for a chat." Leaning into Spain he added, "This laddie here needs time to think about his next ten years in Brixton."

Emilia leaned over her husband's shoulder and clutched his hand. Arthur swung wildly to throw her back. "A big help now, aren't you?" he hissed.

The two men went outside. Gregson offered a cigarette to Holmes, which he declined with a wave. The irascible detective lit a smoke and took two long drags. "On July the thirteenth, a sealed, registered packet, containing an oriental pearl necklace, was posted in Paris to an address in Hatton Garden."

"The jewelry center," Holmes said.

"Yes. It arrived the next day in a wooden case that contained a string of rock candy in place of sixty-one pink-and-white matched pearls in a necklace. Examination showed that the packet was stealthily opened from beneath, and resealed. Lloyds is offering £10 for information."

"I'd imagine that reward might help you in your search."

"It has. And one tip led us to Mr. Arthur Spain here. He happens to be the chief sorter of foreign mail at the Mount Pleasant Sorting Office in Clerkenwell and, on occasion, works shifts on the cross-channel ferry from France to Dover."

"Has he a criminal record?"

"Not he, sir," Gregson replied, "but his sons do. Maybe you've heard of the Spanish Gang."

"I thought them Iberian in origin."

"All English—thieves, confidence tricksters, bookmaking, fencing, you name it."

Holmes nodded. "Pearls can't be cut or reshaped like stones or gold. They'll be difficult to fence."

"Yes, and that's where a chap named Kemmy Grizzard comes in. He handles most of the high-end stolen jewelry hereabouts. The Spain brothers would know him, I'm certain. We've never been able to learn how he disposes of these expensive items—someone abroad, we think. Someone big."

21

KRISCO

"I assume you put him under surveillance."

"Yes, and he's now in custody. Our men saw people from New York and Paris visiting Grizzard's place. It appeared he was about to do a sale. But, we pounced too soon. Grizzard didn't have the pearls, and the two gentleman visitors were from Lloyd's, attempting to negotiate a deal to buy the pearls back. We did find wax samples of fake seals used on the packet in the rubbish. Circumstantial evidence, but enough to hold him, for now."

"And you are certain Grizzard doesn't have the pearls?"

"If he did, he would be making a deal for his release. Lloyds has been pounding vigorously and often upon our door, you see. They'd drop any charges for the recovery of the pearls."

"So, you are back where you began, with Arthur Spain?"

"But, it appears to be a dead end. If Arthur had the pearls he would likely be attempting to make a deal as well."

"*Someone* knows where the pearls are."

"Aye, we just have to find that someone," Gregson said.

"I think you may have already."

The Inspector cocked his head and squinted.

"Emilia."

Holmes motioned the detective further away from the front door. "Did you notice the interplay between them?"

Gregson glanced back toward the kitchen.

Holmes continued: "What would you think if I were to talk with her, as you continue to question Arthur? We might get different stories. I will take Mrs. Spain into the dining room. Continue your interview with Arthur—ratchet up the intensity."

22

"I'm with you, Mr. Holmes."

Holmes escorted Emilia Spain into the dining room and offered her a glass of water. He waited until Gregson began a more bellicose line of questions. The detective overplayed his part, pounding on the table like a madman. With each bang, Emilia winced and closed her eyes. Waiting, Holmes leaned closer and, in a low voice, asked: "You know where the pearls are, don't you?"

Tears trickled down her cheeks. She trembled. "I lost 'em. I lost 'em. My Arty's going to prison, and it's my fault."

Within minutes Holmes had the whole story: As the net closed around Grizzard, he knew that he had to get the pearls off his premises. Arthur was likely being watched, so Emilia was dispatched to take the pearls and conceal them. She frantically searched the neighborhood for a hiding place. She settled on a graveyard in Spa Fields. However, when she knelt down at her father's gravestone to bury the matchbox containing the pearls, she discovered that they were missing.

"We can retrace the woman's steps, but I fear that the pearls may be gone forever," Gregson grumbled.

"It's unlikely that they fell from her pocket. More likely they were lifted."

"A dipper, you think, Holmes?"

"She had to traverse Exmouth Market—a prime location for pickpockets, if I'm not mistaken."

"To be sure. Reports come in weekly from thereabouts."

Holmes popped open his watch. "My lunchtime is gone, Gregson, but I take it you would not object if I were to conduct my own search for the missing baubles?"

"You will contact me if you are successful?"

"Of course, inspector. It's your case."

The next day, Sherlock Holmes strolled in and about Exmouth Market, Spa Fields Park, and vicinity. He left the tip of a silk handkerchief dangling from his left coat pocket, and carried an old empty inkwell in his right pocket. On the second day's outing he sensed he was being followed. He stopped and took out his watch. It sparkled in the sunlight and reflected an image of a boy waiting behind him.

Holmes made his way, in a casual stroll, until he came to a stall selling leather goods set along the edge of the street. He began fingering a collection of belts hanging from the top of the stall. As he reached his arms upwards, his coat opened up, throwing both pockets behind him. Within moments the lad had closed the space between them and dipped both hands, simultaneously, into Holmes's pockets.

Suddenly, Holmes swung around and gripped the lad's hands—which were now holding a handkerchief and an inkwell.

"It's a fair cop, sir," the lad exclaimed in surrender.

Then, just as quickly, the boy swung a huge kick toward Holmes's right leg, grazing his shin and rending his trousers.

"It seems you're no better with your feet than you are with your hands," Holmes remarked.

The lad smiled. But, the boy's smile twisted into a look of confusion as he stared at his right hand. "Blimey! An inkwell. What's all this then?"

"Not much value there," Holmes said. "And, you might also note that the handkerchief has a hole it."

"I made a right pig's ear of it, di'n I, mister?"

"Yes. But, our meeting can be a good thing for you."

"Wotcher mean? Ain't you turnin' me in to the coppers, then?"

"I think not," Holmes replied.

"You're a queer 'un."

"I am that," Holmes agreed. "I simply want some information about an item that a friend of mine lost a few days ago—a matchbox filled with beads."

"Gawdon Bennet! They're valuable then?"

"They are to my friend."

"How valuable?"

"I'll give you two pounds for them."

The boy smirked. "I'm no mug. They're wurf at least ten."

"Ten's too much, and you know it. I'll give you five."

"The pint-sized thief fought a smile. "Can't shake on the deal lessen you let me go."

They shook.

"Mi name's Wiggins."

"Holmes . . . Sherlock Holmes. Can you take me to the beads?"

"It's not so easy. You see, they belong to mi mates—all for one, and like that. Don't know if they'll part wiv 'em for five quid. We'll 'ave to talk about it."

"Can you take me to them now?

"No. Tomorrow. Come 'ere tomorrow evenin' wiv the fiver—and maybe a tad more."

25

With that Wiggins ceremoniously thrust Holmes's inkwell into his hand, dashing off into the thickening crowd.

Holmes grinned as he watched the heads of startled people bob up, like moles from a hole, as the diminutive boy pushed past them.

<•••>

Upon his return the next day, Holmes found himself walking the narrow, rubbish-filled streets of Spitalfields. The matrix of alleys and lanes was so twisted that Holmes was unable to make a mental map—which was his custom.

Dreary women peered from the windows of sagging tenements, gazing out over the bustling street. Casual laborers stood on street corners in the hope of a day's work at nearby wharfs and docks. Despite the unpleasant surroundings, Holmes did not feel threatened. This was not a haunt of criminals.

In many ways, he felt in the thick of life. There was a cacophony of calls from the peddlers: "Apples ha'penny a lot . . . Yarmouth herrings here . . . Eggs fresh from the country." There were costermonger barrows everywhere heaped with green and yellow fruit. A sullen old woman sold cresses as her feet soaked in a tub of some mysterious liquid.

There was significant trading of small animals— pigeons, rats, rabbits, guinea pigs, ferrets, and such, that might be offered for sale at the local Club Row market. Beyond the marketplace, meager industries dotted the neighborhood: upholsterers, matchbox makers, umbrella menders, and chamber masters—knocking out cheap furniture in cramped rooms. It was difficult to believe that this place had once been the home of the celebrated Spitalfields silk workers.

A deep melancholy swept over Holmes as he moved on. It wasn't the dirt and decay so much as a pervasive feeling of hopelessness. This was a place where the future was fugitive. Nowhere was that more apparent than in the faces of the children. The Spitalfields nippers were not lively youths, but apathetic beings set out on their own to scavenge and pilfer. If they had any education it would have been in workhouses or reformatories. But the streets themselves taught the principal lesson: Life is a desperate race where the prize goes to the toughest. Wiggins, no doubt, was at the top of the class.

Holmes found his way to the marketplace and the stall where Wiggins had dipped into his coat pockets. It was a little after the appointed time, but Holmes fully expected the lad would be waiting. He was not.

Holmes scanned the marketplace in search of Wiggins' winsome smile. After nearly half an hour, he headed back to his room.

As he approached his flat at 221 Baker Street, a small girl approached. She looked up with wide, red eyes. Her face and hands were grimy, and the hem of her little dress lay unraveled on the ground. "Mr. 'Olmes?"

"Yes, I'm Mr. Holmes."

She reached into the patch pocket of her dress and retrieved a folded piece of paper. Holmes, upon taking it, immediately noticed the high quality of the paper. He unfolded the missive, and read it:

Holmes -
    We have the lad. Bring us the
pearls, and you can have him back in

*one piece. If you do not come to the
marketplace at noon tomorrow with the
goods, you will have the boy back in
several pieces.*

*The girl will be waiting. Put the
pearls around her neck.*

Don't be late.

Margarita.

Holmes handed the little girl a penny. She uttered an
ejaculation indicative of delight and toddled off. His mind
began racing: This was not the work of common thieves.
The paper, and signature, told him as much—*Margarita*,
Latin for pearl. He never doubted that whoever had Wiggins
would not hesitate to kill him. It was possible they might kill
him with or without the pearls. A person who would use and
endanger small children had few scruples.

Someone had likely been watching Spain's house. They
had followed him. When he encountered Wiggins at the
marketplace, it may have appeared that he had been given
the pearls when the inkwell was returned. They conjectured
that, or Wiggins was wise enough to concoct the story.

Bringing in Gregson now was not advisable, because he
would have been observed at Arthur Spain's residence as
well. Nor did Holmes trust the police to manage the business
without bungling.

After two pipes, Holmes had a plan. It endangered
Wiggins, but the odds of success were good if the boy had
the courage and guile that Holmes suspected he had.

In his hospital laboratory Holmes had all the
ingredients required. He shaped white clay into small balls

and rolled them in crushed mica, which made them sparkle and shine. With a pin, he pierced a hole in each one, and placed them in an autoclave oven to harden the handmade beads over a gas burner. When they cooled, he strung the pearl-like beads on a thread, placed them in a matchbox, and set the remaining spool of thread on top.

Early the next morning Sherlock Holmes took the faux-pearls, thread, note paper and pencil, and set out for the Spitalfields Market. A sanguine sun had just begun to peek over the eastern edge of city. The costermongers were rolling their barrows into place, the flower-women were tying up violets into small penny bunches, and the stalls were being stocked. He stood at the leather-goods stall and surveyed the area. There were only three places where someone could gain enough elevation to see over the crowds to where he stood: The flimsy roof of the market building, or the second and third floor windows of a nearby warehouse that housed a livery stable on the lower level. Further exploration of the stables revealed but one stairway coming from the upper floors.

Holmes scratched out a note, duplicated it, and tacked the messages next to each of the two windows above the stable. He hastily retreated before the sun rose above the horizon.

He waited until just before noon in a coffee shop on Hanbury Street. At precisely five minutes before twelve, he walked to the marketplace and stood by the appointed stall. He opened his watch and waited. Within minutes the little girl was at his heels with another note:

29

Holmes -

You are clever. I pray you are not too clever for your own sake, and the health of the innocents.

Place the pearls around the girl's neck. Look to the top window to find the proof you requested. Do not move from your spot.

The lad will be released when we have the pearls in hand.

Margarita.

Holmes knelt down. "What is your name?"

"Tessa."

She was frightened.

"I want to put some pretty beads around your neck. Would you like that?"

Holmes retrieved the matchbox and opened it. The little girl's eyes widened. She reached out a finger and poked at the necklace as if it were hot coals. Holmes placed it in her hand. She grinned. "For me?"

Holmes nodded. Then he placed them about her neck, tying them together with a hitch-knot. He tied the loose end of the necklace thread to the end of the spool.

He held out a penny.

"Here's a penny for you. I found it on the ground. There are more pennies on the ground if you look for them." He pointed in the direction from which she had come. "Do you understand?"

Tessa nodded. Holmes stood with his hands on the shoulders of the girl, and looked up. Sure enough, there in the top window of the stables was Wiggins. Someone stood behind him in the shadows. Holmes waved to Wiggins. He nodded back.

"Run along, Tessa. Remember—look for all those pennies along the way."

The tiny girl slowly stumbled toward the stable building. As she did so, Holmes let the thread roll off the spool that was hidden in his pocket. He knew that some passerby would likely catch the thread and pull the hitch-knot loose. If they didn't he would yank on it himself.

Holmes could only imagine what was going through the mind of the person, or persons, standing behind Wiggins. Instead of making a swift trip back to the stables, the girl meandered in a slow, jerky stroll with her head bent downward. Wiggins was still visible in the window. They were watching.

Then it happened. The thread caught on a coster's barrow wheel and yanked the knot on the necklace. The pearls burst into the air like roaches fleeing an overturned dustbin. Holmes dashed toward the stables. He grabbed Tessa around the waist, and raced ahead toward the open doors of the stable.

Wiggins was leaping down the stairway as he entered. Two men followed, one brandishing a knife. Holmes put the girl behind him, and picked up a pitchfork. One of the men grabbed Wiggins by the collar, but it tore off in the man's hand. As he ran toward Holmes and Tessa, Wiggins grabbed a bucket of dung and stood by Holmes.

The two men circled. Holmes took off his coat and wrapped it around his left arm. As they were about to pounce, Wiggins yelled, "Fire! Fire! Help!" and flung the bucket of dung at the two men. A burly stable-hand burst out from a nearby storeroom. "What's all this, then?" he demanded.

Seeing the two brutes, one with a knife, the stable hand picked up a block and tackle from the floor and began to swing it around over his head.

With that, the two dung-smattered scoundrels bolted.

Holmes turned to Wiggins as the boy wrapped Tessa in his arms. She was crying and stamping her feet. "Mi beads, Rory!" she cried.

"She's mi sis," Wiggins said, looking up at Holmes with glassy eyes.

Tessa continued to howl as she watched the market-goers crush the shiny beads underfoot. So go childhood dreams in Spitalfields.

Wiggins carried his little sister home. All the way there she stared, red-eyed, at Holmes who silently followed. As they left Brick Lane, the surrounding structures pushed tighter and tighter together. In places, there was barely room for a cart or barrow to pass. No signs or place names were posted in this warren. What had been Dorset Street and Brick Lane had dissolved into a labyrinth of unnamed alleyways and passages branching out in all directions.

Before long, they came to brick steps that brought them down into a tunnel that passed beneath a tenement building. Water and slime dripped from the ceiling. Their shoes skittered through pools of putrid water. Just as the daylight behind was disappearing, a glimmer reappeared at the other end of the tunnel. Another set of steps brought them up and into a small courtyard lined with doors.

Wiggins stopped and turned to Holmes. He pointed to a rickety green door on the far side of the courtyard. "That's our place there. Best stay 'ere, sir. I'll be back."

Wiggins pushed the unlocked door open and disappeared into the shadows with Tessa in hand.

Holmes waited.

A woman exited a door nearby, looked him over with an emotionless glower, spat, and chuckled. "Lookin' a bit lost 'ere, guv'nor." She walked past him into the tunnel, her laughter echoing. He imagined that the expression on his face had been amusing.

"Hey, mister!" a voice called from above. Someone was peering at him through a glassless window. It was a female, he guessed, by the length of her hair. Red arms protruded from a grimy shawl that wrapped around her shoulders, and framed her ample breasts. "Lookin' for a good time, mister?" she asked, with brows flitting up and down.

Holmes found himself unable to speak. The woman shrugged and pulled herself inside.

Sherlock Holmes was familiar with the dingier places in London, but his previous encounters had been in the context of a chase. His eyes and attention, had been on the villains and clues. In this way, his mind had forged a correlation between the slums and criminals. It was black and white, like Charles Booth's poverty map of London, where Spitalfields appeared as a blacked series of city blocks on London's east side. That map had no shades of grey, no color, no faces or names. Holmes remembered filing this map away in his archives, along with the knowledge that one-third of Londoners lived in desperate need and squalor. It was but another scrap of information, like the number of cabs in London—4,142 currently.

But now, he stood in the middle of one of those blackened city blocks. There was a metamorphosis: information had transformed into flesh and blood. He needed to consider this. He would—but not now, and not here. He would walk out of this "blackened block" to his spotless rooms. However, he would never again be able to leave behind the people of Spitalfields.

"Mr. 'Olmes!" The voice of Wiggins shook him from his thoughts. "Mr. 'Olmes, you 'ave mi deepest thanks. I thought you was a bit 'aughty-like, but you're a good bloke, you are."

"I took a chance with your life, Wiggins."

"No needs to worry about me, sir. I can take care of mi'self."

"And your sister, too."

"Tessa 'as the *nous* to take care of 'erself, but she can get in a pickle from time to time."

"She's fortunate to have you as her brother."

Wiggins smiled.

"I trust you remember what brought us together, Wiggins?"

"The beads."

"I still wish to purchase them."

"As I say, sir, they belong to mi' mates. We'll have to wait and see."

With that Wiggins beckoned, and led Holmes back down into the tunnel. A five-minute walk brought them to a timber yard that had a hidden entry. There was a stairway that led to a lower passageway of decaying bricks. This was the gateway into a hidden rookery deep in the bowels of Spitalfields.

Wiggins came to a curtain fashioned from coarse grain sacks. He pulled the drape aside with one hand and, with the other, motioned for Holmes to enter.

The curtain dropped behind them, cutting off the daylight. A lone candle burned on a table in the center of the room. As his eyes became accustomed to the environs, faces materialized out of the gloom. Their eyes seemed to hold a voiceless warning.

London had become a smelter. Dangling over a scorching coal fire, the poor burned in the impersonal flames of starvation, degradation and squalor, becoming hardened inside. The wealthy live in an abiding fear that the melting pot will boil over and spill into their orderly streets. Their minions tend the pot. Politicians' promises diluted their desperation. Bobbies patrolled the margins of their slums to remind the inhabitants where they belonged—as if they could forget. Preachers promised golden crowns awaiting them in the next life. In Spitalfields, every child was unwillingly baptized a Calvinist, inexorably moving toward a wretched pre-determined end.

"This 'ere's Mr. 'Olmes. 'E's a top bloke. Saved mi life, 'e did."

Then, Wiggins introduced his mates: "'Ere we 'ave Ruck. 'E's a fellow Mick. When 'e's not knocking about wiv us, 'e's mudlarkin'."

Ruck was about ten. He had shaggy red hair that wanted cutting. He wore a large checkered scarf around his neck. His bare feet were black as coal.

"Then we 'av Gordi. He's what we calls a "sweeper," and he sweeps 'em pretty clean."

The gang laughed. He looked to be the oldest in the group, about fifteen years. He had a solemn face and dark foreboding eyes that studied Holmes.

"He comes an' goes," Wiggins added, "as his dear muvver don't like 'im hangin' about with the likes of us. Nuff said!"

"Snape here . . . what can we say about Snape?"

"'E's no dam' good!" Ruck snapped.

"Aye, no dam' good—lessen you need an arm broke."

Snape had a short, stocky upper body, thick arms, and hands a size too large for him.

"He worked wiv a smithy before 'e came to the city. Got yer 'ammer 'ave you, Snape?" With that, the lad raised up a three-pound hammer and crashed it on the table.

"Next, over there, behind Ruck is Lickle Mac, his bruvver. He don't do much of anything."

The tiny lad, who was about seven, wrinkled up his face. "Aw-w, Rory."

Ruck turned around and ruffed his brother's hair.

"I'm Rumpty," shouted a chubby boy of about ten or eleven, who wore an expression of permanent eagerness. He was, literally, bursting out of his clothing.

"Maybe you can see," Wiggins said, "Rumpty works for the cook shop of the Convict's Home. He does a great service, as 'e eats most of the food so as no one else 'as to."

The entire company now exploded into fits of laughter—including Rumpty.

Acting the clown, a small lad poked his head out from behind Rumpty and tipped his cap. He seemed to be the youngest in the tribe.

"That nipper in Rumpty's shadow is my cousin, Archie. Gets in the way mostly."

Archie, a plucky boy of near six years of age, threw his cap at Wiggins.

"Now, Mr. Holmes, we know swells like you don't like ladies in your clubs. So, my apologies. Kate, stand up so's Mr. Holmes can see you."

The adolescent raised herself up from the shadows in the corner. The candlelight caught her short-cropped auburn hair. Her tanned face remained shrouded in the shadows. There was little to betray her sex. She wore britches and an oversized man's shirt with the sleeves cuffed up.

"It was near a year before we found she was a girl. By then we didn't 'ave the 'art to throw 'er out."

Kate sat down in the dim corner from whence she'd emerged.

"By way of introduction," Wiggins continued: "Mr. Holmes 'ere did Tessa and me a good turn. He wants the beads we nicked free days ago. He can buy 'em, he says, for five quid. What do you say?"

Gordi was the first to speak: "Seems like to me, if them beads is wurf five quid to 'im, they're likely wurf more to the guv'ner."

They did not trust him. That was clear. Trust might come later. Holmes understood that survival in Spitalfields required a primordial ideology: With each encounter, you become either predator, or prey. Daily deprivation chipped away the thin veneer of civilization that tempered their animal nature. Evolution had put eyes in the front of their heads, like the leopards, raptors and wolves. And, at this moment, Holmes could see, in Gordi's narrowed eyes, a predator waiting to pounce.

Holmes raised a finger. "Well, gentlemen—and lady— maybe they are worth more than five pounds."

His statement brought jeers from the gang.

"However, there is the small matter of the how the beads came into your possession."

"Found 'em," Snape shouted. "What 'ave you got to say to that?"

"I'd say you're talking bosh!" Holmes shot back. Everyone laughed. "But, if we take it to the coppers in just the right manner, they might be good with it."

"Who made you part of our gang?" Gordi squawked.

WHACK! Wiggins slapped the table.

"I say 'e's fine." He nodded to Holmes.

Holmes put his hand on the lad's shoulder. "Wiggins can come with me. We'll both see what we can get for these beads."

Gordi stood up. "Right then. You an' Wiggins. You better be straight, or it'll be the worse for you."

"All right then." Wiggins pointed to Kate. "Give 'im the beads."

Kate walked fully into the candlelight. There, dangling around her neck was the strand of sixty-one milky pearls. She unhooked them, watched them sparkle in her hand for a moment, then slowly placed them on the table. Gordi pushed them forward.

The next day Holmes took a cab to the Spitalfields Market and picked up Wiggins as planned. The lad eagerly climbed into the "growler."

"Never in all mi life, sir, 'ave I been on the inside of one o' these fings!" he remarked, as he took his seat opposite Holmes.

"I suggest you sit over here with me. We have one more party to pick up. And I suggest you hold on to these."

Holmes placed the pearls in the boy's hand. "Put them in your pocket."

They drove to the Bow Street Station where Tobias Gregson was waiting. Holmes stuck his head out and beckoned. Gregson climbed aboard. When we saw the boy he lurched with surprise.

"What's all the secrecy, Holmes? And who's this hooligan?"

"'O's an 'ooligan? I can tell as you're a copper."

"Holmes, can we talk without the boy here?"

"No, Gregson; Wiggins is part of my company."

"You are a most irregular fellow, Holmes."

"And Wiggins here is irregular as well. He's the captain of a formidable platoon. He is the fellow you've been looking for: he found the pearls."

"Ha, I knew it! You're the dip, aren't you, lad?"

Before Wiggins could respond, Holmes cut in: "He came upon them in Spitalfields Market. He asked me to help him get them to their rightful owner."

Tobais Gregson bristled and grumbled under his breath for a moment, then settled himself down.

"All right then," the inspector said. "So be it. Hand them over, lad."

Wiggins began to take the pearls from his pocket when Holmes grabbed his hand. "Inspector, isn't there a reward?"

"This is too much, Holmes!"

"We can take them to Lloyd's directly, if you wish. However, I thought you might like to do that yourself."

"Very well, he can have the £10."

Wiggins eyes widened and glazed over. Holmes laughed. Wiggins immediately composed himself, but his eyes flashed back and forth—no doubt struggling to divide £10 by seven.

— <•••> —

Recovering from his reverie, Holmes reached out with one hand and touched the edge of Wiggins' photograph. He seemed surprised to find that it was flat and cold. "Where are you now, Wiggins?" he murmured. Holmes recalled the note that had accompanied the invitation: "*help me honour and eulogize those that served us.*"

Laughter broke out nearby. This upset Holmes. What was here in this room that could be amusing? He wanted to shout at the rowdy gentlemen: Have you walked the streets shoeless? Ever been hungry?

Holmes speculated, for the first time really, about the purpose of this exhibition. What was S. P. Fields up to?

He turned toward the hallway and hectically searched the jumble of garments for his own coat and hat. He wanted to escape. "You can't change the past," he said, to soothe himself.

Then, he stopped.

The wave of emotions passed . . . as they always do.

CHAPTER III

SHERLOCK HOLMES SPECULATED that if he would return to the gallery, these images from the past might conjure up tender secrets buried within him. Once exposed, he imagined that his secrets might fill the room. Everyone would see them.

His eyes hardened. *This was not an art show. It was a pilgrimage.* S. P. Fields had sent him on a pilgrimage—a quest for a votive purpose that he did not fully comprehend.

Holmes walked on into the gallery. Pulling back from the images on the wall, his legs struck the edge of a bench that marked the center of the room. He sat and looked down—unwilling to focus his eyes on any one particular photograph. But he became aware that his peripheral vision was drawing him to a large, poster-sized image at the far end of the gallery. It took but one glance to send him plummeting, once again, into the past.

UGLY:
ADOPTED AND RAISED
BY THE COSTERS
OF THE SPITALFIELDS MARKET.

The lad was in his late teens, or early twenties, when this picture was taken—a decade after Holmes had made his acquaintance. Ugly looked surprisingly clean and tidy here. He was wearing a black pea-jacket with matching flapped-hat that did not hide his jug-ears. A black silk scarf was tied up close around his neck and sat above a clean white shirt. His outsized mouth and lips were expressionless. He had eyebrows so shaggy they nearly obscured his eyes, which were his most remarkable feature. It was likely a trick of the camera, but the pupils of his eyes did not show. His eyes appeared to be bottomless pools of murky water.

QUEEN AND COUNTRY had recently celebrated the Golden Jubilee that marked the apex of summer for Dr. Watson, and others, who enjoyed the royal folderol. For Sherlock Holmes the highlight of that summer was a case that Watson had never chronicled because he had been absorbed with his practice and family obligations. While hereto undocumented, Holmes referred to it as the *Case of Vishnu's Temple Treasure.*

It was a dull and smoky day, the sort all too familiar in London. Holmes had been summoned by Inspector Lestrade, to the Royal Artillery Barracks in Greenwich, on London's far-east side. He arrived to find the vast estate cordoned off, and the gates closed. Upon presenting his card, he was escorted onto the grounds by a sergeant. An imposing three-story building stretched out across the horizon. A lone figure stood in a courtyard that sat to one side of the sprawling grounds. An obelisk stood in the center of the courtyard surrounded by antique cannons and mortars. One of the larger guns was shrouded with a tarpaulin. There were also a number of smaller veils covering items scattered nearby on the stone pavement. Lestrade was standing near the hefty covered gun with a notepad in his hand. As Holmes approached, the inspector startled and turned.

"Ah, Holmes, I thought you would not wish to miss what promises to be the most remarkable case of recent years."

Holmes was aware that Lestrade was prone to exaggeration but, when the inspector pointed to a pair of dismembered human legs sprawled underneath the barrel of the cannon, he knew that this was no frivolous boast.

Holmes squatted to examine what could only be described as horrendous gore. He stood and turned to Inspector Lestrade who then pointed twenty feet to Holmes's left—to a sheet with a bloodstain the size of cannonball.

"Under that cloth you'll find a human head."

The inspector pointed again. "And there, an arm, and one like it behind the gun."

Holmes stood silently for some time.

"I have read of such things," Holmes remarked.

"In pirate tales," Lestrade conceded.

"This is not a mere murder, Lestrade. It is an execution."

"I call it a mess," Lestrade said.

Holmes noticed a soldier leaning against the barracks entry in the distance. He was smoking and looking on."

"Who is the trooper over there?" Holmes inquired.

"Not sure. The barracks is closed . . . for renovation I was told. Soldiers are billeted elsewhere . . . but not all of them, I suppose."

"Has anyone witnessed this ritual murder?"

"No, Mr. Holmes. The guards were not at the gate at the time. They patrol a huge area. Of course, they heard the cannon fire just before dawn, but no one was about when they came upon this scene—no living person."

"What brought you to this military property, Inspector?"

"The deceased appears to be a civilian. And, as such, the Yard must be brought in."

"Have your men questioned the soldier yonder, or anyone other than the guards?"

"We are getting to that."

"Is the victim identified?" Holmes asked.

"No, you might want to have a look at him," the inspector said, offering Holmes a pair of rubber gloves.

Holmes retrieved his magnifying glass and pencil from his coat pocket, and removed his hat and coat. He folded his garments and placed them in a neat stack on a grassy area adjoining the courtyard. Donning the gloves, Holmes circumspectly approached the ensanguined sheet nearest the gun. The inspector followed.

Holmes casually peeled back the crimson cover lying over the dismembered head. It stuck to the flesh, making removal an untidy process.

"Eyes missing, no help there. Male. Age, thirty to fifty. Unshaven. Long scar on left cheek, probably a knife wound."

Holmes pushed the head to one side with a finger placing the severed head in profile. "Pierced ear, no ring or stud. Possibly a seafaring man. Oh and . . . yes, a small puncture on the back of his neck."

The head rolled to one side as Holmes released the skull. A minute scroll fell from the gapping mouth. Holmes speared the scroll of parchment with his pencil. He took it in hand and gingerly unrolled it to find writing: हत्यारोंकेब्रदरहुड.

"A message," Holmes reported, "in some Indian language. If I might hold on to this, I know where it might be deciphered."

Lestrade bent closer to look at the blood-soaked paper scroll, swatting at flies that had begun to gather. "Holmes, I know you wish to look about, but we must remove the remains as they will deteriorate quickly in the heat. We'll be taking the parts . . . that is, the body, to the local mortuary as soon as the van arrives."

Holmes nodded. "Yes. You may remove the clothing from the appendages as well, but do not disturb the clothing. If you find any items, please make a list."

Lestrade harrumphed. "As is our practice, Mr. Holmes."

"I will be by the mortuary tomorrow morning," Holmes promised, "on Devonshire, I believe. I will peruse the surroundings before I go. It promises to be an interesting day for all of us, Inspector."

Holmes began to circumnavigate the site, spiraling outward. Aware of a strong breeze that was mounting, Holmes knew that, if there were evidence lying about, some of it might well be obliterated in the next few hours.

As he perused the high grass near the courtyard, Holmes was aware that the soldier in the distance was still observing.

There seemed to be few clues until Holmes fell upon a patch of bare ground. He retrieved his hand-glass and bent lower to examine a single bare human footprint. *A rather small fellow*, Holmes thought. He then retraced his steps, closely examining other barren patches of soil. His studiousness bore fruit. More partial, overlapping footprints revealed themselves—*two or more persons*, Holmes speculated. Next to them was a single small print. *Not human. A primate.*

The soldier, who was now very close, nervously flicked his cigarette away and turned into the building. Noting his epaulets, Holmes called out: "Hello there, Captain. May I have a word?"

The man turned back, but did not reply. In partial uniform, the officer was slim, aquiline, and dark—reminiscent of a haughty heron.

As Holmes approached, he noticed a large number of butts on the ground resembling the ends of small cigars.

"Captain," Holmes inquired, "did you serve in India?"

"What makes you say so?"

"The beedies."

"Yes, a filthy habit, I'm afraid." He nodded to Holmes: "Captain McGilney. I'm Royal Artillery, attached to the 32nd Lancers. Recently returned."

"What can you tell me about the goings-on at the courtyard?"

"Nothing. I was asleep."

"Any suspects?"

"Did you notice the gun?" the Captain asked.

"Should I have?"

"It's a bronze cannon—really, quite magnificent—a trophy from the siege of Bharatpur—still in working order . . . obviously.

"India, then?" Holmes confirmed.

"Yes, bloody India!"

The Captain pulled a cloth bag from his coat pocket and retrieved another beedi. As he lit it, the pungent aroma titillated Holmes's senses.

"Betel nut and herbs mixed with leaf, I believe," Holmes remarked.

The man shook another fag out of the pouch and offered it to Holmes who took it in hand. "Thank you."

The two men were quiet as they smoked, watching the body parts being hoisted onto stretchers and loaded into a covered lorry.

"The barracks are undergoing a renovation, I understand," Holmes remarked. "But you're here."

The officer smiled. "Renovation? I suppose. Rats. Rats everywhere—in the walls, floors, ceilings. Filthy beasts. I offered to stay behind to manage the rat-catchers." He gazed into the distance at the departing lorry. "It takes a lot to rid oneself of rats."

"I imagine Scotland Yard will be wanting a word with you."

"And a word is what they'll get."

"You have little to offer, then?"

"Nothing."

As Holmes prepared to depart the barracks he noticed one of the guards at the gate had nabbed a small boy by the collar. The nipper, about nine or ten, was screaming bloody murder. His dog was yelping and biting at the heels of the guard.

"Hey, ya bastard, let me be!" the lad bellowed.

His arms flailed about as he kicked furiously at the guard, who was clearly on the losing end. Holmes chuckled and walked on.

"I'm lookin for mi Da!" the boy yelled.

Holmes stopped and called out: "Set him down Corporal. I'll see to him."

With that, the lad was dropped to the ground, and the dog ceased his caterwauling.

"What's your name boy?" Holmes asked.

"Ugly," was the nipper's reply. And to be fair, the lad was that. Whether an affliction, or accident of birth, the youth had inordinately large facial features and hands. His lips protruded, framing a huge grin. His brows were bushy, and his ears jutted out. All of this combined to give him an otherworldly appearance. "And, this here is Nicki," the lad added.

"Pleased to meet you both. Do you have a Christian name?"

"That's the only name I got. The truth's the truth, sir. Accept it, is what I say."

"I concur with your philosophy," Holmes said."

"You what?"

"I agree with you. So, you're looking for your father?"

"Aye, he 'ad business 'ere, 'e did."

"I see. What was the nature of his business?"

"Him, Nicki an' me do rattin'. Us an' uvvers. Mi Da went back for our money."

"What does your father look like?"

"Just a bloke."

"Where's your mother?"

"She's dead and buried. Just me and mi Da now."

"Holmes glimpsed the lorry disappearing down Repository Road. "Your Da's not here."

"Says who?"

"I can tell you that he is nowhere here about. Why don't you come along with me?"

"Don't think as I will," the lad declared.

"Where will you go?" Holmes asked.

"I have mi mates. Good lads. All for one, an' one for all, is our motter.

"Do you know who said that?

"Mi mates."

"But, before that, it was the Three Musketeers who said those words. Brave fellows who fought for justice."

"I like that," Ugly said. He cocked his head. "How did these mustaters go on?"

Holmes peered into the dirty face of the boy. "They lived happy lives, full of adventure."

The boy's countenance lit up. "Aye—all for one, an' one for all!" he shouted, sticking his fist the air as he turned to go. "Come on, Nicki!"

The tendrils of Holmes's brain were connected to a vast network of common and arcane persons: scholars, thieves, professionals of all sorts, artists, sportsmen, doctors, adventurers, scientists, and craftsmen. Each and every one Sherlock Holmes comes into contact with is filed away in his tidy brain. Some names merit logging into a notebook that waits upon his desk. However, he did not need his directory today. Augustus Stone was not an obscure acquaintance.

With the help of the British Museum, Holmes was able to find the residence of Dr. Stone who had curated the East India Company's Asian collection in years past.

Doctor Stone received Holmes in his library. He was a substantial, pear-bellied man who moved in a confident British style. His eyes sparkled with blissful expectancy.

"Holmes, you are a rare sight, I must say."

"Thank you for your time."

"Time is something I now have in generous quantities."

"Yes, I understand that your collection has been dispersed."

"A few pieces in Kew, another bunch at the Victoria and Albert Museum, the Royal Botanic and the like. A sad affair, if you ask me . . . but, of course, no one did."

"Maybe I can brighten your day," Holmes said, retrieving the bloodstained parchment from his coat pocket.

"Ah, what have we here?" Dr. Stone asked, as Holmes handed him the miniature scroll.

"Hindi or Bengali, I believe."

"Indeed, Hindi. It reads: *hatyaaron ke bradarahud.*" He looked up at Holmes. "And you found it in the mouth of a dead man, did you not?"

"Yes."

"It bears the name of a brotherhood of assassins."

"Indian assassins?"

"Yes, a mysterious society. I was not sure that they still stalked the Earth."

"I can report that they do," Holmes said. "And their handiwork was recently found at a military barracks outside of the city. A man was strapped to a cannon and . . .

"Blown to pieces," the Doctor blurted out.

"Blown to pieces, indeed," Holmes echoed. "Yes, I seem to recall hearing stories about pirates, and sixteenth century Portuguese colonists, employing this form of execution."

"Possibly, but being blown from a gun is a form of punishment which we can credit to the Mughal Empire—a more spectacular version of being drawn and quartered." Stone's eyes flashed eagerly, "The poor soul is lashed to the open barrel of the gun. When fired, the arms are blown off to each side twenty or more feet, the legs drop down below the barrel, and the head flies thirty to forty feet in the air. Nothing remains of the torso. Blown from a gun it is called."

"You accurately described the scene of the crime, Doctor."

"And the victim?"

"A man. We know little more than that at this point."

"On the contrary, you know that the victim perpetrated an egregious act. You see, when someone has committed a terrible crime . . . in India, you see . . . the brotherhood of assassins is often employed. A slit throat is usually the outcome. But, if the crime is judged to be particularly heinous, a more dramatic form of execution is employed. I think you will agree that being blown from a gun does get one's attention."

Holmes's mind flashed to a picture of Captain McGilney tugging nervously on his beedies.

"What might constitute a crime deserving this form of execution?" Holmes asked.

"Difficult to say . . . if someone killed a member of a royal family—or defiled a temple. Any act of sacrilege might engage the assassins."

"Are you aware of any recent events such as you describe?" Holmes inquired.

"I no longer find myself in the flow of recent events, Mr. Holmes. I am quickly becoming part of my own collection of antiquities, but I will look into this further if you wish. Of course, you may be able to learn something from more privileged members of the Indian community."

The Doctor reached for a book from his desk and offered it to Holmes. "Here, you may find something to your benefit in this book by Fergusson."

The title of the battered volume read: *The Ancient Temples and Rituals of India.*

"This may be helpful, thank you, Doctor."

"I'm pleased that I may still be of service. When you have this mess sorted, I should very much like to hear the outcome."

"A promise . . . *if* it gets resolved."

"Don't toy with me, Holmes. You know better than I that it will. When it's over, pray remember me."

Holmes took a Hansom to Green Park, one of those dear and exclusive neighborhoods. He found himself passing the fine portico of Lord Spencer's mansion before the cab stopped at an equally lavish facade. This was the London residence of H.H. the Maharaja of Corvencar, Padmanabh Anizham Thirunal.

Holmes was welcomed at the door by a Bengali domestic to whom he presented his card. Minutes later he was ushered into the morning room where a young Indian man waited.

"Mr. Sherlock Holmes. Your celebrity comes before you. My name is Rama, I am one of the Maharaja's sons. My father is ailing, but I believe he would be disappointed if he were to miss your visit."

The Maharaja was in his chambers at the rear of the mansion. In the mold of his class, the Maharaja was resplendent in Bengali dress, reclining on a chesterfield adorned in gold leaf. His custom, on the streets of London, was to wear the drab black dress of an English gentleman. Today, however, he was garbed completely in white, trimmed in red brocade. His eyes were closed in meditation.

As he entered, Holmes was aware of the pungent aroma of camphor. The source was smoke emanating from a bronze dish next to the Maharaja's settee.

Rama bent low and whispered into his father's ear. The old man's eyes popped open. A pleasant expression visited his face as he blinked and focused. Holmes approached and offered his hand.

"Ah, welcome!" the potentate exclaimed. "I cannot imagine what might bring you to my door."

Holmes's brows lifted in acknowledgement. "I come for your help and advice."

"I will do all in my power to assist you," the Maharaja replied.

Holmes retrieved the small scroll that bore the name of the brotherhood of assassins. Rama accepted it with a look of surprise, and handed it to his father with a knowing glance.

Holmes waited as the Maharaja read the scroll without expression.

"I am told that this scroll bears the name of an ancient brotherhood," Holmes said.

The Maharaja swung himself around to the edge of the settee. "Your information is correct, Mr. Holmes."

"I found it in the mouth of a dead man who was blown from a gun."

Holmes waited.

The Great Detective had many tools at his command—maybe none as helpful as silence. Silence nourished his wisdom, and fed his imagination. Silence allowed him to engage all his senses. However, it was the manner in which Sherlock Holmes used silence with others that validated his mastery: silence left a question mark hanging in the air. It suggested that he knew more than he really did. It gave him credibility when he spoke. Most of all, as in this moment, silence provoked others to speak—oftentimes, to say too much.

The potentate sighed. "One can only hope that the unfortunate victim was deserving of this unpleasant end."

"Unpleasant, you say," Holmes shot back. "No one deserves to die strapped to the barrel of a cannon."

"Mr. Holmes, you should understand that justice is best seen through the eyes of those seeking that justice."

"Are you, either of you, aware of any acts, or events, that might necessitate this extreme form of retribution?"

"Mr. Holmes, I appreciate your interest," the Maharaja replied. "But, there are some things a non-believer cannot understand. Justice finds its own accord in ways we can never imagine."

Holmes nodded. "On that we agree, your highness. However, I fear we may part ways regarding the means by which justice is served."

There was little more to say, and Holmes bid the Maharaja a hasty good-bye.

Holmes returned to his flat. He had no more than shed his coat, when a knock came to his door. He suspected that it might be Lestrade, but it was Dr. Augustus Stone who stood upon his doorstep with a blazing smile upon his face.

"I have it, Holmes! I believe I know what that grisly killing was about—stolen treasure from the Padmanabhaswamy Temple."

Holmes soon found himself bending over a map of India and several dog-eared photographs that the Doctor had spread across his dining room table. Stone pointed to a location near the heart of the Indian continent.

"Have you ever heard of the Padmanabhaswamy Temple, Mr. Holmes? Well, there is no reason you should . . . "

"I believe it is located in Kerala, India—built in an intricate fusion of the Kerala and the Dravidian style of architecture," Holmes answered.

"A-ha, you have been reading Fergusson's book. Yes, within the Padmanabhaswamy Temple, Vishnu is enshrined in the Anantha Shayanam posture, the eternal yogic sleep, on the serpent Adisheshan."

"And there was a recent theft there?"

"Yes, about one month ago—a terrible sacrilege."

"What was taken?"

Stone pulled out two dog-eared photographs of the temple. "There are six sealed vaults in the Padmanabhaswamy Temple. Only one, here in the outer chamber, has ever been opened. It held thousands of years of accumulated treasures—gems and precious metals of all kinds," the Doctor explained. "The other five vaults remain sealed. Even the priests are not allowed access because the vaults are housed in the *sanctum sanctorum*, and must be left undisturbed to enhance the potency of the presiding deity—Lord Vishnu."

"Would the crime have been reported to the authorities?"

"No, Mr. Holmes. It would bring great shame, and enrage the faithful, if word were to get out. This might account for the brotherhood of assassins being engaged. I only know of this theft from a trusted friend—an Indian. But even he does not know the details."

"Who is responsible for keeping the temple safe?" Holmes asked.

"The priests—but it is also under the protection of the local Maharaja."

"The Maharaja of Corvencar?" Holmes inquired.

Stone smirked at Holmes. "You knew this then?"

"You brought the missing piece of the puzzle, Augustus."

"Excellent!"

Holmes's eye caught a person in one of the photographs. He picked it up and looked at a familiar face. Stone leaned over Holmes's shoulder.

"Yes, that's the Maharaja of Corvencar . . . making an annual pilgrimage to the temple."

"I am looking at his jeweled headdress."

"Yes, the Sarpech of Nizamis—part of the temple treasure. It is comprised of more than a hundred carat weight of rubies, and a similar weight of diamonds, with countless other gems, all set in gold. These stones have a worldly value. However, to the faithful of India, its sacred value is beyond imagining. Such a piece is one of many that are kept within the outer vault."

The next morning found Holmes and Inspector Lestrade at the Greenwich public mortuary. It was a grisly affair. Holmes, once again, wore rubber gloves as he examined the remains of the dead man. As he did so, he recounted his conversation with the boy at the barracks gate.

"So, you believe this fellow here . . . what's is left of him . . . was one of those catching rats in the barracks?" Lestrade asked. Captain McGilney would know him, then."

"Yes, he would know him . . . and, he likely knows more."

"You don't suspect 'im . . ."

"Of the murder? No. But there is a reason why this macabre ritual was put on the doorstep of the barracks— Captain McGilney being the sole inhabitant. But let's get on with it, shall we?"

Holmes retrieved his magnifying glass, and poured over the body parts.

"Not much more to learn here," Holmes noted, "except to confirm that this man was a seaman—the bowed legs, you see. I'm almost certain that this is the boy's father."

"How sad, Mr. Holmes!"

"Yes, yes . . . sad. Are his belongings here?"

"On the counter, nothing of particular interest. Here's the list of items."

Holmes ran a finger down the page, then slowly drew the rancid garments from a brown paper sack and spread them out in a neat row. He turned them with his pencil. He requested tweezers and used them to pick a number of hairs from a trouser leg. He examined each hair under his glass, turning them to catch the light. "Notice the countershading— consistent with that of a dog." *Nicki*, he thought.

Holmes then ran his fingers along the cuffs of the trousers and patted the pockets. His hand stopped. He poked a finger down and rolled it around on a hard object. Reaching into the pocket he retrieved a small, shiny object. He held it up to the light, and twisted it in his fingers. "About one carat, emerald cut—unusual for a diamond."

"What!" Lestrade croaked.

"It appears you missed a rather lovely gem."

Lestrade leaned over Holmes's shoulder and peered at the object. The detective turned away and began pacing.

"Yes . . . yes . . . a small part of his swag," Lestrade declared. "The fellow's a thief. Made off with the take, and his mates caught up with him and did 'im in."

"So . . . they find their untrustworthy mate, drag him to a military barracks in the middle of the night, strap him to a cannon, and blow him to pieces . . . rather than simply slitting his throat."

"H'm."

"However, Lestrade, I do believe that there is something to what you say. A single loose diamond in a dead man's pocket likely came from a larger piece of jewelry."

Holmes placed the stone under his glass. "Yes, the grime along the edges reveals that this stone was in a setting. An emerald-cut diamond is rare because it shows every flaw, as well as the true color. This stone is exceptional in both regards."

"I'll run a check on recent jewel robberies."

"I will be surprised if you find any evidence of such. Something tells me this theft occurred five thousand miles from here."

"Five thousand miles?" Lestrade gasped.

"India. Inspector. May I keep the gem for now?"

"You are on to something then?"

Holmes smiled. "I am compelled to make a visit at the moment, but we can exchange information and theories in your office. I will be there at noon."

Holmes went back to Green Park and the residence of the Maharaja. Rama reluctantly welcomed the detective.

"Mr. Holmes, I do not believe that there is anything more for you here," Rama explained.

"Yes. However, it behooves me to return something of value to you and your family."

The heir apparent had a nonplussed expression. "You had better come in then."

"I would like to return the item to your father, if he is receiving."

"My father is, as you British say, under the weather. He can spare you only a few minutes."

"That will be all that is required," Holmes answered.

The Maharaja was, again, waiting on his couch. Holmes reached into his vest pocket and retrieved the diamond. "This small bauble, I believe, is best left in your hands."

Holmes placed it in Rama's hand. His son held it before him.

"The old man glanced at it, sighed, and mumbled: "*Mujhe maaf karado.*"

Rama put his hand on his father's shoulder and turned to Holmes. "This is a most trying time for him."

"I would like to make an agreement," Holmes declared. "I am asking you to give British justice an opportunity to work. I believe you were asking for forgiveness a moment ago. I believe the Vedic literature talks of forgiveness. One need not condone an act, or reconcile with the offender, to forgive. It is something one does for peace of mind."

The maharaja sat in reflection for a moment. "Wise words, indeed. And this counsel is given to me because you assume that I have more influence than I do." The old man stood and looked Holmes in the eye. "When a rock tumbles down a mountain, it does not stop until it reaches the bottom."

"But it could be deflected." Holmes replied.

"That will not change the outcome. The rock will find the bottom. And you, my friend, should not stand in its way. A tumbling rock is an unthinking force of nature."

<•••>

Holmes had ensconced himself in a chair opposite Lestrade's desk. "What have you learned thus far?"

"We interviewed the guards further. The powder used in the gun, and the twenty-four pound ball, were taken from a storeroom attached to the barracks—kept there for ceremonial use. With the discovery of the diamond, we've rattled the door of every fence in the city, made the rounds of all the jewelers in Hatton Garden—all to no avail."

Lestrade grimaced, "We have no solid clues at this point."

"I have taken a more circuitous route, Inspector."

Holmes went on to describe his conversations with Dr. Stone, the Maharaja, and Captain McGilney.

Lestrade listened intently. "Then, you suspect the Captain is involved?"

"Yes. That is the one noteworthy thread that hangs from this morbid tapestry. I suggest you pull on it and see what unravels. The other is the boy. The victim appears to be his father. The lad may have information that could be helpful."

"If what you say is correct, the lad's an orphan now. He needs to be taken in."

Holmes's face took on an icy glare. "You mean deported to Australia, Canada, or some other far flung bit of the Empire! Out of sight, out of mind, eh?"

"No need to get your dander up, Mr. Holmes—it's not my job to manage the orphans."

"I tell you, the lad will be better off in the slums of Spitalfields than in the clutches of our benevolent government."

A silence ensued before Holmes spoke again. "I will find the boy and leave the Captain to you. Please make detailed notes. If the boy turns up at the gate, hold him for me."

"How will you find the nipper, Holmes?"

"I believe soundings are called for here."

"Soundings" was a term used to describe the infiltration of a gang or community of people. It often required Holmes to take on the persona of "everyman"—the art of being invisible in plain sight. These investigative theatrics were one of the ways in which Sherlock Holmes indulged his capricious nature.

The next morning, Holmes made his way to Lumber Court near St. Giles to buy used clothing. The lady proprietors were incredulous when he requested tattered, unwashed men's clothing. His pretext: A fancy dress party.

Holmes took his morning cup before a mirror. His "dramaturgical kit," as Watson called it, was spread before him. He squinted into the mirror, looking for a character that would be at home on Brushfield or Hanbury streets—someone whose queries would not raise alarm.

In most ways, Sherlock Holmes was a man at peace with himself. It wasn't discontent that had him creating a new persona. Rather, he felt a lovely release when he is able to get outside of his own skin. His innate nature could be confining in some ways. Cocaine provided one avenue of escape. However, becoming someone other than Sherlock Holmes provided interesting perspectives, and was often amusing.

There was something else . . . from his childhood. His auntie Beatrix had told him and Mycroft stories about changelings—fairy creatures who put their offspring in place of newborn human babes. At the time, he imagined that *he* was a changeling. That memory haunted him now, as he stared into the mirror, darkening his face with a coffee-colored oil. A changeling. That would explain much.

His beard growth wasn't what he would prefer, but he had matted his hair by combing honey-coated fingers over his head. He would put a pebble in his left shoe to help him affect a slight limp.

Admiring his creation in the looking glass, he baptized him: "Ralph . . . Ralphie—yes."

Within the hour Holmes found himself standing before The Vine Tavern in the center of Mile End. The clapboard building was chipped and peeling. The front door was open to invite passers-by.

Upon entering, Holmes was met with the smell of sour ale and acrid smoke that cast a veil over the patrons. What conversation there had been became muted. The barman looked his way, but the clientele starred silently into their glasses as if to divine the future—which would not be rosy for the likes of them.

Holmes walked to the bar and ordered a pint of bitters, then found a dim corner from where he could make his study. There were costers here, and a city-man with his broken umbrellas leaning against the bar. One patron had a noticeable gift of the gab—a mush-faker. He had a sunken, loose-skinned face punctuated with a waxed ginger-grey mustache. He was using crocus Latin to sell pills that he claimed would cure arthritis, tuberculosis, and measles, among other illnesses.

"I'm not a *medicus licentiatus*," the quack said, "but I found this *medicamentum prodigiosum* in Egypt—completely unknown to modern medicine. Why if this got out, half the physicians in London would be on the street. The inscription in the Egyptian tomb, where I found it, came with a warning from the dead."

"Like as not," replied his would-be customer, "I expect there may be some dead in this country that would, if they could speak, give us a warnin' about your miracle cure. I would as soon swallow a brass knocker as your pill."

Onlookers jeered. The quack closed his valise and stalked off.

Holmes hunched himself over and limped toward the barman. "Pardon me, sir, do you 'ave any need of a rat-catcher 'ereabouts?"

"What are you implying?"

"No offense, sir. I was told that someone was recruiting rat-catchers, and I'm the best."

"Best talk with that dodgy bleeder over there—Alf. He's got 'is ear to the ground hereabouts. For a pint, he'll tell you all 'e knows."

Holmes jostled himself up to the bar next to Alf. The man had swollen eyes, distorted features, and a slovenly appearance that announced that he had done little with his life.

"Mi name's Ralphie," Holmes said. "I'm told you might know of someone in need of a rat-catcher."

"Who told you that?"

Holmes pointed to the barman.

Alf pulled back to better take in the man next to him. "You're a ratter, are you?"

"Uncommon good."

"Well, there was a bloke looking for rat-catchers a week ago. Ain't seen him since."

"Very well. Thank you."

Holmes was aware that, if you wish to engage someone in conversation, shared pursuits or passions are helpful, but shared problems constitute the finest glue for binding and bonding human beings.

Holmes scratched his chin. "I must be findin' work, but I thought I would quench my thirst. Can I offer you another pint? A workin' man can ill afford a little libation, what wiv the new government's tax on beer."

"Aye, but they didn't tax their fine wines," Alf remarked.

"As if we 'ain't got to bear our own burdens, we must carry the rich 'uns on our shoulders an' all."

Thus, a wee bit of whining, and six pennies, put Holmes on Ugly's trail.

"A rat-catchers boy, you say," Alf nodded. "Aye, I recall now. An uncomely little fella as scutters about in Spitalfields Market. The costers an' stallmen 'ave taken 'im under their wings." He flits about like a fly—everywhere an' nowhere. Don't know as I recollect 'is name."

"And he catches rats as well?"

"Aye, wiv 'is good for nothin' fahver. The boy brings 'is pennies to 'is fahver who does naught but 'ang about in the Ten Bells. Give that man a shillin', and he'll melt it into gin."

No sooner had Holmes entered the Ten Bells than he spied Ugly—no doubt expecting his father might show up. Retrieving a hat that had fallen on the floor, Ugly brushed it off with the cuff of his jacket, and presented it to its owner who was drooping over his drink. The man ruffled the lad's hair and presented him with a penny.

Ugly retrieved jackets, brought empty glasses to the bar, propped up gentlemen slouching into their drinks, fetched darts, gathered rubbish on the floor, and found countless ways to make himself useful. Many of these small gestures earned him a penny or two.

Holmes finished his drink and headed for the door. As he had hoped, Ugly was waiting to open the door.

"Thank you, Ugly."

The boy sized up the disheveled man before him. "Hey, you're the toff at the army gate."

From the mouths of babes, Holmes thought. "You've quite an eye, Ugly."

"You're a strange one, sir, if you don't mind my sayin'," Ugly remarked, squinting to more fully to take in Holmes's bedraggled costume.

"Not at all," Holmes answered. "How are you going on? Did your father find his way home?"

"Nah, he's off again," Ugly shrugged. "Not a homebody, you see."

Holmes stood quietly. His mind was spinning. He wondered what it was in the nature of some men that made abandoning a child so easy.

"How do you make your living when your father's not about?"

"A few pence 'ere, a few there. I makes me own way. The rat-catchin' got me a little." The boy looked Holmes in the eye. "Mi' Da comes 'ome wiv the traps an' tells me not to worry . . . we're on the upgrade . . . big, fair, and square, he says. Now, 'e's nowhere to be found."

"When was that?"

"The day afore I seen you at that army place."

"Maybe I can retrieve the traps for you," Holmes said. "In the meanwhile, I could use your help. There's a shilling in it for you."

Ugly's eyes widened, and then, as quickly, narrowed.

"I am looking for some men with a monkey," Holmes explained.

"Like an organ-grinder?"

"No, these fellows would have dark skin, bare feet . . . natives. Have you seen anyone like that?

Ugly scratched his head. "No. Don't reckon you'll find the likes of them in Spitalfields."

"I don't imagine you will. But, I was thinking that you might help me to find them. Maybe your mates could help. There's a half-crown prize."

"They may sir."

"Can you take me to them?"

Ugly balked, "Be'er if I was to take 'em to you. Clapham Common, do you know the place?"

"I do."

"I can meet you there to-morra at noon."

"Very well, then."

Holmes arrived at Clapham Common promptly at noon. Ugly was waiting alone.

"What of your mates, Ugly?"

"There, sir." He pointed.

In the shadows, under the trees lining the park, were a number of undersized ruffians in rags. As Holmes perused the motley crew, Ugly waved them forward. "Mi mates was shocked when I told 'em about you. They think as toffs can't be trusted."

"You can trust me, Ugly," Holmes said.

"Well, sir, what about the monkey men, and the old clothes?"

Holmes smiled, "Think I'm barmy, do you?"

"Rich'uns 'as funny ways."

The boys swaggered up to Holmes and Ugly like legitimate kings. Leading them was a familiar face—Wiggins. He had a red kerchief about his neck. His hands were stuffed into his pockets. A broad grin spread across his face as he spied Holmes.

"Lord above! You're a sight for sore eyes, Mr. 'Olmes," Wiggins exclaimed. "You know these fellows."

Holmes recognized Ruck, Snape, and Gordi.

"Ugly says you want us to find some blokes." Gordi wrinkled up his nose, "Said there's a shillin' for news on 'em, 'an' 'ahf a crown when we find 'em."

"*If* you find them," said Holmes.

"They're as good as caught," Wiggins boasted.

Holmes continued: "The fellows we are looking for are dusky-skinned."

"Darkies," Ugly explained.

"No, Indians," Holmes replied.

"But when we find 'em, we gets 'ahf-a-crown," Wiggins repeated.

"Yes Wiggins. It is safe to say that, if you find the men, you will all share in that compensation. If you find them, leave them to me. They're dodgy devils." Turning to Ugly he added, "You, in particular, Ugly. These men may like to put their hands on you. Be wary."

Wiggins answered: "We can take care of Ugly."

Ugly nodded in affirmation.

"I'll leave you to it, then," Holmes said, holding out his card, "You can find me at this address."

And so, with this tenuous agreement, the Baker Street irregulars were formally enlisted.

As they parted, Holmes whispered to Wiggins: "A private word, if you will, Wiggins."

The leader turned to the boys who were waiting for him. "Need a word with Mr. 'Olmes. Go on now. I'll catch up."

Wiggins' sister Tessa ran to him and grabbed his trouser leg.

"My sis won't be a bother, Mr. 'Olmes," Wiggins said.

Holmes looked into Wiggins' eyes. "I need you to watch out for Ugly."

"We look after one anuvver. Not to worry."

"Yes, well," Holmes paused. "His father is dead. He doesn't know it . . . yet. If I give you a few quid will you see that he has what he needs?"

"We'll take care of the lad wiv or wivout your money. But I'll take your contribution just the same," Wiggins replied.

Holmes took a five-pound note from his pocket and handed it over. "This is for Ugly."

"And Ugly will get the benefit of it. You 'ave mi word."

Holmes nodded. "Thank you. And . . . one more thing . . . nothing about his father for now."

"As you like," Wiggins replied. "You needn't look so grim, Mr. Holmes—there's more orphans than rats in Spitalfields!"

Holmes made his way to 8, Whitehall Place and the offices of Scotland Yard. Lestrade's den was on the second floor overlooking the Thames. It was unusual for him to be in his quarters, for he preferred to be out and about amid the scenes of crimes—"more hands than head!" Holmes was known to remark. But, what he lacked in guile, Lestrade more than made up for in doggedness. When he got his teeth into a case, he bore down with a vengeance.

The broad smile on Lestrade's sallow face told Holmes that the Inspector's interview with Captain McGilney had borne fruit.

"You found your boy?" Lestrade began.

Holmes nodded. "And it appears your interview at the barracks was helpful."

"Captain McGilney walked a thin line between appearing helpful, and being no help at all. And, we caught him in a lie."

"Of what sort?" Holmes asked.

"He told us that he was ordered to watch over the rat-catchers. But, when we interviewed his commander, we were told that the captain requested that assignment. What do you make of that?"

"Captain McGilney does not wish to leave the barracks. Either he is waiting for someone, or he is guarding something there."

"A treasure, you think?"

"Yes, and your visit may prompt him to flee with the goods."

"We didn't have enough to bring him in, but I set a man to watch him."

No sooner were the words out of the inspector's mouth, than a clerk poked his head into the office. "Just got word from Mayfield, sir. It appears there's been another murder at the barracks."

Lestrade and Holmes hurried to the Royal Artillery Barracks. A constable, waiting at the stairway, pointed upstairs. Upon reaching the top, Lestrade and Holmes peered down a long corridor to where another constable was gazing through an open door.

"Mayfield," Lestrade called. The constable turned.

"Here, sir."

"Were you the first on the scene?" Lestrade asked.

"The first from the force, sir. It was one of the guards who found . . ."

Constable Mayfield pulled a notepad from his pocket and flipped it open. "Connelly . . . who discovered the captain here." Now reading his notes: "Corporal James Connelly . . . thought he heard a noise emanating from the barracks. He waited . . . a bit too long, I suppose. When he made his rounds, he found the Captain as you see him here."

The feet of the bloody corpse were tied to the legs of a chair. The torso was lashed to the chair back, and pushed up against a small round table. His mouth was stuffed with a cloth or handkerchief, held in place with a leather belt wrapped tightly around his skull. His left hand lay mangled upon the tabletop. Holmes pushed it to one side revealing a deep gash in the surface.

The dead man's right arm dangled loosely at his side. Below it, on the floor, was a pen. Across the man's bare back were dozens of tiny cuts from which blood had oozed, dripped, and pooled on the floor.

Holmes circled the table and bent lower in an effort to see the face of the victim, which hung mere inches from the top of the table. Holmes pulled out his glass to examine the rope binding the hands of the corpse.

"A manila hemp rope, commonplace in East Asia. It's not tarred, as is the practice here."

As he examined the wounds, Holmes emitted a small exclamation: "Ah-h-h-h, yes." He put his finger to the neck of the dead man and brought it to his nose. "A puncture wound."

"Would you mind," Holmes asked, "if I move the body slightly, there is something strange about his face?"

"Do what you must, Mr. Holmes."

Holmes took two fingers and slowly lifted the head. Lestrade came around and peered over Holmes's shoulder. Constable Mayfield leaned in and jolted with a gasp. The eyes of the wretched captain had been gouged out, and the mucosa dangled down upon his cheeks.

Holmes motioned to the constable: "If you will, Mayfield, please hold his head in place."

The policeman's face screwed up into a sour look as he used a single finger from each hand to balance the head. Holmes bent down with his glass and peered into the gory sockets.

"Inspector, you will notice the small scratches surrounding the eye sockets. His eyes were scratched out . . . by a small animal. And on the scalp there are tears and bites— again, from an animal—a monkey I believe."

Holmes released the gag and pried open the mouth. As he anticipated, a scroll of parchment lay within.

Holmes stood up and began to walk about in the room.

"Look here," he said, pointing to a mottle of bloody barefooted prints on the floorboards.

Holmes turned to the constable, "Constable Mayfield, would you be so kind as to see how far you can follow these footprints? Be careful not to tread on them. They will fade away. Do the best you can."

"A monkey!" Lestrade exclaimed. "This whole affair is becoming more perplexing by the day."

"On the contrary, Inspector. The pieces are coming together nicely. The Captain here was tortured."

"That much is clear."

"Of course, but let's tell this story as it unfolded: The small puncture in the back of Captain McGilney's neck was made by a blow dart . . . tipped with a narcotic of some kind. This incapacitated the Captain while he was gagged and lashed to the chair. A similar method was likely used on the fellow at the parade grounds."

Holmes moved about the table illustrating the process. "The Captain was awakened when his left hand was pierced by a knife that fastened it to the table. His muffled cry was the noise that the guard heard.

"The Captain was questioned. Being gagged, he was given a piece of paper and pen upon which to write his answers. You can see the paper's shape outlined by the spatters of blood around it."

Holmes moved behind the corpse. "He was tortured with tiny slashes on his back. From the looks of it, a very fine, sharp knife was used. As you know the human back has many nerves, and is extremely sensitive. This methodical process amounted to a slow, agonizing scourging."

Lestrade shrugged nonchalantly, "What you say makes sense, and the motive, you believe, was stolen treasure?"

"Yes, I suspect McGilney was involved with the theft from the Padmanabhaswamy Temple. And, I believe it is safe to say that the assassins . . . there are at least two of them . . . have now found the hiding place and secured the return of the treasure."

"How can you be certain?"

"The paper upon which he was writing is not here. If the secret of the hiding place was not forthcoming, why take the writing paper?"

The Constable returned. Holmes eagerly looked up.

"And, what have you discovered, Mayfield?" Holmes asked.

"Well sir . . . Inspector . . . the foot prints go down this hallway here to the left. As you say, they fade away, but there was only one likely avenue—the rear fire stairway. So, down I went. Because they're seldom used, the smudges in the dust on the stairs showed me that someone had been down there recently."

"Excellent, Mayfield," Holmes said. "You will make a fine inspector someday."

Lestrade bristled, "Yes, good work, Mayfield. Did you look further?"

"No, Inspector. The stairs go to the ground floor, then they join a landing with another stairway to the cellar."

Holmes piped up: "I suggest we explore the cellar immediately!"

Holmes strode out of the room with Lestrade and Mayfield in tow. They made their way to a dank, dark and airless cellar. Inspector Lestrade lit a match. Prints in the dirt floor confirmed that the assassins had been there.

"And the monkey tracks again," Homes remarked. "The beast must have ridden upon the fellow's shoulder."

Lighting another match the Inspector peered into the cavernous space beyond. Something near the corner glinted. "There, Holmes!"

Lying along the wall, near the corner, was a small cage. "A rat-trap," Lestrade observed.

"Yes," Holmes replied. "The rat-catcher was here, of course. Look about, constable. The remains of a hiding place are hereabouts. We need more light."

The constable pulled a curtain away from a nearby window. The dust swirled and billowed in the light.

Lestrade coughed and fanned himself, "Damn it, Mayfield! Use some sense."

As the dust cleared, the constable pointed to what appeared to be a pile of rubbish near a boiler. Lying open was an olive-drab trunk with items scattered about it. Holmes lit a match and seized the lid of the metal-trimmed trunk. The union jack had been painted on the top and, on one side, the name: McGilney.

"The lock was easily managed," Holmes observed. Holding his match closer to the hasp he added, "—and recently picked."

"So, the scoundrels have their treasure," the Inspector noted. "They'll be on the run."

"Yes, but two brown fellows with a monkey on their back should be easy to find."

Holmes stepped back and spread his arms wide. "Nearly all the pieces are in place. The poor soul who was blown to bits could not resist a look inside a locked trunk, where he found the jewels. He thought one or two missing items might go unnoticed."

Lestrade's eyes widened, "Yes, and the murderers, who'd been on the trail of Captain McGilney, saw the rat catcher leave early one day and grew suspicious. They followed him, caught him, took his loot, and did him in so that the Captain got an eye-full."

"Yes, we have the story now," Holmes agreed.

"The young boy, Ugly, needs to know."

"Yes," Holmes mumbled, "Watson is marvelous in situations such as this, but I suppose the duty falls to me now."

Holmes was momentarily struck with a realization that the boy had endeared himself to him. His unusual upbringing had left Ugly with a rare purity that appealed to Holmes's quest for truth and authenticity. He wondered if the death of the boy's father would purge the lad's spirit of his innocence.

Then, just as quickly, Holmes shook off his transitory sentimentality. He straightened up, grabbed the rat-trap, and marched toward the stairway. "All that remains is to find the killers."

Holmes had planned to go to Spitalfields Market in search of Ugly, but decided to return to his flat instead—a feeble attempt to put off the grim conversation. However, as it is often wont to do, fate proved implacable.

When Holmes arrived at his address, there, sitting on the doorstep, was Wiggins.

"I've got news, Mr. 'Olmes," Wiggins announced, as Holmes stepped from the cab.

"You found the men?"

"No. But there's a chancer walkin' about Spitalfields, bold as you please, lookin' to find Ugly."

"Who is this?" Holmes asked.

"Alf's 'is name. E's a sly' un. For a little money, he'd sell 'is own muvver."

"I know the fellow. You say he was asking where to find Ugly?"

"Not by name, sir." Wiggins said. "Lookin' for the rat-catcher's boy."

"Yes, it seems Alf is in the employ of the assassins."

Holmes shouted to the waiting cabbie, "Spitalfields Market, with haste!" Then, to Wiggins, "Hurry, get in. We've no time to lose."

As they made their way, Holmes shouted to the driver to hurry up. Wiggins seemed amused.

"Not to worry, sir," Wiggins explained, "Ugly can take care of 'is self."

"Not with these devils."

The cab barely rolled to a halt before Holmes leaped out and flipped a sovereign at the cabbie.

"Where is Ugly?"

"He said he'd wait at our place."

"Take me there now."

Wiggins led Holmes through a labyrinth of streets behind the market into a vaguely familiar timber yard that had a hidden entry. A stairway led to a lower passage of moldy brick. They came to a doorway covered with a burlap curtain. As they approached, they heard voices speaking in a strange tongue. Holmes put his fingers to his lips and motioned for Wiggins to stay put. Quietly, he picked up a board from a nearby pile of warped lumber, and crept closer to the curtain.

Holmes peeked round the curtain, and in the flickering light of a lantern, saw two sinewy Asians on their knees before Ugly. They were chanting. The only word Holmes could decipher was "Vishnu."

The monkey spotted Holmes and screeched. The assassin's heads snapped round.

The dark men's eyes sparkled as they stood in a state of aggressive delight. The bigger one pulled a curved knife from his belt. The other, the monkey on his shoulder, raised his right forearm and twisted his wrist. A sharp metal clank sounded as a blade sprang from a gauntlet strapped to his forearm. It protruded six inches beyond the end of the man's hand.

The smaller fellow gave a sharp command and the monkey leaped from his shoulder toward Holmes. With one swing of his board Holmes caught the monkey in flight and dashed him against the wall.

"A trifle! What else have you got?"

The man lunged his armored fist toward Holmes who side-stepped him, and brought the board down solidly on the back of the assassin's head. In that same moment, Ugly grabbed the lantern from the table and crashed it upon the larger native's back as he lunged at Holmes. The oil splashed and burst into flame.

The fellow's screams brought Wiggins. Before Holmes could react, the two boys began pummeling the assassin who was writhing on the floor in an effort to put out the flames. Holmes pulled the boys off, but not before Wiggins had stamped on the man's chest, driving all the air from his lungs.

Ugly bellowed, "All for one, one for all."

When Lestrade and several constables arrived, the monkey was in a sturdy sack, and the Bengali assassins were bound, hand and foot, sitting against the wall. Wiggins stood guard with an imposing piece of lumber. Holmes was examining the metal gauntlet that he had removed from one of the men.

"This hidden blade is quite a clever device—a favorite of assassins. A particular movement of the wrist and arm releases the blade. You can find drawings of one such apparatus in Leonardo da Vinci's Codex. In early designs, the device required the removal of the ring finger—though not with this particular mechanism."

Lestrade was exasperated. "Holmes, stop prattling on about hidden blades. How did you find these fellows?"

"I didn't find them. These extraordinary boys found them, and their pet. They were after little Ugly here."

"You saved the lad, then."

"Hardly," Holmes exclaimed. "Ugly's looks saved him."

The inspector heaved a huge sigh, "Holmes, please don't talk in riddles."

"These assassins are devout Hindus. The god Vishnu is enshrined in the Padmanabhaswamy Temple. It is Vishnu's treasure that was stolen. There is a legend about the building of Padmanabhaswamy Temple thousands of years ago. A sage prayed for a vision of Vishnu. The tale is an extraordinarily long one, but the gist of it is that Vishnu finally appeared— but in the guise of an ugly, mischievous boy."

Holmes turned to Ugly. "Remember Ugly, whatever others might say, you were once considered to be a god."

"So the assassin, having seen Ugly with his father . . ." The inspector froze. "Well . . . well, we can talk of this later."

"What's all this about my Da?" Ugly asked.

Lestrade turned to the constables. "Best get these blokes put away—and mind that monkey."

The constables took charge of their prisoners and, together with Lestrade, departed.

"Mr. Holmes?" Ugly said, "What's all this now?"

"Ugly, come over here." The lad sat down next to Holmes. "I have some bad news." The boy remained quiet and wide-eyed. The gravity in Holmes's face foreshadowed his news.

"Your father is dead."

"No sir, just off again."

"No Ugly, I am certain that he is dead. It was those fellows Wiggins and you caught who killed him. We've got them now, and they'll be dealt with properly."

Tears pooled in his eyes. Ugly's lip quivered. As the tears began to flow down his cheeks, he sniffed, and wiped his eyes with the cuff of his coat. He reached into his pocket and pulled out a small cotton bag bound with twine.

"Me Da gave me this . . . to 'old for 'im."

Holmes held out his hand. "Let us see what it is, shall we?"

The moment the sack was in Holmes's hand he knew what lay inside. He carefully unwrapped the missing headdress ornament, and held it up to the light. It was fashioned like a necklace, with rubies that sparkled, splashing red glimmers on the walls of the room. Holmes held his breath as he looked upon Ugly's innocent face that now appeared to be spattered with blood.

"I did not know your father, Ugly, but I can tell you that he loved you. These jewels are what the native men were looking for. Your father died keeping that secret keeping you safe. Whatever else he was, your Da was a brave fellow."

"Like the Musketeers," Ugly added.

"Yes, like the Musketeers."

"All for one . . ." Ugly said, half-heartedly.

"And one for all," Holmes replied.

Holmes pressed his calling card in Ugly's hand. "If you need my help . . ."

Ugly nodded.

— <•••> —

For many years hence, a knock at Holmes's door triggered a transitory image of that uncommonly ugly little boy standing before him. When he found himself in the Spitalfields Market, Holmes could not resist glancing over his shoulder. Even today, memories of Ugly mingle with feelings of apprehension and hope.

CHAPTER IV

FOR A BRIEF MOMENT, Holmes felt as if time had stopped—then he impulsively pivoted around, thinking he might catch a glimpse of S. P. Fields.

The crowd had thinned. Only a scant dozen patrons were scattered about the gallery in small groups of two or three. Holmes stood alone.

He had been caught like a fish on the line. The photography exhibition was the hook, and dangling at the end of it were the faces of his irregular army. He had always been the angler—yet tonight, Holmes found himself on the hook.

He casually wandered toward a nearby couple having a quiet conversation before a photograph of young people gathered at the entrance of an alleyway. A large crowd of children were posing—or attempting to do so, as the boys jostled one another playfully. The man was pointing to the scene. He was loosely built and dressed in a casual manner—a collarless shirt, a shabby black jacket, and baggy woolen trousers.

"That's me," he remarked. "I grew up near Dorset Street. We called it Dossett Street, on account of all the dosses."

"Dosses?" the woman replied.

In contrast to her companion, the young woman's presentation was a valiant attempt at respectability. She was nicely turned out in a blue chambray dress. A white silk shawl stretched around her shoulders, which she held in place with both hands. With her delicate features and freckled nose, she had a rather childlike appearance.

"Dosses are large common lodging houses," the man answered, "some had a hundred beds or more."

"And that is where these children lived?" the woman asked.

"Lived? No—most on 'em lived on the street. They would be fortunate if they had tuppence for a night's lodging."

"Tuppence for a room?"

The man laughed. "A room? For a bed, girl—and if you were small, you'd 'ave to share it."

She turned to take a better look at the man, her faced twisted into disbelief. Surbiton had just encountered Spitalfields. This juxtaposition amused Holmes, and pleased him as well. There was a time, he remembered, when no one would have dared mention Dorset Street, which is still haunted by memories of Jack the Ripper.

As the couple ambled off toward the next image, Holmes cautiously approached the photograph that had been the focus of their attention. There were nearly thirty children gathered there—the smaller youths stood in the front, and the larger ones behind. Some of the faces were blurred because they could not hold the pose. His first inclination was to search their faces, but he found himself drawn to their feet. Most had no shoes.

Holmes began a more in-depth study of this photograph entitled: *Miller's Court.* A few of the subjects were smiling, but most wore dull scowls. One woman held a baby high over her head as if to say: *'Ere's mi little Georgie, ain't 'e a bit o jam?* This might well be the only photograph of Georgie. Most of those pictured had long since faded into the moldering bricks lining this alley. But here, tonight, was a testimony that they had once been part of God's creation.

Holmes noticed the just departed young couple standing before another photograph. However, the woman's eyes were not focused on the image, but her companion. *Choices were being made*, Holmes thought. He approached.

"Pardon my interruption," Holmes began, "Do you happen to know if the author of these images is about—S. P. Fields?

The man pulled an invitation from his back pocket and held it out. "I received this invitation. I didn't know this Fields chap, but he stirred my curiosity enough to get Liz and me here tonight."

"Ah," Holmes answered. "Are you enjoying the experience?"

"Enjoying? I was—until I found myself among the subjects."

"Not all the memories are good, then?"

The man drew back and cocked his head. There was something behind his eyes—ghosts or memories held captive.

"You're not Mr. Fields, are you?" the young man inquired.

Holmes smiled. "No, my name is Sherlock Holmes."

He anticipated some sign of recognition, but it did not come. *Not a reader*, Holmes thought.

"Mr. Holmes, I can only say that my experience was not entirely a pleasant one. Not all the memories are good, as you say."

Holmes retrieved the invitation from his coat pocket and held it out. "I quite understand."

The two invitations, side-by-side, put a full stop to the conversation. This interlude disturbed the woman. "Enjoy your evening, Mr. Holmes," she said.

The two men locked eyes for a brief moment, searching from some vaguely understood commonality. What they held in common was not an acquaintance, but a question: *What is happening here?*

The woman tugged gently on her escort's sleeve. He nodded and turned away. Holmes watched them for a time wondering if they might be leaving the show. They crossed the hallway into the next gallery, which was arranged in a similar manner.

Holmes shook off his mood and made a broad, slow scan of the surroundings. It did not appear that Fields was about.

Holmes found himself missing Watson's companionship. His old chum accepted things as they were—reality as it is, not as he wished it to be. Holmes admired this trait that undoubtedly made Watson a good soldier. And so, reflecting upon the good Doctor, he mumbled: "Half a league, half a league, half a league onward," as he strode into the next gallery.

Two men surrounded a portrait at the far end of the gallery. They were chuckling and pointing. Their conversation was garbled, but Holmes picked out a few words: "All hope abandon ye who enter here . . ."

The men laughed.

Holmes approached the portrait that was the focus of the men's feeble jest. *Here's another*, he thought peering at the portrait.

SNAPE:
A BLACKSMITH'S SON,
WHO FORGED A LIFE
FROM THE RUBBISH
IN THE THAMES.

The lad was not quite a man, but already had the muscular torso of an adult. He was resting upon a broken chair leaning near a door, as if guarding it. A staff was clenched in his thick right hand. His scarred knuckles attested to his pugilistic prowess. His back was straight. With one finger on his left hand, he pointed at the photographer as a caution. He appeared, for all the world, like a king sitting upon a throne: his kingdom was a ring six yards square.

PART ONE

IT WAS THE YEAR OF THE WHITECHAPEL MURDERS, and all of London was transfixed and terrified. London after dark was a quieter city, except in those spots where "the fancy" was *en vogue*. Sambo Sutton, the former heavyweight bare-knuckles champion, hung his hat at the Black Lion on Drury Lane. There he took on all comers, promising a shilling for every round an opponent remained standing. Of course, the real money was not in the ring, but around it. The prize-ring was the financial prop of the underworld. There, within dim and dank public houses, gambling, drugs, and vice trades flourished and grew. Foolish Corinthians watched bare-chested, bare-knuckled fighters in the ring spatter their blood upon the canvas. Sharps, pickpockets, and prostitutes circled, scavenging for coin.

Snape said it was the shillings he wanted, but he yearned to, as he put it, "let himself out." As Wiggins had often noted, Snape was built for bruising, not mudlarking. While it was on a whim that he decided to put himself in the ring, he knew, well enough, that he must prepare for the contest. He pulled Wiggins aside one afternoon and told him his plan to take on Sambo Sutton. His friend grinned, and slapped him on the back.

Wiggins "obtained" four leather dog collars that he used to strap two three-pound hammers on the inside of Snape's forearms. Snape wrapped his fists around the heads, and held them up before his face, smiling. He liked the feel of the cold steel in his fists.

"Snape, me boy, your blows are like 'ammers. You'll jammer away at Sambo til 'e crumbles."

"Right-o," Snape smiled, and began jabbing in the air.

Wiggins pulled a watch from his pocket. "Keep 'em up there for three minutes."

Snape continued to shadow-box as Wiggins rattled on: "Move—move, Snape! Stay on your toes. Sambo's flat-footed. Keep moving. 'E'll never land a punch."

Snape raised himself up on his toes and bobbed, weaved and shuffled around in the dirt of the courtyard. His arms grew heavy and his jabs moved more slowly, but he never relaxed. As he felt the pain in his shoulders he let out a groan and smiled, using his pain to propel him on—as he had always done.

"Pick 'em up, Snape. One more minute!"

KIM KRISCO

Snape let out a growl and jabbed faster and faster. He continued to groan and growl.

"That's three," Wiggins said.

Snape kept punching away more rapidly. The pain invigorated him. He liked to feel his body work. It was a wondrous machine that never seemed entirely his. At times, Snape felt like a guest in his own body. He talked to it as it moved and toiled: "Come on. Do your stuff. That's it. That's it."

A young woman entered the yard. She was thin—too thin, some said. She had been ill the last few days. Not bed-ridden, but unable to take her place among the Covent Garden flower-women as her mother had done before her recent death.

Fanny squinted at Snape as he pranced about. Wiggins ignored her, but when Snape caught her eye, he turned to her like a little boy, his arms at his side, shrugging his shoulders.

The woman shook her head. "Ma would 'ave a bloomin' fit if she saw you."

"Ma's gone, Fanny."

"Yes, and so now there's just me. And I'm not abaht to spend my life lookin' after a droolin' cripple."

Wiggins turned.

Fanny put her hand up. "I want nuffin' from you, Wiggins. If Snape follows in your footsteps, he'll be in Newgate before 'is next birthday."

Snape grimaced. "Fanny, it's just a few rounds—a few shillings. I'll be . . ."

She turned away, but not so quickly as to hide her expression of deep disgust.

Fanny's life had not been good since their mother died the year before. The loss of income from their mother's

88

flower sales was bad enough, but worse was the loss of their mother's firm hand—the only thing that had kept Snape from crossing the line into a life of thievery. And, shortly after the funeral, Jack left her. He came and went, but his simple affection had once provided an anchor that kept Fanny from drifting into the rougher seas of life. Now, she felt trapped—imprisoned by class and circumstance.

Wiggins patted Snape on the back. "Fanny's not well. But she 'as the pluck to put you in your place—and me too, come to that."

Later that morning Wiggins brought Snape a bucket of beef brine. "You put your face in this, and soak your fists everyday. It'll toughen your hide. I'll bring some vinegar to-morra. You'll use that too."

When he was not training, Snape walked about with the hammers still strapped to his forearms—now on the outside. This caused curious looks, and more than a few remarks from the other mudlarks on the Thames.

Clutching a sack in one hand, Snape gathered up bits of wood, rope, coal and iron that fell from barges and boats around the wharfs and shore when the tide went out. His take was six to eight pence a day. As he cashed in, he thought: *Every ninety-second round in the ring with Sambo was two days less on the Thames.*

It was a three-mile walk from Spitalfields to Drury Lane. The entourage had grown by two during the last weeks of training. Snape and his brother, Little Mac, and Wiggins with his diminutive sister, Tessa, entered the Black Lion. The two siblings walked in the shadows of their brothers, their eager eyes taking in the motley assemblage scattered about the tavern.

The bar was crowded with men from every class of society, drinking, smoking and chatting. The Black Lion was an austere place, devoid of the adornments generally found in other public houses. The regular patrons groused about the gawkers who had come to witness the P.R. as they called it.

Canvas had been stretched out across the floor between the bar and the fireplace, and four posts fastened to the floorboards were strung with heavy ropes to form the ring. There was a long high balcony running along one wall, just wide enough for a row of chairs to be lined up along the railing. The sun had not set, but the tables were already filled with onlookers waiting for the festivities to begin. They always began the same way.

A small wooden platform was lowered over the center of the ring. A roar arose from the crowd. The gas lamps on the walls around the ring flared higher as if fueled by the multitude's erupting energy. The platform stood eight feet above the floor of the ring.

The barman rang a brass bell, near the bar, three times. The crowd's clamoring diminished slightly. The curtains in the doorway next to the bar parted, and Sambo Sutton pranced into the room—all seventeen stone of him. His dark skin glistened with sweat. His body was thick and solid. His legs were massive, with calves that bulged to twice the size of an average man's. His eyes were wide and eager.

An old, bearded mariner sitting beside the ring arose and ducked into the ring with an antique hornpipe. The crowd cheered as Sambo walked to the ring, lifted the rope, and shifted inside. He nodded to the piper, crossed his arms over his chest, and began to dance. The piper's melody was an odd mix of gay and strange. The piper moved closer to the center of the ring and played louder and louder. The black pugilist positioned himself under the platform, reached his arms down, and slowly lifted himself into an arm-stand. His feet pressed against the platform. The ship's bell rang three times, and Sambo began to dance the hornpipe, upside down, on the elevated platform. A thunderous cheer exploded, hands clapping, cheers and toasts blending in a bizarre cacophony.

Snape and Wiggins settled their young siblings on a table in the back of the room, and slowly pushed through the throng to the edge of the ring. There they got their first real look at the ex-champion. His hands, which where now holding him up, were huge—fingers thicker than Balson sausages. Sweat dripped from the boxer's forehead and puddled on the canvas.

With a flourish of the hornpipe, Sambo pushed himself to his feet and raised his arms high to invite the applause and cheers from the crowd. His body, which had to be nearly fifty years old, was still well muscled. His chest and arms glistened with sweat. He wore black knee britches, and leather shoes that wrapped around his ankles.

There was little doubt that Sambo Sutton would have the crowd in his corner. Wiggins turned to Snape who had a dazed look on his face.

"Dancin' and fightin' is two different things, Snape."

Snape nodded. Wiggins put his arm on his friend's shoulder.

"He's all show. 'E's old. 'E's not got but five rounds in 'im."

"Five seems like a big number, at the moment."

"You're faster. Stay away from 'im. Work his body."

"Yes," Snape replied, clenching his fists. "I'll work it good."

91

The barman jostled his way past the boys and climbed into the ring. He held a leather pouch high in the air and rattled it. "The Champ will take on all comers—a shilling a round, and 'ahf a crown to any man as knocks him down."

"And a busted nose, to boot," someone hooted.

Snape started to move, but Wiggins pulled him back. "Wait."

A hush came over the tavern as heads turned. Nothing. No one. After a minute, rumbling and grumbling began to mount. The barkeep dangled the pouch over Sambo's head. Sambo nodded.

"Two shillings for every round stood against the champ. Two shillings, and five bob if you knock 'im daahhhn!"

"Now," Wiggins said, slapping Snape on the back.

Snape grabbed the rope and ducked under. The crowd cheered. Sambo smiled. Snape wore trousers cut short, and had bare feet. He pulled his shirt off over his head revealing his massive shoulders and arms. The crowd shouted their approval. The astringent "pickle" used to thicken his skin had darkened his face and hands. His white teeth flashed in a bold contrasting smile.

Snape was two stone shy of Sambo Sutton, but his upper body was larger and more developed. He had only recently ceased to wear the three-pound hammers strapped to his forearms. He swung his arms and fists to loosen them. They felt light and quick.

The barkeeper consulted with Wiggins.

Sambo went to an opposite corner. The barman went to the center of the ring, raising his hands to calm the crowd. Side betting had begun—men leaning into one another, striking deals, and shaking hands.

"The challenger from Spitalfields: Snape the Windjammer Hammer!"

The crowd jeered and laughed.

"And, in the opposite corner, the former champion of England and Wales, Black Sambo Sutton from Covent Garden!"

Sutton danced the hornpipe (right-side up this time) doing quick right-left-right jabs. He paused and held up one finger. The crowd shouted "One." Then, two fingers, "Two." And finally, three fingers, "Three," the crowd obediently chanted. He went back into his dance and jabbing as the crowd's count echoed, "One, two, three."

Ovations filled the room. The barman, who was also to function as the referee, sealed the contract: "Two shillings per round—for Snape, The Windjammer Hammer. Two minute rounds."

Wiggins grimaced. They had lengthened the rounds by thirty seconds.

The barkeeper nodded at Snape and Sambo. The bell clanged. The two pugilists cautiously approached the center of the ring.

Sambo's arms and hands remained at his sides. He put his chin up, inviting a blow. Snape knew better than to take a swing that would throw him off balance. Instead, he snapped a jab to the African's gut.

Sambo sprang to life and moved toward Snape, throwing light punches, sizing up his opponent. His right arm was cocked as he continued to jab with his left. Snape easily deflected the punches, waiting for the big one. It came fast! Snape twisted his head and body away as Sambo's fist grazed his left temple.

Sutton immediately closed in and grappled with Snape, delivering jabs to Snape's kidneys. The boy pushed him off with both fists. As he did so Sambo swung another hard right. Snape ducked low and returned a punch to Sutton's ribs. The

Champion realized that this would not be as simple as one-two-three.

Snape had been knocked off his feet twice in the preceding five rounds. Sutton delivered a crushing blow in the fifth, and then walked to his corner as if the fight were over. The crowd, whose mood had shifted slightly onto Snape's side, let out a communal groan. A smattering of applause and table banging was hushed as Snape rolled over and got up on one knee.

Sutton sneered. He walked slowly toward the boy. Under the reformed regulations it was a foul to hit an opponent who was down, or had one knee and one glove on the mat. Snape looked at Wiggins who was waving from the corner. Wiggins held up his hand with his little finger and index finger pointing upward—then sharply turned them down. *Danger.* Snape got the message. He placed his other glove on the canvas and, with one quick push, rose, shoving his body forward into Sutton who was unable to throw a punch.

The crowd cheered as Sutton became incensed and struggled to disengage himself from Snape's hug. The referee pried the men apart. The two men locked eyes as they separated. Blood was trickling from the corner of Snape's mouth. His knuckles were black, blue and bleeding.

"You've never been closer to hell," Sambo Sutton growled.

"And I'm takin' you with me," Snape replied.

It was no longer a minstrel show for Sutton, or a matter of shillings for Snape.

The fighters were sent to their corners. Wiggins attended to the cut on Snape's lip. As he did so, he noticed a woman standing off in a dim corner of the tavern. Fanny had her shawl draped over her head. Tears trickled down her cheeks. She wagged her finger at Wiggins, and put it to her lips.

In the nineteenth round, Sutton, while bending low to dodge a blow, hit Snape below the belt. The boy doubled over and fell to his knees. The spectators bellowed with cries of "foul" as Sutton shrugged his shoulders in seeming dismay. This should have ended the fight in Snape's favor, but the referee, no novice in the prize-fight stagecraft, shot puzzled looks at the crowd and got down on one knee to look at Snape, who was on all fours, and unable to speak.

As the referee began his count over Snape, the onlookers screamed their disgust and brandished canes and clubs in the air. When the referee held up Sambo Sutton's right arm as a signal of victory, boos arose in place of huzzas. Snape had not won many of the rounds, but he had won the hearts of the people. More than that, for the first time in his life, he was proud of who he was. This was not vanity. It was not about what others thought of him. This feeling sprang from a realization that, who he desired to be, and who he was, were now the same.

PART TWO

TWO days later, Sherlock Holmes found himself gazing through prison bars at the hulking boy sitting at the edge of the bunk in his cell. As the locked turned, Snape looked up. His face was bruised, and his eyes where outlined in a greenish-blue cast. The jailer swung the door open and motioned for Holmes to enter.

"Thank you," Holmes said.

"Mr. 'Olmes?" the boy said in disbelief.

"Wiggins told me you were in a pickle."

"A pickle?" Snape replied. "They've nicked me fer murder, Mr. 'Olmes."

Holmes remained silent.

"I didn't do it," Snape added quickly. "I couldn't 'ave."

Holmes grabbed a small stool from the corner and sat down in front of Snape.

"Tell me everything you can recall," Holmes said.

Snape rubbed his face with both hands as if he were waking from a dream. "Did Wiggins tell you about . . . Fanny?" he began.

Holmes nodded. "She died."

Snape bolted. "She was murdered. That devil killed mi sister!"

"The doctor you're accused of killing?"

"Yes." Snape look down in a sheepish manner. "Fanny was . . . expecting."

"With child?"

"Yes."

"And, she went to this man?"

"First to a fellow by the name of Brevos. He said as 'e couldn't help, but passed 'er on to Dr. Dransfield—the devil as they say I killed."

"You saw Dransfield?"

"Yes."

"And, you beat him," Holmes said, pointing to Snape's bruised fists.

"Nah, nah, Mr. 'Olmes. These hands are a gift from Sambo Sutton. Nah, nah, I saw this doctor and . . . yes . . . I hit 'im . . . hit 'im good in the chest. But he was alive when I left." Snape's head dropped lower. "Perhaps I did. Perhaps I did . . . kill 'im."

Holmes knew more than a dozen ways to kill a man with a punch: a chop to the temple—or the bridge of the nose, or the Adam's apple. Snape just admitted that he had hit Dransfield in the chest. Holmes was also aware that a hard punch to the heart could stop it long enough to bring about death. And a punch to the ribcage could break ribs, and cause internal bleeding.

Holmes leaned closer. "How many times did you hit him?"

"Twice, I swear. Twice in the gut. 'E fell dahn. I kicked 'im and left."

"Where was this? When?

"A shop in Lumber Court, near St. Giles—after dark yesterday."

"Were you seen there?"

"Aye, there was anuvver poor soul—a young girl—waitin' in his office, like my poor Fanny. I told 'er to run. Get away before Dransfield killed 'er."

Snape's lips trembled. His eyes grew glassy. "You didn't see 'er, Mr. Holmes. Fanny was in agony. The bloomin' blood—everywhere!"

Holmes was disquieted. He had always been uncomfortable around expressions of strong emotion. Emotions clouded intellect. As such, Sherlock Holmes had little use for them.

Snape banged his fist into the wall. "'Er funeral's on Friday."

<•••>

"Watson, I need your æsculapian eye," said Holmes. "I have received permission to examine the body of a man who has recently died."

Dr. Watson was always pleased when he found himself helpful to his friend. Holmes was good about inviting Watson's ideas and expertise. However, as the Doctor had learned over the years, Holmes's generous invitations were sometimes an artifice. Holmes would listen patiently to Dr. Watson, and then, almost invariably, launch into an exposition that negated nearly everything the good Doctor had said. This was frustrating, but hardly surprising, as Sherlock Holmes was like most other human beings in one regard: he needed to be right. However, unlike other human beings, Sherlock Holmes usually was. This was fortunate, because Holmes's existence required that he be right. It was an enormous burden, but one that Sherlock Holmes bore well.

"Certainly, Holmes. Who is the fellow to be examined, and on whose behalf are we conducting this examination?"

"It's on behalf of Wiggins' mate, a youth called Snape."

"Is he that rather stout lad who waddles about?"

"No, that is Rumpty. Snape is the ham-fisted youth—fifteen stone, or so, of solid muscle."

"Rumpty, Dumpty, Snape," Watson muttered. "These names mean nothing to me. Why do you meddle in their affairs? *Noblesse oblige*, I suppose."

"I should not use that expression," Holmes shot back. "It carries a dreadful stigma. Those who use it seldom see their societal obligations extending beyond their pocketbooks. They offer the less fortunate a hand, while keeping a foot on their neck."

"Really Holmes, are you beating the drum for William Booth?"

"I am—but will you help me just the same?"

"No question of that, my friend. I suppose I'll never understand you."

"Nor I, you. Fortunately, a lack of understanding does not preclude friendship."

"Well said, Holmes. Whither are we bound?"

"Bethnal Green Mortuary."

The house of the dead on Turville Street was a grim building befitting its function. It had been hurriedly constructed to manage the cholera outbreaks that periodically plagued London's east end. Holmes had arranged, through Inspector Gregson at Scotland Yard, to gain access. A necropsy had been completed, and the coroner was not pleased to learn his examination might be challenged. That is how he interpreted Holmes's request; and, to be fair, his assessment was correct.

A caretaker ushered Holmes and Watson in. The coroner, Dr. Shipman, was waiting next to a marble slab bearing the body of the former Dr. Eric Dransfield. Holmes introduced himself and Dr. Watson with few extraneous words. Dr. Shipman had a vacant look, devoid of life's juices. He was the kind of fellow who would look at a great oak tree and see only wood.

The coroner pulled the sheet away for viewing. The chest of the bloodless corpse had a violet cast. A deep Y-shaped incision had been made in the chest, which extended from each shoulder, down over the breastbone to the abdomen.

With obvious resentment, Dr. Shipman handed Holmes his summary, which Holmes passed on to Watson. Watson read over the brief report.

"Dr. Shipman, I see you only examined one organ, the heart. Why was that?" Watson asked.

"If you notice the bruising of the chest and abdomen, you will see that enormous blows were delivered. There was internal bleeding. The cause of death was *commotio cordis*."

"Agitation of the heart," Holmes said, "resulting in heart failure."

"Yes, Holmes," Watson replied. "The blow disrupts the rhythms of the heart—causing ventricular fibrillation."

"I see," Holmes replied quietly. "Dr. Shipman, may I ask as to how many cases of *commotio cordis* you come across in your . . ."

"Thirty-one years," the coroner answered, assuming an expression of mingled affability.

"In your thirty-one years, then, how many cases of *commotio cordis* have you encountered?" Holmes restated.

There was a long pause that told Holmes and Watson what they needed to know. The silence went on until discomfort moved Watson to speak: "It's very rare indeed, is it not, Doctor?"

"Yes," Dr. Shipman conceded.

Holmes took the report in hand and read it. "Other than the bruising in the chest and abdomen, what else did you notice on the body?"

"Nothing of consequence," Shipman answered.

"And you would not mind if Dr. Watson and I took a few moments to look for ourselves?"

"There are no wounds, if that is what you are implying," the coroner spat. "The cause of death was heart failure."

"That may be so," Holmes said, "but there are many things that can stop a heart more quickly than a fist."

Dr. Shipman was silent. He realized, in his haste to dispatch the autopsy, he had not examined the kidneys and liver. The police report all but indicated that the murderer had beaten the victim to death.

Holmes removed his hand-glass from his pocket and proceeded to examine the body. Through the glass he studied the face of the deceased. The nose was interesting. He bent lower.

"Dr. Watson, would you please look at the nose, and the membrane inside, and tell me what you see?"

Watson did so. "Ah, yes, I see what you mean, Holmes. The nose cartilage has been undermined, and the nose is collapsed."

"Indeed, and inside you will also notice a deterioration of the membrane caused perforations."

"Yes, Holmes," Watson concurred.

Dr. Shipman stood silently. He took on a similar appearance to that of the gaunt cadaver before them.

"What, in your opinion, could cause this deterioration?" Holmes asked Watson.

Watson opened the eyes of the dead man and peered at them. "Dilated."

The coroner shrugged his shoulders. "Eyes are always a little dilated upon death."

"Not to this degree," Watson noted.

"Regardless," Holmes interjected. "I invite you to look at the forearms."

Watson picked up the stiffened arm. Dr. Shipman leaned closer.

"So, the man had some injections recently," the coroner said. "He was likely vaccinating himself. He worked in a disease-ridden warren."

"Ah, yes, a disease-ridden warren that required—what would you say—twenty or more vaccinations? Poor fellow! I believe, if you examine the liver and kidneys, Dr. Shipman, we might discover that your assessment as to the cause of death was partially correct. He did die of heart failure. However, the cause was an overdose of cocaine taken nasally or intravenously."

"Tachyarrhythmia," Watson added.

PART THREE

HOLMES was ensconced in his Morris chair, thoughtfully sucking on his pipe. Dr. Watson did not engage him when he was in a pensive mood. The room was filled with offensive smoke from Holmes's coarse shag. The Doctor had endeavored to improve Holmes's brand of tobacco by giving him expensive tobacco mixtures. His gifts were graciously accepted. For a time, Watson was hopeful, as he observed the stack of tobacco tins piling up on the bookshelf adjoining Holmes's desk. Sooner or later Holmes would find himself without his shag, and he would open one of the tins. So thought his friend.

However, just the previous week, Watson had knocked one of the tins from its place while retrieving a book. The tin sprang open, revealing a collection of dead beetles. The remaining three tins contained collections of other members of the *coleopteran* family. For a moment, Watson amused himself with the thought of Holmes stuffing desiccated insects into his pipe.

Watson retrieved the latest edition of the *Daily Mail* and took a seat on the settee opposite Holmes, who took several minutes to register his presence.

"Ah, there you are!" He exclaimed at last, as if Watson had just materialized before him. "Wiggins promises to stop by this morning. I believe we should forego our breakfast in favor of a hearty lunch at Wilton's."

"Their sole *Meunière* is delectable," Watson concurred, making the point with his thumb and index finger closed in a pinch. After a while he asked, "What's Wiggins coming for?"

"I promised Snape that I would pay the cost of a coffin for his poor Fanny. Perhaps you will join me in attending her funeral tomorrow?"

"To be honest, old man, I don't think so."

"You were invited."

"It was you who was invited, as you gave the woman's brother his freedom—and because you are paying for the coffin."

"To the living we owe respect, and to the dead the truth," Holmes quoted, cryptically.

"What *is* the truth?"

"That the less fortunate among us deserve as much respect as the greatest. And while it matters nothing to the deceased, it seems disrespectful to her memory that Fanny should be buried in a cardboard coffin filled with sawdust."

"Fanny's reward is surely to come in the life hereafter: she will wear a crown."

"You don't still believe that, surely?"

"Yes, I do, Holmes. I believe that human beings have a soul or a spirit—call it what you will—that goes on from this life to reward or punishment in the next."

"You never did finish *The Martyrdom of Man*, did you? Nor look at D'Holbache? Well, just consider, my dear Watson: if the soul did exist, how would it see without eyes, hear without ears, or think and perceive without a brain and a nervous system? The idea is absurd. Death, my friend, is the bold full stop which finishes all of our stories."

"To me it is merely a comma—a pause before another story commences."

A knock intruded into this awkward moment. Holmes arose and looked out of the window to the stoop below. Mrs. Hudson's feet shuffled in rat-tat-tat steps to answer the call. Within moments the single knock on the parlor door brought the captain of Holmes's irregular army.

As the door was opened, Wiggins swept the cap from his head. Mrs. Hudson stepped back and away. It was only then that Holmes saw Wiggins' sister, Tessa, standing as a diminutive shadow behind him.

"Come in," Holmes said.

"It's abaht . . ."

"About the money, yes," Holmes completed. "I have it for you, Wiggins. Come in."

Wiggins' stood, hat in hand. Watson rose and offered his hand to Wiggins.

"My condolences to you and your kin. Fanny's spirit lives on—in our hearts," Watson said, with a nod toward Holmes.

Holmes picked up the gauntlet. "Yes, Wiggins, Snape and your brothers have our support in this difficult time."

"Thank you Mr. Holmes, and Dr. Watson. Your help 'as bin most welcome. A proper burial is a comfort to Snape." Conscious that Holmes's gaze had turned on little Tessa, Wiggins added. "I hope you do not mind that Tessa came."

"Brave little Tessa!" Holmes recalled.

With a motion from his hand, Holmes offered Wiggins and Tessa a seat. "I don't wish to intrude upon your grief, but the doctor and I were, just now, speaking of what it is that brings us comfort in times such as this."

"I'm not much for the Church, and all that, Mr. Holmes," Wiggins answered. "The grim reaper is a close neighbor of ourn in Spitalfields. I've thought on death more often than's good, I reckon. We come in weak and whimperin', and we should go out bellowin' and blazin'. Those old Vikings 'ad it right."

Wiggins' eyes glimmered as he looked off into the light from the window. "To be on a boat—a flaming boat—sailin' into deep waters. And, on the shore, your friends and family watchin' the last of you rising up in the smoke and flames until you're nothin' but a speck of light far, far away."

Holmes was momentarily swept up in Wiggins' visualization before the little voice in his head reminded him that this type of Viking funeral had, like the horns on their helmets, more to do with myth than reality. However, understanding that reality offers little comfort to the grieving, he did not mention this fact.

The old soldier also enjoyed Wiggins' romantic evocation of the pagan past. And, for a brief moment, Watson pictured himself as a dead chief on the flaming longboat, disappearing over the watery horizon.

"Yes, I know what you mean, my boy," Watson said to break the trance.

Holmes gave Wiggins a five-pound note, and then put a penny in Tessa's hand.

"She calls you the penny man, Mr. Holmes," Wiggins noted with a proud smile.

Most people have no idea what to wish for when they throw a coin in a fountain, Holmes thought, *but put a penny in a child's hand, and the hope we once held for ourselves is rekindled.*

"This is too much, Mr. Holmes," Wiggins said, looking at the fiver.

"Holmes stayed Wiggins' hand. "Maybe you could put the rest toward a meal for everyone after the funeral."

The image of a flaming boat arcing over the horizon was one that stayed with Holmes. It was as close as he could permit himself to go regarding the question of life after death. And so, Sherlock Holmes's imperfect belief lay suspended between a boat sinking downward into oblivion, and a spirit rising, ever upward, toward heaven.

CHAPTER V

LOOKING AT THE PORTRAIT OF SNAPE, Sherlock Holmes could not help but wonder what had been done with the life that he had helped to preserve. Snape's arrest for a murder—a murder he did not commit—surely marked a turning point in the lad's life. The question remained, however, as to which direction Snape had turned in.

As Holmes pulled himself away from his recollections, he ran his eyes over the other stark black-and-white images in the gallery, recalling that, in just the last year in Britain, there had been over 1,300 burglaries, 800 assaults, 200 robberies, and 180 murders. *Were any of these the work of Snape, Ugly, or Wiggins?* A child born in Spitalfields had but two choices: poverty or crime. *Why would anyone follow the "right path,"* Holmes wondered, *if doing so left him frequently unemployed, exploited and humiliated? Was that the point of this exhibition?*

Holmes had received a personal invitation. For some reason, the photographer wanted him to attend. S. P. Fields could be looking for him at this very moment.

Holmes straightened his jacket and made his way to the entrance hall. He carefully extracted his coat and hat from the jumble on the table, and donned them. As he strolled out the door, he half expected to hear a voice beckoning to him, but none came.

Curiosity gnawed at him as he made his way to Watson's flat on Sheen Lane. The ten-mile ride brought Holmes by the Hurlingham Club, which was lighted up with some exclusive event. He noticed a Mercer *Limousine* entering the front gate. In that moment, Holmes felt himself standing in the center of the chasm that separated Spitalfields from Fulham. The rich dallied and danced on the disinfected banks of the Thames, while the mudlarks looked for a penny's worth of coal in the mud.

Watson brought himself to the window as he heard the cab pull up to his flat. He had expected that Holmes might have arrived much later, given the near hour-long drive to and from Russell Square. As the car pulled away, Holmes retrieved a cigarette from a case and lit it. He climbed the first of three stairs to the front door, and leaned against the railing. The cigarette cast a crimson glow on Holmes's features, telling Watson that his friend was troubled. Watson decided not to retire.

Three cigarettes later Holmes found his way to the parlor. Watson was making a good show of reading, with a book spread open in his lap.

Upon entering, Holmes contained a small smile when he noticed the book in Watson's lap lay upside down. "Your book has kept you from your bed," Holmes said, "tell me about it."

Watson clutched it to his belly. "No, no, my friend. I want to hear about the photography exhibition. What did you think of Field's work? Did you meet him?"

"Fields was conspicuous by his absence. The images themselves were well done, I suppose. The portraits in particular were . . . engaging. I believe that would be the word."

Holmes went through the motions of retrieving and lighting another cigarette as a way to make space for himself. He appeared unable to describe the evening's experience.

"There were many memories for you, I suppose."

"Memories," Holmes repeated dispassionately. "Memories are peculiar things, are they not? Always there, yet one is not aware of them. They remain below the surface, surviving for decades in deep waters, like a shipwreck lying on a broken coral reef."

"An apt metaphor, but rather grim. Are you saying that it made you feel awkward?"

"Not awkward so much as surprised . . . "

"Surprised?"

"Yes. I did not respond as I had anticipated. I expected to feel a vague joy—some satisfaction even. The irregulars did good work for me, and I always treated them fairly. I helped them on several occasions—as you know."

"As they helped you."

"Oh, no question of that," Holmes agreed. "They helped us, and we rewarded them."

"They provided a service, and they were properly paid," Watson summarized.

"Exactly so."

Holmes crushed the cigarette in an ashtray. "I fear I am keeping you up, Doctor."

"On the contrary. I would be interested in knowing about the photographs themselves. What was the quality?"

"Quality? Good enough, I suppose—although one or two of the prints were tinted ever so slightly—not well washed. No, the purpose of this exhibit was not to demonstrate mastery of the camera or darkroom. It was about the subject matter."

"It included your irregulars, then."

"Yes. Wiggins, whom you know—Snape—Ugly . . ."

Holmes was caught in a pensive state.

"I was much too weary to attend the whole of the exhibit," Holmes remarked, walking to the hearth.

"Are you are going back?"

"The only thing that would draw me back would be the photographer—S. P. Fields. As I say, he was not present. You saw the invitation. It addressed me in a personal manner. I thought I should like to meet the person behind the lens."

"Yes, I agree, it was strange that he was not there to greet you."

"We concur on that point."

Holmes sprang to life, retrieved the invitation and note from his pocket, and read it:

" . . . *with thanks to you and my mates, a fortunate few were able to find a footing on clean pavement.*"

Watson reached out. "Let me see it."

Holmes handed the invitation to him, and Watson read it through again. "Obviously, he is well educated. But more than that, Fields has a poetic turn of phrase. *The lives of the deprived hover barely off the ground. Their accomplishment lies at the bitter end—the fact that they survived at all.* That is well said, is it not?"

"You have put your finger on the nub of the mystery: It is the clearly pseudonymous 'Mr. S. P. Fields' who interests me. Who the Devil is he, and what's he after? Why did he want me to attend the show?"

"Perhaps he felt that you might enjoy it."

"Enjoy it?"

Holmes sounded upset.

"I should have thought that our memories of the irregulars would be gratifying. You have cause to feel proud of the way you looked after them."

"So full of artless jealousy is guilt, it spills itself in fearing to be spilt," Holmes quoted.

"Queen Gertrude had good reason to feel guilt. You have no such reason."

"Watson, a man is not only guilty of those things that he has done, but of those things that he might have done."

The following day Holmes and Watson set out for Russell Square, then the headquarters of the Royal Photographic Society. The building's sandstone and brick façade took on a warm and welcoming appearance—unlike the prior evening.

Holmes pulled his friend to one side as they approached the front door. "Watson, I believe an indirect approach to our inquiry is called for here, as the R.P S may well wish to guard the privacy of its members."

"As you wish Holmes. I will follow your lead."

The doors were closed and locked. Watson pulled on the bell-chain. The locks rattled, and a white-headed gentleman poked his head out of the door. "Yes—may I be of service?"

Holmes removed his hat. "We have come about your society. We have questions pertaining to membership."

The gentleman looked delighted. "Certainly, I am alone at present, but I may be able to answer any questions that you have. I've been a member for nearly fifty years."

"We feel most fortunate to have you to ourselves," Holmes replied, "May we come in?"

The black door opened. Holmes and Watson entered and followed the stoop-shouldered fellow who was motioning for them to come along. Holmes glanced into the galleries on either side of the hallway. The distant images seemed benign in the daylight.

The hallway led to an office area that, at one time, had served as the dining room for this residence. The elderly man wore a tight-fitting herringbone suit. His snow-white hair was combed back with no attempt to cover his shiny scalp. Expectation was held in his eyes.

"My name is Barrenger—Neil Barrenger. I'm the serving secretary for the R.P.S." His genial nature was immediately apparent. His watery blue eyes had a hazy magic about them.

"Holmes—Sherlock Holmes, and this is Dr. Watson."

"My, my, are you the detective fellow?"

Holmes nodded.

"And you are interested in membership?"

"Dr. Watson here is." Holmes declared, turning to Watson. "Isn't that so?"

It was a frequent ploy of Sherlock Holmes to make Watson the focus of attention during an interview, so that he might be better able to bring all his senses to bear on the subject. Watson had ceased to be surprised, or put off, by Holmes's spontaneous misdirection. However, there was a moment of panic as Watson recalled that the sum total of his photographic knowledge could be exemplified by a Brownie cardboard box camera with its simple meniscus lens. His 2¼-inch-square photographs looked as if a slipshod impressionist had painted them. His £1 investment had been used only once, when he was on holiday in Blackpool.

"I consider myself an amateur," Watson began.

"Aren't we all?" Barrenger said. "If I may be so bold, I was wondering about your cameras?"

Watson was wondering also—as was apparent by his open-mouthed grin.

Holmes leaned forward. "Don't you feel, Mr. Barrenger, that photography has more to do with the photographer than the camera?"

"I concur completely, Mr. Holmes. Take our current exhibition. The images were created with any number of, what some might call, inferior cameras."

Holmes could not believe his good fortune. "I have heard about this exhibit. It has been described to me as having rather unusual subject matter."

"Indeed, sir. Our previous exhibitions have been primarily focused upon advances in photographic technology. The subject matter was secondary, if you will. *Irregular Lives* is a dramatic departure for the R. P. S."

"That is the exhibition we passed on the way in?"

"Yes, would you like a tour?"

Holmes and Watson waited in the hallway as their host fumbled in the darkness of the gallery for the light switches.

"Please come in, gentlemen. You may wish to take a few moments to enjoy these extraordinary images. I'm afraid the public has not been as receptive as we might have hoped."

"I'm sorry to hear that," Holmes said, as he began to circumnavigate the gallery.

Watson took a seat on one of the benches near the center, and was craning his neck in a feeble attempt to look interested. And, something did catch the Doctor's interest—but it was not the images. Holmes moved cautiously, in a trance-like state. Even their host, Mr. Barrenger, took note of Holmes's peculiarly reverent manner. It was as if Holmes did not wish to disturb the people in the pictures.

Seemingly oblivious to his outward behavior, Holmes moved toward a portrait that appeared to be taken at dusk. Grey tones surrounded the faces in such a way as to blur the edges. The elemental features of the two faces emerged from the gloom as if they floated on the surface of dark waters.

KATE & ARCHIE:
ORPHANED AT THE AGE OF SIX, KATE FOUND A FAMILY, AND MADE HER WAY WITH ARCHIE.

The young woman was leaning against a poorly lit stone wall. A handsome young man, beaming with pride, stood next to her. He had his hand on her shoulder, which was wrapped in a thick shawl. Her eyes were looking down to the street at a tattered basket of flowers. She held a small bouquet that was wrapped in tissue paper. The penny spray, clutched in her hand, was wilted.

WEDNESDAY

WATSON LOOKED FORWARD to the bi-monthly publication of the *Illustrated London News*. He had marked the date on his calendar and, like clockwork, marched down to a makeshift newsstand, little more than a glorified crate, at the entrance of a mews near Porter and Baker Streets. Archie, the newsboy, made it a point to hold a copy of the *Illustrated News* for the Doctor.

Watson was surprised to find a junior version of Archie there—his head just above the crate. "Where's your brother, Benjie?" Watson inquired.

"Kate's gone missing." Benjie leaned closer, and in hushed voiced added: "Kidnapped, I reckon."

"How long now?" Watson asked.

"Near two days."

"This is serious, then," Watson said, picking out four pence and placing it in Benjie's hand.

The boy pulled the periodical from the stack inside the crate and placed it on top. Watson glanced at a thrilling full-page illustration of a lifeboat in rough seas with a sinking ship in the distance—*18 Rescued from Doomed Schooner*, the headline read.

"If there is something I can do, ask Archie to see me. You know where I can be found."

Watson walked off deep in thought. Benjie called out: "Your paper, sir."

Watson returned to his flat to find Holmes adjusting books and papers on his desk. He had been doing this for the last three days. When Watson entered, he eagerly turned to greet him.

"Is that, perchance, *The Daily Mail*?"

"No, Holmes, the *Illustrated London News*."

Holmes muttered something under his breath. Watson would not be drawn in by Holmes and settled himself down immediately to read this edition that he had anticipated for a fortnight.

Holmes continued to shuffle the objects on his desk.

"It appears you are making the most of this rather fallow period."

Watson meant this as a jest, but as often happens, the canard eluded Holmes.

Sherlock Holmes lurched in his chair. "*C'est n'importe quoi!* Do you believe that the criminals of our fair country have gone on holiday? Possibly I should go to Yorkshire, and take the waters with holiday-making thieves and murderers in Harrogate!"

"You don't have to go that far to find a case," Watson said. "Archie's girl Kate has gone missing—for nearly two days now, and the irregulars can't seem to lay hands on her."

"Missing girls—a lover's quarrel," Holmes expostulated.

Holmes paused, caught in thought. "Yet—if Wiggins and the rest have not been able to find her—then it may be serious. Watson, if you find yourself at Archie's stand, ask him to come by."

"I did so, Holmes. But let me make a point of it. I can pick up *The Daily Mail* as well."

Watson returned with the newspaper, along with some news of his own.

"Archie has not yet returned. It was his brother Benjie—I may not have told you, who could offer little more news. However, I made a point that Archie should come by. Benjie did not seem encouraged. What do you make of that?"

"It suggests that our urchin army has, once again, been up to mischief."

"Mischief? Felony or larceny, more like. I suppose you think that your intervention in the lives of these young hooligans will set them on a better course in life, but I don't believe it."

"Neither do I, Watson. No one saves us but ourselves. Our life's journey is merely a string of decisions. We do something, or we stop doing something. My presence—our presence, in their lives merely offers them a choice that the streets cannot."

Holmes's caring usually showed itself in ways that were rational, rather than emotional. This made it seem as though Holmes had no emotions. Living with Holmes, one had to

117

appreciate that having emotions, and expressing them, were two entirely different things.

Watson was drawn to the window by a commotion in the street below—an irate cabby cursing a coster whose barrow had overturned. Looking up, he noticed Archie standing in the street.

"Holmes, the prodigal son is lurking across the street. No doubt debating whether or not to call upon us."

"As I said, a string of choices."

"Ah—he has chosen, Holmes. Archie approaches."

Archie's usually bubbling countenance was absent. Watson invited him to come in and take a seat. He had been in 221B several times before—sometimes shinnying up the drainpipe late at night. Being older than the other boys, Wiggins had commonly selected Archie to bring messages to Holmes when the irregulars had been engaged.

"Benjie tells me that Kate has gone missing," Watson stated.

"That's right, Dr. Watson.

Archie had yawned several times. There was grit in his eyes, and an almost imperceptible tremor in his right hand. *Sleep deprivation* was Holmes's diagnosis.

"Two days now," Holmes added. "You haven't had much sleep."

"I ain't had none, sir," Archie replied.

Holmes waited.

"I'm frightened, sir."

"You suspect something or someone, don't you, Archie?"

"Yes, sir."

Once again, Holmes sat in silence.

"It might be the bloke we nicked three days ago."

"You stole from someone."

"In a way," Archie said. "'E left 'is things behind and dashed off, sudden-like."

Holmes dropped his head. "Archie, don't play word games with me. Tell me exactly what happened, in plain English."

THREE DAYS AGO—SUNDAY

AS Kate ceremoniously dressed, Archie watched her from the bed. To Archie, she embodied the best of femininity without any hint of frailty or vulnerability. Her strength was apparent in her sure movements and piercing green eyes.

Uncomfortable and flattered at the same time, Kate chided Archie: "What you lookin' at, boy?"

"The most beautiful gel in Clerkenwell."

"I'd best be beautiful, as I'm the bait," Kate answered.

"And I like the shape of your 'ook, gel."

Kate wiggled her hips. "'Ere fishy, fishy!"

Archie laughed, which made Kate happy. She had been happy since the day she realized that Archie cared for her. Prior to that, her family had consisted of a rag-tag gang of boys who had befriended her a dozen years ago.

She had been attracted to Wiggins, the leader of the gang, not with a grand passion, but with affection. She screwed up enough courage one day to kiss him. He looked hurt. "Aw-w, Kate! Don't seem right—you and me bein' pals, an' all."

He was right, of course. Wiggins usually was. Her motivation, she realized then, was not to charm the man himself, but rather to ensure his continued care and protection. Spitalfields was a dangerous place for a girl coming of age. She was aware that, unless she snagged a fellow, she would likely find herself strolling the streets and alleys at the upper end of Haymarket. She had seen herself in the faces of the prostitutes who waited, bare-shouldered in daring *décolletage*, for a graceless young gentleman to buy them a drink and more. Kate knew that she teetered on the edge of that life, and was determined to maintain her balance. She even dreamed of finding herself in Mayfair, or some other posh neighborhood in London.

The last touch was a comb she placed in her auburn hair that pulled her curls to the side of her left ear. She did not have delicate features, but her eyes were large and fierce. Her body was thin and tanned, which gave her a sultry appearance.

She swung around to face Archie. "There, wot do you think?"

"You beauty! I pity the poor men of the city. 'Elpless they will be before the charms of lovely Kate, the Siren of Swinton Street."

She laughed and walked to the bed, bent low, and kissed Archie. He reached up and pulled her closer.

"Stop it," she scolded. "You'll wrinkle mi dress."

Archie swung around to place himself on the edge of the bed. He put his arms around Kate's waist and pulled her between his legs. "I'll wrinkle more than that, mi lovely."

A knock came to the door at that moment.

"Of course," Archie said.

Kate put her hand on Archie's chest and pushed him away. "That will be Wiggins and Snape."

Kate answered the door.

"Fish beware," Wiggins said, as he grabbed Kate by the hand and looked her over, head to foot. She put her finger to the side of her mouth in a coquettish manner.

Snape smirked, which was about as demonstrative as he could get.

The group gathered around Wiggins, forming a circle.

"You know how this goes. You must put the fish in a compromisin' situation, Kate."

"I'll not take mi clothes off for some strange fellow."

"So, Archie ain't strange then," Wiggins jested.

Archie nor Kate seemed amused.

"All right then, Wiggins said, "but in your bloomers or your little—nightshirt fing."

"It's called a step-in," Kate said.

"We'll be at the door," Wiggins assured. "No need to worry."

"If you scream," Archie said, "We'll be on 'im like flies on jam."

"Right-o," Snape added.

Snape was in love with Kate. He had been since they were children. She would nurse his wounds, which were many, as Snape was a brawler. His hulking body seemed always to be covered in bruises and scrapes. His out-sized hands were rough. His knuckles scarred. Snape made no overtures toward Kate. He knew they would be rebuffed, and his fantasy could not survive that certain rejection.

"Knock the glass over there on the floor," Wiggins reminded Kate, "and we'll come rapping on your door."

Wiggins put a bottle of cheap wine next to the two glasses on the table by the bed. "Get at least one glass into 'im, but no more. You drink none of it."

121

Kate nodded. "Very well. We all know what to do. Let's do it."

She wrapped a gold-fringed blue shawl over her shoulders and made for the door. Snape dashed to open it for her. The longing in Snape's eyes was obvious to anyone who cared to look.

The boyos, as Kate called the men in the gang, went in various directions as they exited the lodging house. Kate walked with them for a while, until she turned toward Farringdon Station.

The boys took their places along Swinton Street. It would be a long wait. Archie didn't like the idea of Kate flaunting herself at the coffee shop adjacent to the cab-stand at the train station. She would sit at a sidewalk table sipping the same cold cup of tea for hours.

A year of experience had told her what the ideal "fish" would be: One, a male out-of-towner—so he would be carrying luggage. Two, a foreigner, if possible—but one with a little English. Three, middle-aged and undersized—so he was not likely to put up a fight. It was a bonus if he were married—and so, perhaps, wearing a ring.

Immigrants had lately beset London. Italians, in particular, flowed into Saffron Hill, where their comrades had cloistered themselves for decades. Most Londoners were familiar with the penny ices they peddled about the streets of the city. This singular confection was popular, and those pennies seemed to have compounded quickly. Many Italians now had shops of every variety. No sooner did one countryman gain a foothold, than a *cugino* or *nipote* came to join them.

Wiggins had learned that a freighter was coming into Southampton from Italy. It had arrived late last evening.

Typically, the freighter carried a dozen or so passengers for the thirteen-day journey. Wiggins had calculated that it would take the better part of the day for these passengers to find their way to Saffron Hill. They would be tired and confused. When they finally arrived at Farringdon Station, they would feel a sense of ease. They would let their guard down. Danger was behind them—or so they would think.

Kate could tell that a train had just arrived as passengers began to pour out of the white stone archways of the station. The foreigners would lag behind, and so most of the cabs would be gone—and she would be waiting.

There he is, Kate thought, as she watched a man emerge from the station dragging a huge carpetbag, and carrying a satchel over his shoulder. He wore a substantial wool coat with huge pockets and horn buttons the size of a penny. His shoes were badly scuffed and appeared to be a size too large for him, which caused him to shuffle his feet when he walked. The foreigner had sunken brown eyes that showed lack of sleep. A bushy mustache could not conceal a cruel mouth. His face was unshaven, and his coarse black beard gave him a gloomy appearance. Nonetheless, his delight was obvious in his eyes.

He approached the sign that read: "Transportation," gazing at it—his mind translating: *Trasporto*.

Kate called from her table: "All the cabs are taken. We'll 'ave to wait, I'm afraid."

In his confusion, the man did not think that Kate was addressing him.

"Good day to you," Kate beckoned. "You're from Italy, aren't you?"

He nodded. "Yes—I am from Napoli."

As a rule, Italians in London style themselves as Neapolitans. Probabilities were that this fellow had never seen Naples. His skin tone put his origins further south.

"You may get a cup of coffee here." Kate said. "Do you understand?"

"*Sì, caffè*. May I seet wid you?" he asked.

Kate shrugged her shoulders. "If you wish. I must be on mi way soon."

Kate pulled her shawl over her shoulders as if preparing to depart. She knew men, especially Italian men, loved the chase. An indifferent response would likely be irresistible to Mario Giotti—and so it proved.

Archie was the first to see Kate and "the fish" strolling down Swinton. Kate walked slightly ahead of Mario. His eyes bounced between the strange surroundings and Kate's *derrière*—here fishy, fishy. He was hooked, now they would reel him in.

Catching Archie's signal, Wiggins and Snape pulled back from the doorway that led to the lodging house where Kate had rented a room. Mario was struggling with his huge valise, all of which pointed to a good take for the boys and Kate.

Mario hesitated as they came to the entrance. His eyes flashed about. He had become leery. The situation required *finesse*. If Kate yanked on the line too hard, he might become frightened. If she was too timid in her invitation, he might let his wariness take over. Either way, he would bolt.

Kate stood looking at Mario quizzically. Ever so casually, she retrieved a handkerchief from her sleeve and wiped the perspiration, first from her upper lip, then the cleavage that peeked above her dress. A smile visited his face.

"*Bella*," Mario mumbled, as he followed Kate up the stairs.

Archie, Wiggins and Snape converged on the stairway in the same moment. Wiggins pointed to Archie and motioned for him to go up. Snape followed two minutes later. Wiggins took one last look around and quietly climbed to the second floor. Archie was standing next to Kate's door with his head bent toward it. Snape was cracking his knuckles. Wiggins pointed to his ear to hush Snape.

Five minutes . . . seven minutes . . . ten. Archie wore a look of concern. Wiggins smiled. Then, *CRASH!* The signal.

Snape pounded on the door, and pushed it open.

"*Madre di Dio, che cosa è?*" Mario screamed, as Snape, Wiggins and Archie entered.

Kate wrapped her arms around her step-in in false modesty.

Snape confronted Mario, whose trousers now encircled his ankles. His shirt was open and hanging loose. Archie and Wiggins stepped in close behind Snape. The plan was to give the victim just enough room to run. All that was needed now was to get him moving.

Snape gave Mario a long slow look.

"*Mi dispiace, non lo sapevo!*" Mario bleated.

Snape turned to Kate. "Is this fella your customer?"

Kate slapped his face. Snape cocked his fist. Archie and Wiggins grabbed Snape, who struggled fiercely. The three men tumbled to the floor and thrashed about screaming and yelling.

This was Mario's cue to exit—stage left. Which, he did. He pulled up his trousers, and ran through the open door, tripping down the stairs.

The boys laughed.

"Welcome to London!" Snape shouted.

Kate hurriedly dressed as the boys continued to jest. Wiggins looked out the window. He could see no sign of London's newest citizen.

"Good job, Kate," Wiggins said, as he turned to the other men.

Archie picked up the large carpetbag and set it on the table. "Wot 'ave we 'ere."

Snape grabbed the satchel and sat down, opening it in his lap.

"Ah-h," Wiggins said, as he took a sterling silver shaving kit from the bag. "Belonged to his papa, no doubt."

Snape riffled through the satchel frantically. "Nothing here but a bunch of letters and books. O, now this is more like it." Snape pulled out a bottle of brandy and a large pocketknife. "Books and letters in Italian, not much there, but the knife and brandy are worf somethin'."

Five minutes later everything of value was sitting in a pile on the bed.

"Anyone want 'is duds?" Archie asked.

"No!" Wiggins shouted. "The clothes are a give-away. Burn 'em—and the carpet bag."

Archie gathered up of the clothes and began stuffing them in the bag.

"I'm keepin' this satchel," Snape declared.

"All right now, Wiggins said. "Kate—you go first. Snape, follow Kate and make sure that the cove don't find 'er. Later, Kate, near the end of the day, come back and remove all your things from 'is room. Be watchful. I'll bring the swag to the office. Archie, you see to the clothes and bag. We'll meet up tonight. Go on now—go."

WEDNESDAY—BACK AT 221B BAKER STREET

"I imagine you're disappointed in us—in me, Mr. Holmes," Archie said.

"In several ways," Holmes answered, "including your overwhelming lack of originality!"

"It's an old ruse, I know, Mr. Holmes."

"I fear that is exactly what Mario thought. Yet kidnapping a woman is an extraordinary action, particularly for a foreigner. It's not logical."

Holmes went to the mantel to retrieve his pipe and pouch.

Watson intervened. "Archie, did you find a note or a letter in the rented room—something to suggest a kidnapping?"

"You mean where our little ruse took place? How should I know?"

Holmes swung around. "So you haven't gone back there?"

"We asked the proprietor, and 'e told us as 'e'd seen nothing of Kate, nor the Italian neither."

"Yet Kate was expected to return to remove her belongings, was she not?"

"Yes, Mr. Holmes. It does seem strange."

We need more facts," Holmes said. "Tell me about the man. What did he look like?

Archie pursed his lips and looked down, closing his eyes. "Well, see, 'e was a short man—about five foot three or thereabouts, a typical Italian, you know, with dark hair and eyes. He 'ad a big moustache, and a bit of a beard comin', for 'e can't 'ave shaved in a week."

"Did he have any scars, or unusual features?" Watson asked.

"One of 'is eyes was closed down more than the uvver."

"Which eye?"

"The right—no, I'm a liar, the left," Archie said, holding out his arms in front of him for orientation.

"Anything else—anything at all?" Watson inquired.

Archie tilted his head. "'E 'ad a tattoo on 'is wrist. I only saw part of it—a V or a W maybe."

"Very good," Holmes said. He took a long drag on his pipe and walked toward the light of the window.

Holmes was caught in thought. The conversation was over—his side of it, at least.

"Archie," Watson said, I suggest you continue your search. If you have news of any kind, report back."

"Thank you, sir," Archie said to Watson. "Thank you, Mr. Holmes."

It appeared that Archie's acknowledgement had gone unnoticed. Then Holmes swung around. "We need to go back to the room."

"We can go anytime you wish, Mr. Holmes."

"Dr. Watson and I will be at your stand in twenty minutes."

The lodging house on Swinton Street was a cut above the low lodging houses of Spitalfields. It was mostly inhabited by broken-down clerks and businessmen, and occasionally, by derelict clergymen or lawyers. Lodgers had a room to themselves for half-a-crown a week. Holmes, Watson, and Archie led the way, with Benjie following. It had proved impossible to leave Archie's younger brother behind.

The Warwick Inn, as it was named, was a three-level brick building carved out of a larger warehouse property. It had no real lobby to speak of, but rather a caged counter stretched along one wall. Sitting behind it were two men playing cards. Holmes motioned for Archie to make the overtures.

"Wotcher donin', gents? I was wonderin' if we could 'ave a dekko at room B, upstairs."

Neither man moved to address Archie. Finally, the larger of the two turned. "It's half-a-crown a week."

"I know," Archie said. "I rented it—that is, Kate rented it, a couple days ago. We left something behind."

"Nothing's there," the innkeeper interjected. "I cleaned it myself."

Holmes approached the counter. "May we see the room?"

Startled by Holmes's presence, the innkeeper became more attentive. "Of course, sir. I'll be most happy to show it to you."

"We require only the key," Holmes said, placing a shilling on the counter.

The key was forthcoming and the *entourage* found their way to the room. The furnishings and *décor* were sparse. No carpets—a stained mattress without bedclothes. A thorough search confirmed the innkeeper's report. There was nothing to be found.

Upon returning the key, Holmes asked about a red-haired girl who had rented the room recently.

"You mean Kate, sir? Yes. I believe she returned here to retrieve some belongings."

"She did!" Archie jumped at the counter, but Holmes held him back. "You said you 'an't seen 'er!"

"Did I? My apologies. I must have been confused. I sometimes am, sir, on account of an old injury to my brain going back to the Zulu War."

"No matter," Holmes interjected. "What we need to know is, when Kate returned, did you notice a man with her?" He wagged his finger.

"Ah," said the innkeeper, evidently thinking, quite mistakenly, that he understood what was happening. "There was no man with her. However . . ."

The innkeeper's hesitation had the sound of a purse being opened.

Holmes placed another shilling on the counter.

"However," the innkeeper continued, "A rough sort of fellow inquired after 'er."

"Short, brown eyes, black hair?"

"The very fellow, sir—an Italian if ever I saw one."

Holmes nodded solemnly. "You saw Kate with this man?"

"No, sir. As I said, he inquired as to her whereabouts."

"But he waited outside."

"I saw him there—yes."

"Thank you."

Archie and Watson looked grave.

Holmes turned back to the innkeeper. "Did you notice the tattoo on the man's hand?"

Holmes did not reach for a coin, but instead laid his cane on the edge of the counter with a loud crack.

"No, sir."

Holmes turned back to the trio.

"Why would 'e want Kate?" Archie exclaimed.

"Not Kate," Holmes replied. "Something Kate had. Archie, what happened to the things that Mario left behind?"

"We took the valuables, and the rest went into the dustbin."

Holmes turned back to the innkeeper. "You said that you cleaned Room B. Did you find anything there?"

"Nothing of consequence, sir, I assure you."

"Letters or papers?"

"Something of that sort. It went in the bloomin' dustbin."

Holmes smiled. "And, that dustbin is—where, exactly?"

"In the alley, sir," the man said, pointing to the hallway on his right.

Holmes dashed into the alley and poked a finger into the rusty dustbin. There, on top, was a folded sheet of paper. He opened it and read aloud:

The woman for my
borsa. Return here
to-morrow with my
property or she die.

"That was two days ago!" Archie screeched. "We're too late."

"Perhaps not," Holmes said. "He wants the contents of his satchel."

"The *borsa*," Watson confirmed.

"Yes," Holmes said. "Do not think the worst. This devil is smart. If he kills Kate, the contents of the satchel would find their way to the police. He does not want that. Moreover, he knows that a live hostage might prove useful."

"Wait," Archie said. "Snape took the satchel. It had only a pocket knife and some brandy—and some letters and books."

131

Snape did not answer Archie's knock.

"'E's lookin' for Kate," Archie said. "We can go in."

Before Archie could ask, Benjie grabbed a hidden key cleverly wedged in a floorboard near Snape's door.

Upon entering, it was clear this was a young man's abode. The pile of rubbish in the sink revealed that Snape's dinner usually came in tins—Fray Bentos Corned Beef being a particular favorite. The bed was a mattress on the floor. The only decoration was a tattered poster hanging on the wall, showing the champion John L. Sullivan posing, ready for action.

"Here's the bloody satchel," Archie shouted, pulling it from the corner. "The brandy's over there—or what's left of it."

Holmes grabbed the satchel. He quickly inspected the exterior, and then pried it open. He turned it inside out. Empty.

"What happened to the letters and books?" Watson asked.

Benjie, who had been silently tagging along, stopped. "There!" He pointed to the grate. There among the ashes were what remained of a dozen or more letters and two books. The books had not burned, and several of the letters had fallen off to the side, but were charred.

"Carefully now, bring them here, Benjie." Holmes ordered.

Holmes cleared off a portion of the only table in the room, and made way for the burnt remnants. He tapped one of the books on the edge of that table and examined the cover. It read, *Il Testamento Politico di Carlo Pisacane*.

"I have read the works of Pisacane," he said.

"What was your impression?" Watson asked.

"Shocking. He provided much of the philosophy behind the anarchist movement as it is practiced today in Paris— especially the terrible idea that they call *propaganda of the deed*—or, to put it bluntly, the use of random violence as a political act."

Holmes ignored the second book in favor of one letter that remained intact. He opened it and read aloud, translating from the Italian as he went along:

> Mario,
>
> There are anarchists who believe they can gain power by expressing threats or publishing pictures of weapons. This is naive, in light of the destruction and slaughter that the armies of the oppressor exact every day.
>
> There is need for destructive intervention. We will sabotage the machinery of capital and authority. Our arsenal is propaganda, agitation, attacks, and riots. We must attack the symbols of authority. Our actions will inflame the hearts of the oppressed and spread the seeds of revolt.
>
> You and I carry a history of revolution inside of us. The responsibility to act falls to us to bring down the towers of the mighty.
>
> Luigi

"This is Mario's plan," Holmes said. "He is not here to sell ices, but to orchestrate a murderous attack on the city."

"And that bastard has my Kate!" exclaimed Archie, in horror.

Holmes stiffened upright. "Gather up everything here— every burnt scrap. Archie, see if you can find the clothing and other things you discarded."

"Getting those things back may be trickier than you think," Archie replied.

Holmes handed him some coins, saying, "See what a few pounds can do."

As ever, in a crisis, Holmes became a thinking machine, delivering orders faster than a Bonham's auctioneer.

"Benjie, find Snape. Bring him to Baker Street. Watson, we must bring other forces to bear on this situation."

"I quite understand," Watson replied. "I'll go to Gregson or Lestrade."

"Neither," Holmes shot back. "Mycroft. My brother is needed to untangle the bureaucratic knot in Whitechapel. At this time of day, he'll be at the Diogenes Club. Go to him and explain the situation. Ask him to meet me at Baker Street. I will take the charred remains there. We must *rendezvous* as soon as possible."

Within minutes of arriving at his flat, Holmes retrieved several bottles of chemicals from the cupboard. He made a solution of alcohol, glycerin, and water. He laid the charred papers in a tray and poured the mixture over them. With tweezers, he placed the re-hydrated fragments on a sheet of glass. He then held the glass over a bright light. By twisting the glass at various angles, he could control the reflection of light in such a way as to read various fragments of the letters.

Watson was the first to arrive. He found Holmes with newspapers scattered about the floor. He was huddled over his desk, thumbing back and forth in an Italian dictionary. His understanding of Italian would help in deciphering the text—which, Holmes knew, would be an arduous process. Holmes began scanning the charred paper for English words, and oft-repeated Italian words. He compiled a list, putting strokes next to a word every time it was used.

"Mycroft was alarmed," as you might suppose," Watson reported." He is alerting the Special Branch, and promises to be along soon."

"Too many cooks, Watson—too many cooks! I have here a couple of pieces of the puzzle."

Holmes handed Watson his list of English words:

Windsor ////
Tower ////
Fenchurch //
Hart //
Byward //

"These are street names, Holmes," Watson noted.

"Yes, or place names."

"My God, you're right! The Tower, Windsor Castle—the Queen!"

"A possibility, Watson, as Windsor and Tower were used four times. However, the Queen is not in residence at Windsor presently. I have only examined some of the fragments, but I believe that the frequency of the words is noteworthy."

"So, you believe that Windsor Castle or the Tower of London may be targets for a bombing?"

"Yes, that is a strong possibility. I will examine more fragments, which may point to other places.

Holmes had barely recommenced his forensics when Mycroft arrived. Holmes laid out his findings to his older brother whose clockwork mind immediately grasped the current reality.

Mycroft smiled as Holmes concluded his report. "I know the target."

Holmes and Watson waited.

"The Crown Jewels."

"Of course," Watson said. "The Tower!"

"The jewels are not in the Tower," Mycroft said. "They have been removed—temporarily—while a new enclosure is being constructed. They are at Windsor Castle."

"But they will be returning to the Tower."

"Tomorrow," Mycroft answered. "They will leave from Windsor on a special train, non-stop to Fenchurch Street Station. From there they will be transported by unmarked wagons to the Tower."

Holmes bolted up and retrieved a map of the city. Mycroft and Watson gathered behind him. Holmes traced the route with his finger: "Seething—Byward—Trinity Square—Hart. There are various routes."

"Yes, you are correct," Mycroft answered. "I'll suggest that we delay the real transfer, and send a false shipment as scheduled. Our people will be ready to pounce on the anarchists."

"Not so quickly, Mycroft," Holmes said, holding up an admonishing finger. "There is the life of a woman at stake here, let us not forget. It is important that we move with caution, and take the alien gang alive."

"We'll do what we can, of course," Mycroft said, "but you know the risks as well as I. If a bomb is involved, it takes but one pull of the wire, or strike of a match, to detonate the device. These people put their cause above their lives. We must put Queen and Country first."

"I understand that you will do what you feel you must, Mycroft—as you have always done. I will do what I must—as I have always done. I am bound to protect my client."

"The woman—Kate—is your client?"

"She most assuredly is."

"Very well, Sherlock. But please do not interfere. Doing so will put you at risk," Mycroft warned. "I must be off."

As the door closed behind Mycroft, Holmes turned back to the fragments.

"What are we going to do?" Watson asked.

"Mycroft has the luxury of covering the many routes between the train station and the tower. You and I, Watson, must pinpoint the place where Mario and his henchmen will attack. That information, I am certain, lies somewhere in these fragments."

Watson pitched in, managing the soaking of the remains of charred paper—preparing them for Holmes. Holmes placed the pieces on a sheet of glass and, standing over a bright lamp, read the faded lettering, continuing to make note of word frequency, and also the manner in which some words were written. They worked well into the evening. Holmes and Watson were glassy-eyed and tired.

"I think a cup of tea is called for," Watson said, as he took off his rubber gloves.

Holmes nodded and sat down, rubbing his weary eyes. As he waited for his cup, his eyes scanned the new list of words he had jotted down. He paused.

Holmes retrieved the Italian dictionary and began to translate.

"Watson," he called. "There are two Italian words that have occurred more than twice: *chiesa* and *bara*."

Watson came into the parlor carrying two steaming cups. "Church and cheater," Watson stated.

"Close, my friend. Church and coffin."

"Church and coffin," Watson repeated. "A funeral!"

"Indeed, a funeral."

Holmes rushed to the pile of newspapers that were in a heap by his Morris chair. He flung the pages away as he leafed through them. "It occurs to me that the target of the attack might be the funeral of a dignitary. The routes we identified earlier include churches—All Hallows' and Saint Olave's."

"No one noteworthy?" Watson inquired.

"No one . . . Wait a minute," Holmes exclaimed. "A funeral—any funeral—would provide the perfect cover for an attack. The casket . . ." He leaped to his feet. "That's it!" he shouted. "If there is a funeral at one of these churches tomorrow, I'll wager that we shall find Mario and his comrades in attendance."

Kate found herself laying in a fetal position on a musty mattress. There were no windows, but the sun peeked through a dirty skylight. She was imprisoned in a dingy room devoid of decoration.

She could remember walking down Threadneedle Street after removing her belongings from the lodging house. A wagon came up alongside her. Men jumped out and dragged her into the back of the vehicle. Her last memories were of a sweet chemical smell. Her head spun and—nothing.

Kate stretched and went to the door. Locked. She listened carefully, and heard muffled voices speaking in Italian. Kate recognized one of the voices from the next room—that of Mario.

<•••>

The next morning, Holmes arose early to don his costume. He was dressing in clothing so tattered that it did not appear it could bear the weight of a needle. His mismatched suit was one size too small. He matted his hair, and blackened several teeth for a dreadfully bedraggled appearance.

After a quick cup of tea, Holmes and Watson made their way to Fenchurch Station. They hailed a cab, asking the driver to go to All Hallows Church. In fun, Holmes practiced the part of an inveterate drunkard whom Watson had taken under his wing—and straight to church. Watson had to agree that the look on the cabbie's face was amusing as Holmes feigned heaving before entering the vehicle.

Along the way, Holmes noticed members of the Special Branch, barely incognito, scattered along the streets that intervened between the station and the Tower of London.

Before they arrived at the church, Watson ordered the driver to stop and wait at the Pinnacle Hotel on Seething Lane, just north of the church.

Watson's nose wrinkled. "I understand the need to dress the part of a drunkard, Holmes, but must you adopt the aroma as well?"

"*Eau de* Thames, I call it."

"I believe you enjoy this too much—taking on the persona of a drunken lout!"

"Anything for Queen and country," Holmes replied. "The vicar, a C. H. Lambert, confirmed that the church is scheduled

139

for a brief memorial service that will take place less than an hour from now," Holmes said, as he checked his watch. "If our suppositions are correct, the funeral party should be arriving soon."

Watson looked worried. "A detachment from the Special Branch is posted all about. I fear they will put a spanner in the works."

"Yes," Holmes agreed. "Entirely too many cooks! We need to act quickly and decisively."

"I'll be at your side, Holmes."

"You must hang back and distract Mycroft's contingent."

"I assume you are armed," Watson said.

Holmes produced a jackknife. Watson laughed and reached into his coat to produce his Webley revolver. He handed it to Holmes.

"I'm not certain it was a wise decision to let that young man—Archie—participate."

"Short of locking him up, it would be impossible to stop him. He would come with his mates and cause a stir. No, I told him to meet us here well after the attack. That will keep him and the others away."

Watson lurched in his seat as the sound of vehicles approached.

Holmes poked his head out and quickly withdrew it. "They're coming."

A black and white curved-top carriage passed, followed by two more carriages. The hearse was from a well-known business.

"It is doubtful that Stevens and Sons know the true nature of their cargo," Holmes said.

"Nor the nature of the mourners! So, you believe the explosives are in the coffin?"

"It would offer the perfect way to maneuver a bomb close to the street," Holmes noted.

"If so, they will have a timer, or trip wire."

"Trip wire," Holmes stated decisively. "A timer would require that they know the precise time the delivery is being made."

"But, a trip wire would put them in the path of the destruction."

"There are ways to delay an explosion."

As the funeral carriages came closer, Holmes directed their driver to go, with haste, to the church.

"Be conspicuous with your presence, Watson, just before the convoy reaches the church. That will serve as a momentary distraction for the convoy, Mycroft's agents, and the funeral party. Do not move in a threatening manner, but merely watch the parade intently."

A small shaft of light struck Kate's chest. It shot through a hole in the box that confined her. A wave of fear washed over her when she realized she was a helpless bundle: her mouth was gagged, her hands and feet lashed tightly.

She could feel vibrations, and hear the sound of movement and hushed voices. Then, the movement stopped.

Holmes and Watson watched from across the churchyard as the rear doors of the hearse were opened. The other funeral carriages moved to the curb ahead. Six men, all dressed completely in black, exited and took their places next to the hearse. The vicar came out of the church wearing white bands and a loose knee-length cassock. Holmes and Watson watched as the vicar approached, raising his arms as if to say, *Are we ready?* After a few words, the vicar returned to the church.

"They are waiting for the convoy," Holmes noted.

Watson pointed a finger in the air as he heard the wagons approaching. "Here we go," he whispered.

Holmes turned to see three large wagons jostling down Byward Street. He pulled an opened bottle of gin from a bag, ruffled his hair, and adjusted his moth-eaten jacket to make it drape sloppily about him. He nodded to Watson, exited the cab, and began stumbling and swaying down the street toward the entrance to the church.

At first, the six men standing outside the hearse paid him little attention. However, as he got closer, they turned to watch him. Holmes stopped and gaped. He took off his hat and put it over his heart as a supposed gesture of respect. At that moment, one of the men alerted his comrades to the approaching wagons.

Holmes walked on as if he were moving past the church. All the while the detective's eyes were riveted upon the coffin now resting just outside the hearse. The convoy came to a momentary stop as it passed Dr. Watson, who was now standing at the curb—just as Holmes had predicted.

A long pause, and the convoy moved on. Holmes could hear a collective breath of relief emanating from the members of the fictitious funeral party.

When the caravan was one hundred meters away, the six Italians positioned themselves around the coffin. As they slowly began to lift it, Holmes turned and moved back toward the hearse—his eyes still scanning the casket. The movement of the pallbearers told him the coffin was heavy. As it rose, Holmes could see a loop of wire protruding from under the lid.

He pulled his jackknife, opened it, and secluded it inside his hat, which he now carried in his hand. When all eyes were on the approaching vehicle, Holmes made a mad dash toward the coffin. One of the pallbearers turned and tried to push him way. *"Adare—scappa!"* the man hissed. Holmes twisted past the hand and threw himself upon the coffin, bringing it to the ground. Two of the men grabbed him and threw him to the pavement.

The convoy was now twenty feet away. The men abandoned the coffin, but Mario stayed behind. A panicked look came over him as he ran his hand over the edge of the casket. The others were rapidly moving off in many different directions.

Holmes jumped to his feet.

Mario dropped to his knees behind the coffin, frantically feeling along the lid for the tripwire. He screamed in frustration, rose, and began yanking on the coffin lid.

Holmes pulled the revolver and pointed it at Mario, who ignored the threat, baring his teeth in a simian grin. He gave one last pull on the lid.

The last nail was coming out. The lid was rising. Holmes leaped for the coffin and threw himself on the lid.

Before Mario could react, police surrounded the hearse. Distant curses came from the terrorists as they were rounded up and dragged away. Holmes was draped over the casket. He noticed Archie running up the street.

As Archie and Watson converged on Holmes, he held up a finger to stop and still them. He then began to slowly open the lid of the coffin. Hushed alarms rose from the lips of the onlookers as they saw Kate lying, wide-eyed, in a bed of dynamite.

Archie ran toward Kate. Watson held him.

"A bomb!" Holmes said. "Everyone—back."

Haltingly, everyone moved backward.

"Back a hundred yards. Find protection," Holmes ordered.

Holmes felt around for the end of the trip wire. He found it and traced it to a bundle resting under Kate's left arm.

He gingerly uncovered the bundle, and found a small corked bottle resting on a thick piece of paper. Under the paper were several blasting caps. The trip wire was tied to the cork.

"Acid," Holmes said, talking himself through the process.

Kate was bug-eyed and breathing heavily. He gave her a forced smile.

Holmes removed, first the bottle, then the blasting caps. He signaled to Watson.

Archie and Watson ran to the open casket. Watson removed the gag from Kate's mouth.

"Thank God," where her first words. "I thought . . ."

Holmes put his finger to her lips. He cut the bonds that held Kate inside the coffin, and lifted her out. Archie took Kate from Holmes and set her on her feet.

Holmes signaled for the police to return. He gave a few brief instructions and then turned to Watson.

"Holmes, you're a hero!" Watson exclaimed, incredulously, "How did you do it?"

"I cut the tripwire," he said, holding up his jackknife.

Watson laughed. "A bold act, indeed."

"As you know, in the heat of battle, one merely does what needs to be done."

"You saved Kate," Watson said, as he watched Archie and Kate in an embrace. "And saved many other lives, not to mention this old church and the Crown Jewels."

"All Hallows may be the greatest treasure. This ancient building survived the Great Fire. It would have been a supremely iniquitous event that would allow a handful of fanatics to bring it to ruin now."

"Do you suppose Mario and the others thought about that when they made their plan?"

"No doubt. They were obviously striking at the symbols of power and government, naïvely believing that the incident would incite the masses to revolution."

"Revolution? Absurd! What is there to revolt against?"

"You might well ask Archie and Kate," Holmes said.

Watson turned to see the young couple kissing in the distance. "I believe that revolution is the last thing on their minds."

Holmes became uncomfortably aware that his fixation on the couple in the portrait had brought an abrupt stop to the tour. As he turned to Neil Barrenger and Dr. Watson, he wondered how long he had taken to travel so far back in time.

"I'm sorry, gentlemen," Holmes said. "There is something captivating about these images."

"There seems to be," the curator agreed. "We have noticed that some of our patrons are drawn completely into these portraits. While the work is remarkable in some ways, I find its subject-matter . . . a little distasteful."

Watson nodded: "You probably haven't met many people like those, have you?"

Barrenger's brows rose. "Indeed, I must admit that I've spent a good deal of my life avoiding such people. The East End is a strange land to me."

"I cannot say the same," Holmes remarked. "My work has often brought me into such places."

"I'm sorry to hear that."

Holmes's head cocked as a novel thought came to him. "I cannot say that I regret my association with the more dismal side of London. Finding myself in strange places, with unfamiliar people, has allowed me to know myself better."

"Ah, yes, and if Socrates is to be believed," Barrenger added, to brighten the mood, "your experiences created an uncommon wisdom."

Holmes offered a smile. "Uncommon wisdom," Holmes reflected. "I have enough vanity to believe that that describes me. However, it occurs to me that it is the persons in these portraits that possess uncommon wisdom—and the photographer, of course. What can you tell me about him—a Mr. Fields, I believe?"

"I have not met the man," Barrenger replied. "The offer to sponsor an exhibition, and subsequent negotiations, were conducted by a representative of his."

"A representative, you say. Who might that be?"

Barrenger's face wore a look of confusion. "I'm afraid I can't recall. Is it important?"

"I simply wish to pass on my appreciation," Holmes said, "although I must confess to some curiosity as well."

Their guide nodded.

Watson intervened. "Would it be possible for you to put us in touch with Mr. Fields' representative?"

Good old Watson, Holmes thought.

Barrenger shrugged his shoulders and looked around. "My time is my own, as you can see. I believe the information you seek is in the office." He got a worried look. "I'm not sure . . . Well, it may take a few minutes for me to lay my hands on the proper letters."

Watson approached him. "Would you mind if I accompanied you? A few moments in a comfortable chair would do me some good."

"By all means, Doctor. Mr. Holmes, you are welcome as well."

Holmes twisted around, scanning the perimeter of the room. "If you don't mind, I should like to take in more of the exhibition."

CHAPTER VI

HOLMES WAS ALONE. He turned his back on the portrait of Archie and Kate and walked away. A few steps brought him to one of the benches in the center of the room. His head was still, but his eyes scanned the images on the walls. He became aware that his heart was racing, as if he were running. His mind was indeed running: voices, faces and places were rising up, like some dark phœnix, from the ashes of his past. He seized his head between his hands to still the onslaught.

Fear was not an unfamiliar emotion for him. He was a human being, and fear is the oldest, and strongest, of mans' emotions—which may account for the success of the species. What distinguished Sherlock Holmes from others was what he feared.

For most people, death is at the top of a long list of fears. Holmes was satisfied that his instinct for survival would suffice. It was the unknown that headed his own short list of fears. This was the fear that compelled him to gorge himself on information—facts—knowledge. He could never possess enough information. At the same time, he was aware of the vastness of what he did not know. This gave him an

149

advantage over others, because he seldom stumbled into situations unprepared. Not knowing, but thinking that one does, is the cause of most failures.

Holmes now found himself facing an unknown. But that was not the sole reason that his heart was racing. There was also a rare moment of regret that gripped him now. The kind of regret that is often found hiding in death's shadow.

Holmes bolted to his feet and paced the perimeter of the gallery. He had, long ago, learned that the antidote to fear was action. As he circled the room he beckoned: "Come, come to me."

As he approached each photograph he stopped and peered at the image, forcing himself to watch it for a full minute—then, on to the next one.

You invited me to your exhibition, Fields. I accept!

Holmes circled the room in a mechanical ritual. Most images had a vague familiarity that he acknowledged with a nod. Then one photograph caught him unprepared.

BENJIE:
A BOY ABOUT
THE BUSINESS OF LIFE
ON THE STREETS—
WHERE EVERYTHING
IS FOR SALE.

The small boy sat on the curb with a calico cat in his lap. His oversized jacket drooped into the gutter, and his rolled-up trousers revealed shabby shoes. His hair was little more than stubble upon a head recently shaved—no doubt to rid him of lice. And, in counterpoint to everything surrounding him, his blazing smile created a lovely paradox.

BENJIE WAS MESMERIZED by the silver florin spinning in the gentleman's fingers.

"My boy, this is yours for a few minutes' work."

"What d'you want?"

"A small thing really, Benjie. I'm . . . a doctor of sorts. I need a tiny vial of your blood for a patient."

Benjie's body recoiled.

"Just a thimbleful, is all."

Benjie nodded, hesitantly. "For two bob, then."

"Good boy. Let's tell the dustman outside that he need not wait for you, shall we?"

The angular man put his arm around the ten-year-old boy's shoulder and led him out to the street where Tux, a flying dustman, was waiting to collect the ash, rubbish and *débris*.

"What's this then?" Tux asked, as Benjie approached, empty handed, toward the waiting horse and cart.

The doctor held out a shilling. "I have a small task for the lad. I'm sure you can do without him for the rest of the day." He pressed the coin into Tux's palm.

The ageing dustman looked askance at Benjie, who nodded.

"Very good, guv'ner," Tux agreed. "You can find your way home, can't you, Benjie?"

"Yes, Tux."

The dirty refuse-collector shrugged his shoulders and, grumbling under his breath, grabbed the reins of his nag and urged it onward.

Benjie was led back into the doctor's elegant home, and soon found himself lying on his back atop a narrow padded table.

"I'm going to prick your arm with a needle. Hold it still and steady. Close your eyes."

Benjie shut his eyes; but they suddenly flew open when the doctor's hand clamped his arm against the tabletop.

"Ow!" Benjie yelped, as the needle struck his vein.

"Quiet. This will only take a moment."

The sting in Benjie's arm lessened, and his body relaxed.

"There," said the Doctor.

As the needle was pulled out, Benjie watched a bead of blood cut a scarlet track down his forearm.

"Wait here. I have to see to this blood now. I'll be back directly."

"Wiv two bob," Benjie added.

"Yes—with your money."

A short time later, the doctor returned to find Benjie sitting on the edge of the table. He twisted a silver coin before the youngster's eyes, and then placed it in his outstretched hand.

"You are a singular boy, Benjie. I have a friend who is looking for a lad just like you. She would pay you well for your help."

"'Ow much?"

"A half-crown per day."

The boy's eyes widened as if the gates of El Dorado were opening before him. "You're 'avin' me on now, ain't you, sir?"

"Not at all, Benjie. Would you be willing to go with me to see my friend? She is presently some distance away. I could have you back just after nightfall."

"Before nightfall, sir. Mi muvver will worry if I'm late."

In May 1889, Sherlock Holmes and Doctor Watson had just returned from Africa. As they made their way from Marylebone, the elegant brick and stone façades in Kensington peered at them through the December fog, creating an ethereal effect. The mist thickened, and an acerbic scent announced that they were approaching the Thames. The hansom offered a ghostly view of a waterman conducting a clumsy barge down the silent highway beneath Hammersmith Bridge.

"It will be jolly to share rooms again Holmes—I appreciate the invitation," Watson said.

"I could not very well leave you on your own while Mary is in Switzerland. After all, a man can live only so long on canned beef and shortbread," Holmes jested.

"You don't know how close to reality your little jibe is, Holmes."

"Very well then, let us make a few stops along the way, beginning with the newspapers. How I've missed the *Daily Mail!*"

When the distant cry of someone shouting headlines pierced the fog, Watson rapped on the roof. The cab slowed down. An adolescent boy began to materialize before the cab.

As the lad hurried to the carriage, a voice piped up: "Dr. Watson—Mr. 'Olmes."

"Ah, it is good to see you so well, Archie!" Watson exclaimed.

For several years, Archie had filled the shoes of his older cousin, Wiggins, as leader of the back-street brigade.

"We've been away," Holmes said.

"Yes, sir, I've noticed. Mi muvver and me 'ave bin lookin' for you."

Archie baulked.

"Something's wrong then, Archie?" Watson asked.

"Yes, sir. It's mi bruvver, Benjie. 'E's gone missin'. Can't find him nowhere, sir."

"If *you* cannot find him," Holmes remarked, with surprise, "then he is surely lost! Give the good Doctor and me time to get settled, and come by. It appears you know the address."

"I surely do, sir. Can I bring mi muvver? It'd be a comfort to 'er to know as you might 'elp us."

"By all means," Holmes answered. "Your mother is most welcome."

Archie handed Watson the newspaper, and stepped back from the curb. "Thank you, sir."

The clip-clop of the horse's hooves on the cobbles was the only sound for some time before Holmes spoke: "It is important that we look after our urchin army, since we have been absent from our command, Watson. It would be only sensible to keep an eye on them, you know."

"Holmes! A drop of compassion wells up in you, and you pass it off as pragmatism."

As they drove to Baker Street, Watson leafed through the *Daily Mail*.

"Anything of interest?" Holmes inquired.

"Let me see—the *Exposition Universelle* has opened in Paris, with the completed Eiffel Tower—that hideous monstrosity in the heart of the city! But this is more in your line, Holmes: the body of a young boy was found in the Irwell River. Authorities are seeking information as to his identity."

Holmes nodded. "There is a mystery there to be sure, but one which is unlikely ever to be solved. What do you find on page three?"

Watson turned the page and scanned the columns with his finger.

"*King of Cottonopolis Missing*, it says here. Sir William Hyde Gregston, whose family sits prominently on the board of the Royal Cotton Exchange, has disappeared. It seems as though his twin brother is suspected of foul play, and has been questioned by the police, who are continuing to search for Sir William. And, over here we have—well . . ."

Watson's review of the *Daily Mail* was halted by their arrival at 221, Baker Street. Within minutes, the driver delivered the trunks, marking the end of the adventure that Watson would later entitle *The White Goddess*.

However, there was little time for rest, for many of the troubles that unceasingly bubbled up from London's melting pot took the form of a knock upon the door of Sherlock Holmes.

"That must be Archie," Watson said, in response to the banging downstairs.

"That is not Archie's knock," Holmes observed. And, of course, when Watson opened the door, Holmes's words proved correct.

A footman stood on the porch. He nodded toward a carriage at the curb. An immense gentleman stepped onto the pavement, and steadied himself. He stood like a portrait by Sargent, looming over everything around him. The Victorian fussiness of his dress, however, could not conceal an anxiety that worked its way through the twitching features of his face. The footman bolted down the stairs to take the gentleman's arm, stabilizing the corpulent body during its sluggish journey to the door.

He waddled to the threshold, lifting a multiplicity of chins. "Sir George Talbot Gregston to see Mr. Sherlock Holmes." A card was presented.

Watson ushered the distinguished guest into the parlor, where they found Holmes sitting at the desk, hunched over a newspaper.

"Holmes, Sir George Talbot Gregston is here to see you."

"Yes, yes—Sir George." Holmes looked up. "A fair trip from Manchester! But I expect that you have a house in London as well."

"Yes, Mr. Holmes—and others in Paris, Zurich, and Cadiz."

"I suppose that great riches are difficult to contain in only one home."

The man smiled. "I am uncertain as to how to take your remark, Mr. Holmes. I was told that you were inscrutable—

and so you seem to be." The man removed his topper and placed it on the table near the door.

"Please have a chair, Sir George," Watson offered, as Holmes rose from his desk to take a place near the hearth.

Once seated, the visitor spoke in quiet, measured words: "I am here to seek your aid in finding my brother, William Gregston. His recent disappearance has found its way into the newspapers. So, I suspect that you may have already heard about it."

"Only minutes ago, as a matter of fact," Holmes replied. "The *Daily Mail* had him as *Sir* William Gregston."

"Ah, yes, Mr. Holmes. The contributions of my brother and I to British industry were recently recognized."

"No doubt your contributions to the coffers of the Conservative Party were recognized as well," Holmes remarked.

Gregston's scowl was barely concealed by a feigned look of amusement.

"Mr. Holmes, it seems to me that it behooves us to graciously accept honors that others might bestow upon us. But I digress."

"At the risk of digressing further, I have, for some time now, felt that the honor of which you speak has been debased." Holmes paused and leaned back in his chair. "But, I suppose this honor has whatever meaning one may wish to attribute to it."

Their guest remained stone-faced for a moment as he took in the full measure of the man sitting across from him.

Holmes continued. "And, as you say, we digress. May I assume the efforts of the police are proving unsatisfactory?"

"Nicely put. They are not satisfactory. As you might suppose, their efforts are being directed by my sister-in-law, whose goals run counter to my own."

"Surely, you both share a concern for your brother's well-being?" Watson remarked.

"My concern is *about* my brother's well-being—not necessarily *for* it." He withdrew a handkerchief from his coat pocket, and dabbed the corner of his mouth where some spittle had accumulated.

"There is ill-will between you, then," Holmes surmised.

"Exactly, sir. Our fraternal relationship was, I fear, destined to be oppositional from the start. Our father accumulated the great wealth that my brother and I now enjoy. We tend to the business, but that requires little genius, and only modest effort on our parts. The great mechanical looms grind on day and night with little active attention from us."

The man shifted forward to the edge of his chair, and stretched himself upward in a prideful manner. "My brother and I are twins—fraternal twins—born minutes apart. Remarkably, during a difficult birthing process that led to our mother's death, those in attendance did not make note of which of us was the first-born. And Samuel Hyde Gregston's staunch religious beliefs precluded his simply declaring an heir."

"Most unusual, but one might think the matter would have been sorted out by now," Watson remarked.

"Quite so. However, our father died at the age of eighty-three—when my brother and I were fifty-one years old. His singular last will and testament stipulated that we should have equal shares in the mills and related enterprises. However, the great bulk of his personal wealth, which is scattered over the globe, was to be held in trust for the son that survives the longest . . . with one stipulation." The gentleman's grim gaze turned inward as his mind grasped at some chiseled memory. "If my brother and I should both live to our eighty-third birthday, the remainder of our father's estate will be divided into equal parts between us."

"May I wager a guess as to your current age?" Holmes followed.

"Exactly so, Mr. Holmes. My eighty-third birthday, and that of my brother, is on December the twenty-first—eight days hence."

"Your brother has disappeared at a most inopportune time for you," Watson noted.

"But a most *opportune* time for Lady William Hyde Gregston," their guest observed.

His insinuation caused an unpleasant pause before he continued: "My brother has fallen into ill health recently. Liver difficulties, I am led to believe. He's looked yellowish for some time, and has been losing weight in recent months."

"You believe, then, that your brother is ill, dying—or already dead," Watson said, in summary, writing in his notebook.

The gentleman smirked and raised his brows. "I will pay you handsomely, Mr. Holmes, if you can report the whereabouts and condition of my brother to me before the twenty-first of December."

Holmes clasped his hands together in front of him, and stretched back in his chair.

"I'm afraid your case falls outside my scope," Holmes declared.

"How much would it cost for it to fall *within* your scope, Mr. Holmes?"

"As remarkable as it might seem, more money than you possess."

Gregston grimaced. "A pity! I shall not waste any more of my time—nor yours."

159

And with that, the pompous gentleman rose, retrieved his hat, and left the apartment.

As he watched Gregston's carriage depart from the parlor window, Watson commented: "So much for brotherly love!"

"Yes, they are hardly Castor and Pollux, are they?"

"No indeed, Holmes. With some, when they succeed in this world, all that they possess is money."

Then, as if to emphasize the extremes of Holmes's and Watson's social circle, Archie and his mother arrived, even as the dust from Sir George's carriage settled in the street.

Archie's mother wore a mouse-colored dress and a dingy white apron. As she tidied her salt and pepper hair behind her head, Holmes noticed that her rough hands were corded with blue veins. *She wears the indelible stamp of a woman stooped under the weight of a hard life*, Holmes thought.

"Mr. Holmes, and Dr. Watson—I'm most grateful as you're takin' the time for the likes of us," Archie's mother began. "It's Benjie, sir. 'E's gone missin'."

"We're worried, sir," Archie added. "Scoured the city, we did—me and the rest."

Holmes studied the unassuming woman. "We took you from your work," Holmes observed. "It must have been a particularly difficult stain that you were cleaning."

The woman's eyes widened. She glanced at her son Archie, who was nodding. "As I told you, muvver, Mr. 'Olmes can see what ain't there."

"Smelling the lingering scent of ammonia, and knowing that you hail from St. Giles, I surmised that you were cleaning and patching clothing to sell," Holmes explained. "No mystery there! When did you last see Benjie?"

Archie chimed in again, "About two days ago, Benjie took up with a flyin' dustman—a fella by the name o' Tux. The old codger hurt 'is self, and needed help wiv 'is collections."

"All seemed good, sir," the woman said. "My boy was grateful t'ave a few pennies to share. So proud as 'e could help to put food on the table. But, at the end of the day, it weren't Benjie coming home, but Tux—the grimy old geezer, telling us as a gentleman 'ad offered Benjie a fine bit of work along the way."

The woman's eyes brimmed with tears. "We waited for Benjie—but 'e never came, sir. I'm frightful worried. There's bin a couple o' young boys gone missin' lately from the Dials, and thereabouts."

"You went to this gentleman's home?" Watson intervened.

"That very evenin', Doctor," Archie assured. "To the *front* door. Told 'em as 'ow I was lookin' for my bruvver, and wanted to talk to the gentleman of the 'ouse."

"But he never came," Holmes concluded.

"Right again, Mr. 'Olmes!"

Holmes's alarm was revealed only by the insistent tapping of his forefinger on the arm of his chair. "I think it important that we make further inquiries." Then, turning to Archie's mother: "At the moment, it may be best for you to return to your home. If you have no objection, I should like Archie to accompany us. He will be able to make a report."

"Oh, bless you, kind sir! Your words 'ave given me new hope."

<∙∙∙>

BENJIE stared out the train window as the cobblestone streets of London dissolved into muddy roads. The doctor's face was buried in his newspaper during most of the long journey from London to Manchester. The boy's uneasiness increased when he was told that there would be a carriage ride from Manchester's Piccadilly Station. He was moving farther and farther from home.

"So, your friend is not in Manchester?" Benjie asked, as the train pulled into the station.

"She is waiting just a short ride away."

They walked to a trap that was waiting for them outside the station. The lad started when the steam-whistle blew its farewell. As the train moved out, Benjie had the unfamiliar feeling of being utterly alone in the world.

As the doctor stepped onboard, he gave an order to the driver: "To the lodge, Brodie."

The carriage moved at a swift pace. Benjie's eyes flashed side to side as the factory-dotted horizon of Manchester disappeared into empty rolling hills. The sky blackened with clouds. A slight drizzle added an increasing chill to the air.

Thirty minutes later, the carriage slowed as it came upon a stately white, two-story house some distance from the road. "Braunmoss House," the doctor said, as the boy peered at the ivy-covered hunting lodge.

The carriage moved into the driveway, then lurched to a stop before a large green door flanked with shutters. As the door opened, a tall, angular woman in an austere black gown emerged, and walked to the edge of the steps overlooking the driveway. Her murky eyes were set deep into her loose-skinned face. A grim delight was barely concealed in her features.

As Benjie and the doctor climbed the stairs to the porch, the gaunt woman held out a gnarled hand. "So, this is Benjie!" she said, almost to herself.

Her hand, suspended in the air, reached out toward Benjie and twisted, palm up, as if she were envisioning the boy's head in her hand. "We have some cakes waiting in the dining room. You must be hungry," she cooed.

The doctor whisked Benjie toward the somber lady. "This is Lady Gregston, Benjie."

The lad nodded, and touched the brim of his cap, "Ma'am."

Her leathery hand pointed toward the house. Benjie obediently walked into the gaping doorway. As he crossed the threshold, Lady Gregston's smile vanished. She turned to the doctor. "He is what we've been seeking, you say?"

The man nodded. "A perfect match."

"What of the others?"

"Their usefulness is limited, as you know. That is why we need Benjie."

"Yes, of course. And, you will take care of the others—as you have before?

The doctor paused in mid-stride.

"For an additional fee, of course," Lady Gregston hastened to add. "Whatever you require."

Upon hearing this, Benjie turned to see the two forms silhouetted in the dimming gray light of the day. His smoldering fears ignited. His first thought went to his older brother.

"Archie!" Benjie gasped, *sotto voce*.

The door slammed shut.

<‹•••›>

HOLMES, Archie, and Watson departed almost immediately for 11A, Aubrey Walk, the home where Tux reported last seeing Benjie. *En route*, Holmes shared his plan.

"Watson, you will go to the front door, with Archie in hand, and make a forceful inquiry. Keep the person who answers at the door as long as possible. When your inquiry is rejected, as I suspect it will be, raise your voice in a shrill manner as a signal."

Archie and the Doctor parted ways with Holmes, and made their way to an enormous black enamel door. Centered on the door was an ornate brass knocker—a gryphon clawing its way inside. A maidservant answered their raps.

"I wish to see the master of the house," Watson announced, presenting his card. "I am Dr. John Watson."

The maid bent over Archie. "You've been told. Your brother's not 'ere."

"I insist upon seeing your master," Watson said. "Our business is with him."

"He is not at home," the woman replied.

"Where has he gone?"

"I have no particulars, sir."

Watson interrupted the closing of the door with an insistent cry: "Please—I am a colleague. I must know of his whereabouts!"

The woman cocked her head and squinted. "As I say, I don't know, sir. I'll give him your card when he returns."

As the door moved again, Watson raised his voice. "Look here, my good lady, I must leave a message. Bring me a pencil and paper at once!"

This masquerade continued for some time as Archie and Dr. Watson waited for the notepaper, and methodically scribbled a cryptic note. Then, from the corner of his eye, Watson spied Holmes stepping from the path beside the home onto Aubrey Walk.

"Thank you," he said. "I will wait for further word."

Once settled in their flat, Holmes retrieved paper and pencil, and made a hasty sketch. "Look at this, Watson. What are your thoughts concerning this apparatus, which I noticed at Aubrey Walk?"

Watson studied his drawing. "How big is it?"

"The India-rubber hose is approximately five feet long. I believe that the three-inch tubes at either end are silver. The black bulb in the middle of the hose is a pump of some kind."

"Yes—yes. This apparatus is a medical device. It can be used in a variety of ways, but primarily for transferring blood from one individual to another."

"As I suspected!" Holmes exclaimed.

"The fellow is a doctor, then?"

"Not a physician," Holmes remarked. "Medical research, it would appear from his laboratory. Are you acquainted with an individual called Reuben Rottenberg?" Holmes asked, holding a card to Watson's eyes. "I found his box of cards in a desk drawer."

"No. However, a trip to the Royal College of Surgeons may tell us something."

"Excellent, Watson! I should appreciate it if you would explore that avenue."

Turning to Archie, Holmes gave further orders: "I suggest you put two of your lads on Aubrey Walk. Ask them to report here if the man in residence returns. And, of course, follow him if he leaves again." As Archie waved off, Holmes added, "When your sentries are in place, Archie, return here. We must find Tux. Hurry!"

The adolescent turned a worried face to Holmes. "You fear for mi bruvver, don't you, Mr. Holmes?"

"I do, Archie."

<••>

"BENJIE, it is time to earn that half-crown we talked about," his furtive benefactor said. "Enjoy the cakes in the dining room. I will come for you soon."

Lady Gregston swooped in behind Benjie, prodding him toward a long mahogany table bearing plates of cakes and confections. Benjie's stomach growled. It had been nearly seven hours since he had eaten.

"Young boys like milk, don't they?" Lady Gregston asked, pouring a glass full.

"And ale," Benjie replied.

"Milk will do, for now. You must be strong and healthy if you wish to help Sir William and me. Eat your fill, Benjie."

Dark passions swept over her face as she watched Benjie consume the pastries. She nudged a plate of delicacies closer.

"None for you, ma'am?" Benjie asked.

"No, Benjie, I will dine later."

"Where has the doctor gone?"

"He is preparing the room for you and my husband."

"Then, my work is for your 'usband?"

"Work? It is not really work, Benjie. We simply need some of your . . ."

Benjie turned. "Mi wot?"

There was no reply.

166

Benjie moved back in his seat. "I don't want this work, ma'am," Benjie said, pushing his chair back.

The lady remained motionless.

Benjie stood, grabbed one more cake, and strode toward the hallway—immediately colliding with the doctor.

"Benjie, Benjie, slow down—there's nothing to fear here. Come along." The cake dropped to the floor as the doctor's hand grasped Benjie's neck and steered him into the hallway toward a wide oak staircase. The colorless daylight forced its way through a stained-glass window above the stairs. The muted crystalline tableau depicted a fair-haired knight with his foot upon the throat of a dying dragon. The hero's sword had pierced the neck of the beast, and blood poured from the wound.

The man and the boy were soon padding silently down a dark corridor toward a room at the end of the second floor hall. The door was open. Someone was waiting.

Benjie's feet did not obey his mind that told him to flee. Like the ticking of a clock, his measured steps mechanically brought him toward the waiting chamber. A putrid smell permeated the air. In a dim corner, an old man lay under a canopied bed. His eyes were closed, and his breathing was labored. A long, narrow table stood next to the bed.

The doctor cleared his throat. "Sir William, this is Benjie."

With one last shove from behind, Benjie stumbled to the bedside. The old man's eyes opened narrowly. He raised his right hand, and beckoned.

Benjie moved closer.

Suddenly, the old man's hand struck out and grabbed the boy's forearm. The vice-like grip belied the man's seeming frailty. The youngster attempted to break the grip with his

167

other hand, but could not. Benjie pulled away, but the bony hand, like that of death itself, held firm.

The old man's lips trembled as he spoke in a dry, hoarse tone: "Hmmm, So young!"

The doctor came forward and touched the old man's arm. His hand relaxed, and Benjie jerked free.

The Docter pressed a half-crown into Benjie's hand. "Here. Now, as you did before, I want you to lie on this table. There will be a small prick again. You must be quiet and still for a while longer this time."

A muddled feeling overtook Benjie. It was as if he were in a dream—watching himself climb onto the table. It was someone else's arm being strapped to the tabletop—not his. It must be another's eyes staring at the water-stained ceiling above.

The doctor opened a black bag resting on a nearby dresser, and extracted a hose with shiny needles on both ends.

"Close your eyes, Benjie," came the command.

Benjie braced himself for the stab. The puncture came once—then again, before his arm was released. The boy turned to see the doctor open a tiny valve at the other end of the hose and slowly squeeze the black bulb. Blood spurted from the end of the tube, spattering across Benjie's face and lips. It tasted like wet pennies in his mouth.

HOLMES was perusing a notebook he had taken from the Rottenberg home, and making notes, when Dr. Watson returned from his investigation at Lincoln's Inn Fields. Archie was quick upon his heels, having posted members of his urchin brigade around the house at Aubrey Walk.

"There may be a few threads upon which we can pull, Archie, but Tux is our best hope. Let us find that antiquated dustman."

Then, he turned to the Doctor.

"Good hunting at the R.C.S., Watson?"

"Yes, the library provided some useful information for us."

"Join Archie and me, if you will, and make your report while we search for Tux."

As the carriage departed, Watson shared what he had learned: "Rottenberg calls himself a hematologist. He's published several papers on the typing of blood. Are you familiar with the practice, Holmes?"

"Yes. An Austrian—Landsteiner—is attempting to classify blood into several types. Certainly, such a process would prove useful in criminal investigations."

"Indeed, the theory is that there are three or four types," Watson added. "In addition to blood-typing, Rottenberg published an article in *The Lancet* with a rather novel and fantastic theory that new blood can revitalize degenerating organs in the human body."

"Fantastic, possibly, but the idea is far from novel. In the late sixteenth century, Pope Innocent VIII was said to have been given the world's first blood transfusion to keep him from aging."

"A legend, surely, Holmes!"

"One would hope so, for it was said that Innocent drank the blood of ten-year old boys."

Watson's body stiffened in fear.

"Yes, Watson."

Holmes's eyes shot to Archie, who seemed lost in thought.

As Tux was an itinerant, finding him was no simple task. However, the three seekers were not surprised when the costermongers, and the Covent Garden flower women, pointed them to a public house set in the center of Whitechapel Road. Sitting as it does, at the great east-to-west artery of the city, this ancient establishment served as a hub of dubious commerce.

As Archie, Holmes and Watson approached, they observed a mixture of good and evil countenances lined up along the benches outside. Leaning against one corner of the public house stood a gentleman sporting a brilliant red scarf and a slouch hat. A steel hook protruded where his left hand should have been.

"'Ooky, we're lookin' for' Tux," said Archie. "'Ave you seen 'im?"

The man twisted himself around. "Yes, Archie—round the back. Is Benjie at 'ome?"

"No, Alf. That's why we need the old geezer."

They stepped around to the rear of the inn. There sat Tux hunched over a mug of ale—foam dripping from the ginger-gray whiskers that wrapped around his jaw. His once white jacket was smudged, torn, and buttoned high upon his chest, as it was too small to enclose his great pear-shaped belly. When he saw Archie, he lowered his head and made himself small.

"Tux, these are my friends, Mr. 'Olmes and Dr. Watson. We need to talk to you about Benjie."

Tux shook his head, and pushed away the mug. "Poor Benjie. I can tell you, guv'ner, this 'ole business 'as knocked me off my perch."

Holmes and Watson took seats adjacent to the musty man. Archie stood behind them. "Tell us what you know about the house where you left Benjie."

Tux's head lifted, and his brows knit together. "It wasn't me as left him, guv'ner. 'Twas Benjie's choice. Gotta respect a man's choices, Doctor."

"Benjie is a boy," Holmes said. "Nonetheless, what can you tell me about what you found at the house on Aubrey Walk?"

Tux settled back in his chair. "Not what you might call fancy goods—but first-rate glass, fine cork from an old ice box one time, an' clo'es like new—soiled is all."

"Soiled how?"

Tux took on a look of confusion. "I dunno, guv'ner. Blood, could be."

"Blood!" Archie exclaimed. "Tux, if one drop of Benjie's blood gets spilled, you old splodger, you'll find yourself in the chutes with the other rubbish."

"Was it the blood then, or something else, that caused the householder to bring you, rather than the parish dustman, to their home?" Watson asked.

"I can't say. I makes me own way in this world, guv'ner. I believe as what happens to a man's stuff before it goes into his dustbins is no business of mine."

Holmes leaned in. "I suggest you make it your business, or you may find the law coming down on you."

Tux screwed himself further down into his chair. "Among the dust, I often found empty bottles—for medicines, I believe."

"Did you ever notice anyone visiting the house?"

"Well, once, a carriage were outside whilst I gathered the dust. It 'ad a crest on it, as I recall."

171

"What was on the crest?" Holmes asked.

Tux's weathered face screwed up into a knot, and his eyes closed. "A shield of a kind—blue and yellow, it were, and—sitting atop it, a great silver 'elmet."

"Can you recall any words?"

"There was words written on it, but not so's I could read 'em."

Holmes cocked his head and squinted. "I have a proposition for you, Tux," Holmes said. "What would it cost me to rent your cart and horse, and borrow your jacket and hat?"

Tux chortled. "You're a bit long in the tooth to be takin' up in the streets, aren't you, Mr. Holmes? I'm not sure as I can stand the competition." He laughed, obviously enjoying his rough jest more than Holmes did.

"My career will be less than a day in length, and I will make but one call," Holmes answered. "All will be returned to you tomorrow."

Tux assumed a serious look. "A good day can bring me as much as a pound, would you believe, sir?" he said, nodding his head.

Holmes smiled. "You may be a good dustman, but you're a dreadful liar, Tux. You can have your pound—however, it will cost the loan of your trousers and shoes as well."

Tux's eyes flashed upwards, and his mouth hung open for a moment. "It's a bargain, sir," he said, holding out his grimy hand for a shake.

Holmes grasped it loosely, and sealed the deal.

Archie was sent to fetch Tux's garments to Baker Street, and the cart and horse to Holland Park, near Rottenberg's home. Holmes planned to masquerade as Tux to gain entry to the Aubrey Walk residence once again, and to put his own keen eyes on the dustbins therein. Watson and Holmes headed home to await Archie's return. Upon entering, Holmes immediately bolted toward the bookshelves behind the desk.

"Do you have a book on heraldry, Watson?"

The Doctor pointed. Holmes retrieved it, and began leafing swiftly through the pages. He stopped, and poked his finger sharply into one of the pages. "Yes—yes, of course!"

BENJIE found himself emerging from a somber gloom— dizzy and disoriented. He was lying down, but not in the bedroom. He heard a wee voice: "You'll be fine in time. They'll bring you broth soon."

Benjie turned his head to find a pale face framed in the darkness. "I'm Jake. I've been 'ere a long while. What's the day—d'you know?"

Jake had a boy's body, but his face was wizened. The muscles of his cheeks were twitching, and his eyes blinked rapidly.

"They're takin' blood from all of us, you know," Jake said.

"Us?"

Jake turned back. Huddled against the far wall of the dank room was another form.

"Tom and me. What do they call you, eh?"

"Benjie. Where are we?"

"Manchester, or nearby . . ."

"No," Benjie interrupted, "this room."

"Cellar—under the big 'ouse."

173

Benjie sat up. His head spun, and his eyes struggled to focus. "I'm thirsty."

"Yes, yes—we're always thirsty, aren't we Tom? Don't matter how much we drink. Always thirsty, we are."

"We have to get out of here."

"There's no way out, Benjie. One door—one window above it. That's all."

"The three of us can . . ."

"No. Tom ran. They put the 'ound on 'im and messed 'im up somethin' 'orrible," Jake said, pointing to Tom's feet.

Benjie's eyes had adjusted to the darkness, allowing him to see the skinny youth pressed against the far wall. Tom's legs were pulled up tight against his chest. His arms were clutched around his knobby knees. His bare feet were bleeding, black and blue. Raw flesh oozed where his toenails had dropped off.

"Beat 'is feet with a club. Tom can't walk now." Jake began to shake. "We're gonna die."

Benjie grabbed Jake by the shoulders. "Nobody's dyin'!"

HOLMES had just shed Tux's grimy clothes, and was standing before a long mirror removing his false beard.

Watson, with his face twisted in disgust, used a broom to push the pile of tattered garments onto an open newspaper spread on the floor alongside the clothing. "I feel as though I should call the public disinfectors, Holmes. I don't know how you can tolerate having these horrid rags on your body."

"Soap and water is all the hygiene required," Holmes assured. "Please be careful not to discard that sack there. Inside we may well find some pieces to this puzzle."

Watson went down to speak with Mrs. Hudson, and returned with a tray of tea and sandwiches. As he came into the parlor, he saw that Holmes had already spread a newspaper on the desk, and was carefully placing objects from his dustman's sack thereon. He began poking each item with a pencil.

"Dustbins," he said, "write the most truthful biographies. The challenge here is to know which of these items might best put us on Benjie's trail."

He continued his incessant prodding, occasionally examining an object with his glass. Within five minutes he had put four of the objects to one side. "Here are the telltale clues, I believe."

Watson approached as a dutiful friend. For, while Holmes was a singular man in most regards, he shared a trait common to consummate craftsman and artisans: he relished an audience—not for adulation or approval, but in the way a magician enjoys revealing his sleight of hand to an apprentice.

"Object one," Holmes began: "blood-stained cotton—fully in keeping with the work of a hematologist. Object two: an old railway timetable from Euston Station. And, related to this, there were three recent entries in his expense ledger for 16/6 under "train.""

Holmes reached back into the pile of previously discarded items, and retrieved a bit of old cheese in a torn wrapper. "H'm. This is not a local cheese. Let us add this to the mix."

Prodding several small pieces of badly soiled fabric the size of a calling card, Holmes asked: "What do you make of these, Watson?"

Watson picked up one of the pieces, and held it to his nose. "Ah, yes, flannel patches used to clean a gun—a large bore. Most likely a shotgun."

"Exactly so," Holmes remarked. And then, pointing to each of the patches in turn, "This one had tow and oil on it— this one, turpentine—and this one, sperm oil, I believe. This might also explain the whistle I discovered in a canvas jacket hanging near the rear door."

"He hunts—the whistle calls the hounds," Watson confirmed.

Then, Holmes stuck his pencil into the neck of an empty bottle, and held it up. "And, the real prize—a bottle that once held sodium citrate. What do you make of all this?"

Watson gazed upon the five objects. "The blood, we are agreed, relates to blood typing. The man is a hunter, most likely of game fowl, and he recently cleaned his shotgun."

The Doctor then picked up the bottle and smelled it. "Sodium citrate is a common alkalinizing agent. It's used to treat kidney stones."

"How might it be used with blood?"

"Possibly as a preservative—or an anti-clotting agent."

"Genius, Watson! And, what of the cheese—you are a gourmet, are you not?"

"I enjoy my cheese more than the next fellow, but I am not an expert."

Watson picked up the dried chunk of whitish cheese, along with a scrap of the wrapping. "A white cheese—semi-soft. As you say, the blue and green wrapping is not familiar to me."

"Exactly, Watson. It is not a common cheese in this city. I think we can put Archie and his band to work with regard to this cheese."

Within an hour, Archie returned with the last piece of the puzzle.

"Mr. 'Olmes, look 'ere." Archie held up a bright blue and green package in one hand. "Eden Glenn cheese."

"Made in Manchester?" Holmes queried.

"It's a witch you are," Archie replied. "Near Manchester, sir, in Leigh."

"A Leigh Toaster," Watson exclaimed. "Makes me rather peckish. What did that package of cheese cost you, Archie?"

Archie presented a sly smile. "Cost me, sir?"

"Well then, what will it cost *me*?" Watson inquired.

"A gift, sir," Archie said, as he presented the cheese.

"No time for dining, fellows," Holmes shouted. "We're off to Manchester!"

"Then you believe Benjie is in Manchester, Holmes?"

"Yes, probably near the Gregston Estate—on the basis of the coat of arms, you know. You might check your wallet also. I am certain that 16/6 is the fare from Euston to Manchester. If your pistol is well oiled, I suggest you retrieve it, and grab a warm coat and hat."

Holmes put his hand on Archie's shoulder. "We need you here, Archie. If your lads report that Rottenberg has returned, you must wire us at Manchester Station. Take these coins for a telegram. The extra money will help you make payment for the cheese."

BENJIE crouched on the narrow ledge of the window above the storeroom door.

"He's comin'," Jake whispered, "with the broth."

Benjie waved Jake away from the doorway, and put his finger to his lips. The lock clicked, and the hinges hummed as the door swung open. Jake and Tom shielded their eyes from the glaring lantern light splashing into the room.

A man's voice could be heard just outside the portal. "Benjie? Benjie? I have some broth for you. No need to hide from me."

Jake pointed to a dark corner. The man stepped inside, lantern in one hand, bowl in the other. He squinted into the darkness.

Benjie leaped from the ledge onto the back of the man. The bowl of broth shattered on the floor. Benjie gouged his fingers deep into the man's eyes. The devil screamed, twisted, and swung the lantern back and forth in an effort to dislodge the cat-like boy.

"A-a-agh, blast you, you bloody bastard!" he yelled. The man reached over his head and seized Benjie's neck, ripped him around, and cast him to the floor. Jake leaped forward to block the kicks being directed at Benjie.

"Get 'em, Jake!" Benjie screamed. The desperate man dropped the lantern, grabbed Jake by the collar, and tossed him against the wall. The lantern flickered out. In the darkness, the desperate man groped along the floor for the boy. Then came Benjie's foot—violently smashing into his face.

"Argh! My nose!" Blood gushed between the man's fingers and streamed down his neck. A second kick caught the man in the groin. He rolled onto to his side moaning.

"Hurry, Jake, quick! Help me with Tom."

"You'd best go now, Benjie. Bring help."

The injured man struggled to his knees and made a feeble attempt to grasp his assailant. Benjie punched him hard, again in the nose. The man bellowed and collapsed on the floor.

Benjie rushed from the room. Scrambling up the wooden cellar stairs, he burst into the kitchen.

"What's all this!" a wiry cook said, as she poked her head around the pantry door. "You there . . ."

Benjie ran toward the light of the rear door. He leaped into the garden with only one thought—*run!*

SHERLOCK HOLMES gazed through the train window at the weather-beaten moors that lay between London and Manchester. He had wrapped himself in a tight silence for nearly an hour before he turned to his companion.

"You are comfortable with silence, Watson, a rare virtue which makes you an ideal companion."

Holmes's gaze turned back to the passing landscape. "There is something bestial and cruel at work in the human race—something I have never been able to fathom."

"Or to accept, thank heaven. Don't worry, Holmes. We will find him . . ."

"Find him, Watson? Benjie has less than eight pints of blood coursing through his young veins. The loss of more than three will put him at death's door."

"Rottenberg knows this."

"Yes, and that is what makes him such a hideous beast."

As soon as the train lurched to a stop, the duo rushed into the station. Holmes found no message from Benjie at the telegraph office. A governess cart pulled up to the curb as Holmes and Watson emerged. As they opened the rear hatch, Holmes spied a large black curtained carriage waiting in the distance.

"The vulture circles, Watson."

"The carriage?"

"Sir George Gregston, I am certain. Clever fellow! Waiting and watching us."

"He may have known all along, but kept himself free from suspicion whilst we did his dirty work."

Holmes addressed the carter: "We are looking for a cottage, or hunting lodge, in the countryside—near the Gregston Estate. The house of a Londoner, I believe."

"I imagine you're speakin' of Braunmoss House, sir. It's there you wish to go, then?"

"We do," Holmes said.

The cart splashed down the road. Watson pulled his collar up around his neck as a frosty drizzle began.

"There will be no place for subtlety or politeness when we arrive, Watson. Have your revolver at the ready."

A little more than half-way into the journey, the driver pointed and remarked: "Most unusual, sir."

He was referring to another set of wheel tracks in the mud ahead.

"Few travel this way in winter, sir."

This confirmed Holmes's suspicions. Upon arriving, Holmes and Watson paid the driver, and made the journey from the road to Braunmoss House on foot. Racing onto the front porch, Holmes pounded on the door. No answer. He thrust it open.

A woman, gowned in black lace, scurried into the hallway toward the door. "How dare you!"

"Where's the boy?" Holmes demanded.

The woman stopped in her tracks. Holmes confronted her. "The boy, Benjie—where is he?"

She hung her head in resignation, and took a deep breath. "Run away. The others are in the cellar."

"Others?" Watson exclaimed.

"Watson, to the cellar. I'll find Benjie!"

BENJIE knew a dog was hunting him when he heard it baying in the distance. Spying a hollow log, he ripped off his shirt, put it on a long stick, and poked it into the hollow. He grabbed nearby brush and jammed it into one end of the log. He frantically searched the area for something else to close the other end of his trap.

Holmes had heard the dog as well, and followed the retreating yelps into the woods. He came upon an ageing handler trotting well behind his Herrier. Holmes beckoned sharply: "Hello there!"

The man stopped and turned toward the unfamiliar voice.

"Call your dog off, at once!" Holmes ordered.

The man grimaced. "Who are you?"

"I'm the man who's saving you from hanging."

The man paused but a moment before he blew two short blasts on a silver whistle slung around his neck. "Skyler! Skyler, come."

The yelping ceased, and the hound returned, panting heavily at the side of the old man.

"Benjie! Benjie!" Holmes called out. "It's Mr. Holmes, Benjie."

After repeated calls, amid the rustle of brush, Benjie burst forth into the waiting arms of Sherlock Holmes.

"Mr. 'Olmes, bless you, sir!" he exclaimed. "We must see to Jake and Tom."

"Dr. Watson is no doubt doing just that. Come along."

HOLMES and Benjie returned to Braunmoss House to find Dr. Watson in the parlor, nursing Jake and Tom.

"Good man, Watson. Are the boys all right?"

"They're alive, Holmes. Poor Tom here must go to hospital quickly."

"The Gregstons?"

"Upstairs."

"Rottenberg?"

"Secured in the cellar, a bit worse for wear, thanks to Benjie, I believe."

Holmes ruffled the hair of the lad. "Well done, Benjie! Come along."

Holmes and Benjie hurried up the stairway, following the dreadful sobbing coming from above.

Watson heard a carriage pull into the driveway, and waited downstairs for the twin to enter. Sir George Talbot Gregston appeared triumphant in the open doorway. He looked at the Doctor and the boys momentarily, then silently walked toward the mournful sounds of Mrs. Gregston above.

As he climbed the stairs, Watson settled the boys down and followed him, patting the revolver in his pocket.

Gregston approached Holmes, who was waiting at the bedroom door. The room was plain, austere, and stripped of color. Mrs. Gregston was on her knees, weeping at the bedside of her husband.

Sir George entered.

Watson joined Holmes and Archie, as they stepped inside—standing back a respectful distance.

"Is he alive?" the twin enquired.

With that, the dark woman's head swiveled. She arose and swept in like a harpy to confront her brother-in-law. "You vile man! Leave my home!"

"I've come to pay my respects."

"Respects? Your brother still lives—no thanks to you. Your blood could save him."

"Save him from Hades? For what—another seven days? You cannot cheat death. And, really, what is the point? You will have little need of the Gregston fortune in Broadmoor."

The ghastly man then walked to the deathbed. He leaned over his brother, turning his head to better hear the gasping breaths. He retrieved a nearby chair and placed it next to the bed. Then, lowering himself onto the chair, he waited for his brother's life come to its blunt, and predictable, conclusion.

Holmes motioned Benjie and Watson toward the door.

The next morning, Holmes and Watson took Benjie to his mother's shop in St. Giles. Archie was there as well. As they approached, Benjie pulled away. He stood silently on the threshold of the shop. His mother gasped with relief when she saw her son.

Immediately, Benjie was crushed against the bosom of his mother in the most tender regard. He bided there for some time.

When Benjie pulled away, he turned to Archie, who had been waiting off to the side. Tears welled up in their eyes as the brothers embraced.

Holmes and Watson stood as privileged interlopers.

"It takes more than blood to make a family, Holmes."

Barrenger, letter in hand, began to reenter the gallery; but Watson held out his arm to stop the curator, took the letter and waited.

Holmes remained motionless before the portrait of a young boy sitting on the curb of a dirty street.

After several moments, Watson intentionally shuffled his feet to announce his presence as he approached, motioning for his companion to wait.

Holmes started and turned.

"Ah, there are you are, Watson. You were successful?"

"Yes, Holmes. Mr. Barrenger was able to locate the correspondence related to this exhibition, but it may not be as helpful as you might have hoped."

As Holmes turned, Watson was able to get a closer look at the subject in the photograph. "Ah, is that little Benjie?"

"Yes. You recall our last meeting with him?"

"How could I not, Holmes. Those ghastly brothers still haunt my dreams."

"Indeed, my friend. Ghosts come in all varieties—as S. P. Fields knows too well. What have you and Mr. Barrenger conjured up for us?"

As Holmes walked toward Mr. Barrenger, his body relaxed and his gentle smile returned.

"As I told the good Doctor here, I was not actively involved in arrangements for this singular exhibition. However, I worked with an emissary of Mr. Fields to arrange the gallery and hang the photographs." Watson handed the letter to Holmes as Barrenger continued: "Here you see the instructions that the young man brought with him from Mr. Fields."

Holmes took the letter in hand and read it silently.

"As you can see," Barrenger noted, "it is all rather technical in nature—lighting, the order of the photographs, how they are to hang, and so on and on."

"As you say, Mr. Barrenger," Holmes replied. "However, there is certainly something to be learned here, particularly with regard to the order, and where the larger portraits are to be placed."

"Yes, yes, Mr. Holmes. It would seem that some of the images are more important to Mr. Fields."

"Quite so, and you will note that the larger images are all portraits."

"Indeed, I noticed that as well."

"What can you tell me about the gentleman who carried these instructions? Will you describe him for us?"

"He was a bright young fellow. In his early thirties, I would think. Nothing particularly remarkable about him."

"His name?" Watson inquired.

"Mr. Jacobson."

"Did he say from whence he hailed—was he from the city?" Watson continued.

"He did not say, but his manner of speaking would seem to put him in the city."

"Where in the city?" Holmes asked.

"Well, it's difficult to say." Barrenger hesitated. "I—I have little upon which to base an opinion."

Holmes moved closer. "I would think you could venture a guess."

Barrenger was disconcerted. "It's not for me to say. But, I might be lead to believe that Mr. Jacobson might, at one time, have been at home on the very streets that are the subject of this exhibition."

"Thank you." Holmes replied. "In your communication with Mr. Jacobson, did he, perchance, leave an address?"

"No, sir. But it is interesting that you should ask."

"Why so?"

"Mr. Jacobson, on one occasion, said that he expected someone would inquire after him. And, if they did so, I was to tell them, using his words—I wish to recall it exactly—I was to tell them that . . . like many of his tribe, he was a ravenous wolf. And, that the time had come to divide his plunder."

Their host paused. "I believe it is a Biblical reference. He is a patron—a benefactor of the R.P.S, so it would not be proper for me to add more."

Watson cocked his head. "Benefactor?"

"Mr. Jacobson made a sizeable financial contribution, you see."

"You need not be embarrassed," Holmes assured him. "Mr. Jacobson engaged you as a messenger, and you have discharged your duty admirably."

"Most kind of you, sir."

Holmes added: "Would it be reasonable to assume that Mr. Jacobson's generosity ensured this singular exhibition?"

The old man's head bent low. "It is not for me to say, Mr. Holmes. That is all the information I can give you."

Holmes offered his hand. "That is all we require."

Barrenger shook Holmes's hand, and turned to Dr. Watson. "I'm afraid I have neglected your membership, sir."

Watson's mouth gaped. "Membership?

I sly grin crept over Holmes's face. "Doctor—I cannot imagine how you would be able to incorporate membership in the R.P.S. into your exceedingly demanding schedule."

Watson gave Holmes his irksome *we'll talk later* look.

PART TWO

RECOLLECTIONS AND REUNIONS— GOOD & EVIL.

CHAPTER VII

NO SOONER HAD HOLMES entered Dr. Watson's flat on Sheen Lane than he marched to the shelves that lined the wall behind the Doctor's desk.

"The Bible is on the second shelf," Watson noted. "I'll put the kettle on."

Watson had not had time to put a flame under the kettle before he heard a shout from the parlor.

"Benjamin," Holmes exclaimed. "Benjie—little Benjie."

Watson returned to find Holmes sitting at the desk chair with the Bible in his lap. Holmes turned to Watson and poked his finger into the page.

"Genesis chapter forty-nine, verse twelve: Benjamin shall ravin as a wolf: in the morning he shall devour the prey, and at night he shall divide the spoils."

"Jacobson's message—yes, I see."

Holmes laughed. "Jacob's son—do you see. Jacob's twelfth son was Benjamin."

"Indeed, Holmes. Very clever."

"Benjie was always a clever boy. Now he's a clever man. But, the fact that he references the Bible mystifies me. It's not the Benjie I have known."

"He has matured, Holmes. What age do you make him now? In his thirties—mid thirties, I should think."

"How is it that barefooted Benjie, in the span of twenty-five years, finds himself in a position to bestow a sizeable monetary gift on the Royal Photographic Society?"

Holmes poked his finger into the Bible, "at night he shall divide the spoils. His spoils. It does suggest that he has accumulated some wealth."

"Yes, Holmes. And what did the original invitation say?"

Holmes patted his pockets for the invitation. "Something to the effect—ah, here we are:

> *with thanks to you and my mates, a fortunate few were able to find a footing on clean pavement.*"

"Clean pavement, and a fatter wallet, it would appear."

Holmes shook his head. "Little Benjie—of all the irregulars."

"So, you believe Benjie is Fields?"

"I believe he and others created Fields."

"And again, we come to the central question: to what end?"

"To repay debts, it appears."

Watson looked askance at his friend. "Debts?"

"Debts come in all varieties, Watson."

"And, regarding Mr. Fields, is it a debt owed, or one to pay?" Watson asked.

Holmes's eyes glazed over. "Yes—I wonder?"

The post waiting in the silver tray in Dr. Watson's hallway had been overlooked in their hasty return from the gallery at Russell Square. But, once fortified with a brisk cup of Ty-Phoo and a bite of shortbread, Watson saw to his only other afternoon ritual, and shuffled through the waiting mail.

"I think you'll find this interesting Holmes. A missive addressed to you."

"At your address?"

"Exactly," Watson confirmed, carrying the envelope to Holmes.

No sooner had the letter touched his fingers, than Holmes exclaimed: "Ah, the drama continues!"

He turned the envelope in his hand and held it up to the light. "Familiar stationery. I venture Mr. Fields has something more in store for us."

"Us?" Watson asked. "I believe these events revolve about you alone."

"Never alone, my friend. Mr. Fields knows full well that we are a dyad. We were observed at the R. P. S. exhibition today, and that is why the invitation came here. Notice there is no stamp upon it."

"Well then, what does Mr. Fields have to say?"

Holmes carefully unfolded the envelope and produced a familiar engraved invitation.

S. P. FIELDS
INVITES YOU TO A DINNER
TO REUNITE, CELEBRATE, AND
HONOUR BOTH THOSE WHO CARE,
AND THOSE WHO CARED.

8.00
SATURDAY, MARCH 22, 1919.
7, CHAPEL STREET,
BELGRAVIA, LONDON.

Again, a small note was enclosed. Holmes read it aloud:

> *I could not hope to mystify you for long. My invitation was never intended as a puzzle, but merely as a prologue.*
> *As the French might say, "Qui vivra verra." If you can abide not knowing a little while longer, a rare treat awaits you.*
> *This invitation includes Dr. Watson. It is our fervent wish that you should have all your friends with you on Saturday.*
> —S. P. F.

"It appears," said Watson, "to be a rather elaborate way to bring you and others together."

"Yes—and did you note the address?"

"Indeed, he has friends in high places, it would seem. You are welcome to stay here, of course."

"Thank you, Watson. I think it best if I return to my cottage for the intervening days. I cannot leave my garden unattended. I may return early on the twenty-second and, together, we may decide if we should partake of this purported 'rare treat'."

Watson knew well that it was not the garden, nor the bees, that beckoned to Holmes. Men with great minds, like eagles, build their nests in lofty solitude.

When they were younger, Watson had judged Holmes's efforts to seclude himself as unfortunate. He had believed that solitude and loneliness were one and the same. And, to be fair, when he was younger, solitude had been unpleasant for Watson. But now, in his golden years, he found it increasingly agreeable. For Holmes, solitude was never a preference or a choice, but rather a necessity. The Doctor had always respected Holmes's need, even when he did not understand it. The best companions enjoy each other's company, and respect each other's privacy.

No doubt Holmes would use some of his time in Sussex to do research. It was not like Holmes to walk into any novel situation unless he held in custody a goodly number of facts and factors. There was a file among his boxes entitled "Irregulars." Until now, the more than two-decade old file had been opened only to add a note or clipping. These scraps of information and notes awaited Sherlock Holmes.

Holmes laid a file labeled: *London's East Side / Irregulars* before him on his desk, and eyed it as though it were a tasty meal. He bent low and blew the dust from the cover. Taking a kerchief from his breast pocket he waved it about to clear the air. He had only himself to blame for the dust, as Mrs.

Thornton had, on numerous occasions, been cautioned never to clean or move his file boxes—or anything on his desk.

As he pulled on the faded blue ribbon binding the file, the cover sprang open, and a barrage of pages, notes and tawny newspaper clippings poured onto the desk. Holmes's eyes twinkled as he fingered the items. The acquisition of information was therapeutic for Sherlock Holmes. If he were to accept the dinner invitation, he intended to walk into S .P. Field's dining room as a confident guest.

Number seven, Chapel Street, was set in a stylish neighborhood, adjacent to Buckingham Palace. As their cab pulled up to the ornate limestone portico, the misty windows scattered a golden light from every window in this three-story home. Watson paid the fare and turned to Holmes.

"S. P. Fields at last," Watson exclaimed.

Holmes pulled a photograph from his pocket and offered it to Watson. "Do you recognize this little girl? I wonder if you recall meeting her."

Watson lifted it closer to the window. "Difficult to say in this light. But if it's one of the irregulars, I suppose it must be Kate."

"No, it's not Kate. I'll wager it is S. P. Fields."

Watson squinted at the image of a small girl sitting on a donkey. He turned it over, but could not read the scribbling on the back. Watson handed the photograph back to Holmes and exited the car. Holmes followed.

The polished red granite railings of the stairway and portico glistened in the mist. The door swung open even before they reached it. Gay music could be heard in the distance as the attendants took their wraps and gestured toward the end of the hallway.

Holmes and Watson moved forward. They could hear voices mingling with a dulcet Brahms melody. Rounding the corner, their eyes were dazzled by huge crystal chandeliers that spanned an enormous hall. A string quartet was bowing away in one corner, while a small gathering of people huddled near the center of the hall. As they approached, a hush fell over the gathering. Heads, then bodies, turned to greet them. There were seven in all, two women among five gentlemen.

One young fellow pushed to the front of the assemblage, and began to clap. The others joined in as Holmes and Watson approached. Every face was smiling, save one—that of Sherlock Holmes.

Holmes held up his hands in a cautioning gesture. The music stopped. "It's not my birthday, is it?" he exclaimed.

A few chuckles rippled through the gathering as the obvious host stepped forward with his arms held wide. "A birthday is one thing—but I, for one, am grateful you were born. Welcome, Mr. Holmes and Doctor Watson!"

"Thank you, Archie," Holmes replied. "It seems the alleys of Spitalfields are far behind you. I am eager to hear your story."

"And, so you shall. But it is not just my story, but also the story of every person here—and many of those stories include you. I can say, personally, that I consider you the author of my story," Archie said, offering his hand.

Watson stepped forward and shook Archie's hand. "So you're S. P. Fields?"

"If you mean the talented photographer, I am not." He placed his hand on the arm of an elf-like woman in a drab dress. "Mr. Holmes, Dr. Watson, it is my profound pleasure to introduce S. P. Fields."

The slender woman had deep-set green eyes that were wide and soft. Although over thirty, she possessed the look of a guileless lassie, and wore the black uniform of the Salvation Army. She stepped forward and extended her hand.

"It's my penny man," she said.

Holmes's face softened. He patted his waistcoat pocket. "I'm afraid I have no pennies, Tessa—or is it Sister Tessa?

Tessa reach out and grasped Holmes's hand in hers. "It wasn't the pennies, Mr. Holmes. You know this. It was what they represented. And yes, you may call me Sister Tessa."

"I take it you're one of William Booth's tribe?" Holmes asked.

"Yes, Mr. Holmes; and proud to be a soldier in the Salvation Army. Some call us Slum Sisters."

"Ah, yes—midwives and such," Watson said, taking Tessa's hand. "And you're S. P. Fields?"

"Yes, I must plead guilty again," Tessa said. "But it was Archie's generosity that transformed an idle pastime into an exhibition that we hope will stir the hearts of our brothers and sisters."

Holmes retrieved the small photo from his pocket and handed it to Tessa. Her hand went to her mouth, and tears formed in the corners of her eyes. "You knew. You knew—of course."

Watson reached out for the photograph. "May I?"

She handed him the tattered photograph. "My first photograph—taken by an itinerant photographer in Clapham Common. It cost my brother an extra four pence to put me on the donkey. That remains one of the best days in my life."

"Astounding," Watson said, as he returned the photograph.

"And your brother?" Holmes remarked. "I don't find him among the gathering."

Tessa hung her head. Archie stepped forward to deflect Holmes's attention. "I suppose you know that Wiggins is not apt to roam the local thoroughfares. However, I suspect he may find his way here before the evening ends."

Holmes's eyebrows rose.

Archie continued: "In the meanwhile, other members of the irregulars eagerly await you. Shall we go on to dinner?"

Hardy conversation and robust laughter enveloped the congregation as they made their way into the dining room. Waiters were at their stations. Archie motioned for Holmes and Watson to take up places on his left. Kate sat on his right. When the guests had taken their seats, Archie clinked his wineglass with a knife. As he did so, the waiters began pouring champagne. Of course, Tessa demurred.

Archie stood. "Ladies and gentlemen, as I look around this table, I find meself—awestruck." Chuckles bubbled up around the table. "Lawd above, Wot are you laughin' at?" Archie smiled. "You might take a boy out o' Spitalfields, but . . ."

A long pause ensued in which Archie methodically looked into the eyes of every guest. He swallowed hard. "We're missing one, at the moment. But I have hopes that he will be here soon. I see it as nothing less than a miracle that most of us—most of the irregulars—are here."

"By hook or by crook," came a shout from one of the guests.

"Yes, it almost makes me religious, thinking about it. Kate promises me that a great dinner is in store—bangers and mash, is it Kate? But before we're served, I want to welcome our guests, Mr. Sherlock Holmes and Doctor Watson."

Applause and cheers arose: "Here, here—bravo!"

"It will be an evening of toasts and boasts," Archie declared. "And, I believe it is appropriate to direct the first round of toasts to Mr. Sherlock Holmes."

Archie raised his champagne glass. The others took their glass in hand and stood. When silence was complete, Archie turned to Holmes.

"I stand here tonight, only because of the support and affection of all of you. The people that make the biggest difference in our lives are those who care about us, when we do not care about ourselves. I'm speaking of my Kate, of course, but especially of Mr. Sherlock Holmes. I can still recall the time we met. You saved my brother's life, and probably mine as well. Thereafter, you helped along the way." Archie raised his glass high. "As Tessa said: We, the fortunate few, have found our way from the rancid gutters of Spitalfields, to cleaner pavement—thanks to Mr. Sherlock Holmes!"

Glasses were uplifted as Kate, Benjie, Ruck, Snape, Ugly and Tessa turned to Holmes.

Holmes, who had always brushed away adulation, and gratitude, was lost in the moment, until self-awareness finally obliged him to offer a nod in acknowledgement.

Kate caught the eye of the head waiter, and signaled for dinner to be served: Dressed stone crab with toast, roast loin of venison, garden lettuces with mint-shallot dressing, and lemon sponge pudding with Pippin apples were on the menu.

Holmes, who sat on Archie's left, directed his conversation to Archie and Watson. Benjie, who sat on Watson's other side, bantered with the good doctor almost non-stop. Finally, heavily laden with food and drink, Benjie lost steam. This allowed Watson to make a clumsy attempt to prod the proverbial elephant in the room.

"Benjie, my boy, it seems that the irregulars have come into money."

"Not in the least. It's Arch who's in the money, but he is quite liberal with his friends, as you can see," Benjie replied. "If it weren't for Archie and Kate, I'd still be selling my blood for half-a-crown a time. You remember that, do you?"

"I do, Benjie. If I may, I would like to inquire about your mother?"

"Our mother died three years ago. I wish she could see us now."

Holmes overheard this interchange and turned to Archie. "You are the founder of this fine feast, Archie," Holmes began. "You are a benefactor extraordinaire. I don't wish to be a poor guest—but while my appetite is more than sated, my curiosity is left wanting."

He laughed. "You have a peculiar way of almost saying what's on your mind. Are you asking me from whence my newfound wealth comes?

Holmes waited.

"I am employed at Vickers."

Holmes was stunned. "The armament company?"

"The very same," Archie confirmed.

"It seems they pay extremely well."

"More than a shilling a day, plus expenses," Archie parried.

Holmes twisted his chair around and leaned in toward Archie. "You know I will not condone ill-gotten gain."

"Is it ill-gotten when one steals from a thief?" Archie replied.

The host turned away and stood at his place. He clanged on his glass with the handle of his knife. The glass cracked, and red wine spread a crimson stain across the table. A hush fell over the gathering.

"I apologize," Archie said, too much in his cup. "Good wine should not be wasted. While the dinner is over, the evening is not. As I noted earlier, a night of toasts and boasts." He nodded to the waiters who removed the dishes from the table as he continued.

"As you know, I have come into some money recently. And, while I wear a Henry Poole dinner jacket, I have not forgotten the boy who bought his second-hand clothing at St. Giles. I remember the cry—nay, the command—with which our dear friend Wiggins would end every meeting: all for one, and one for all!"

Archie signaled the waiter behind him. The man nodded and opened the service door. Waiters marched into the room bearing domed silver serving platters that they placed before each guest.

"A dessert is something sweet at the end of a meal. The lemon pudding was lovely, but for the irregulars, the sweetest dessert comes in coin.

This singular ritual captivated Holmes and Watson. Holmes pulled his chair back as if the covered silver serving dish set before him held a serpent.

Archie spread his arms wide. "I want you to take this dessert home with you as a small token of gratitude. I have no doubt . . ."

A shrill voice boomed from the dining room doorway. "I have no doubt most of you will melt it into gin, and drink yourself into your graves."

The guests were shocked—not by the words so much as the voice.

CHAPTER VIII

WIGGINS STOOD AT THE ENTRANCE to the dining room, glaring at Archie. "The new aristocracy! You should all be ashamed of yourselves."

His clothing hung loose on his frame. His face was gaunt, set off by his dark eyes filled with tears.

"What 'appened to you? 'Ave you forgotten where we came from? 'Ow it felt to have the heel of the English on the back of your neck? Irish or not, you know how this country treats its children."

Wiggins' eyes bore into Archie. Tessa rose and walked toward her brother. As she approached, Wiggins' body began to tremble. Tears carved paths down his dirty cheeks. He sunk to his knees.

Tessa knelt down before him and wrapped him in her arms. She tried to speak, but her sobbing made it impossible. A fragile stillness enfolded the room. One of the guests, Snape, rose and walked over to the brother and sister. He grabbed Wiggins by the shoulders and lifted him to his feet. With Tessa's help they walked him to Snape's former chair and set him down. In the light, his frailty was apparent. His cheeks were sunken. Cords stood out in his neck. His lips were dry and cracked, and his shaggy hair was in disarray.

Kate grabbed hold of Archie's arm, her stunned expression mirroring that of the other guests. Archie cleared his throat.

"Wiggins, you more than anyone else—more than I—deserve to sit at the 'ead of this table. You made this gift possible. What lies upon these silver trays was taken in retribution—but it was taken in greed as well. For that I am sorry."

Wiggins looked up at Archie and his old comrades. He clutched the handle of the covered serving dish and lifted it. A simultaneous intake of breath from the guests echoed as everyone stared at a pile of gold sovereigns. He grabbed a handful and let them fall through his fingers, clanging on the silver tray.

"We can put this booty to good use. It can buy freedom, and save lives."

He rose to his feet and threw the coins across the table at Archie. "This booty—this retribution, as you call it—can return Ireland to its owners—the Irish people!" He swayed for a moment, and then collapsed on the table.

Wiggins was carried to an upstairs bedroom. The shock caused by his appearance subsided as the guests adjourned to the parlor. But, whisky, cigars and cigarettes could not stifle emotions that were broiling within the guests.

Tessa attended her brother, washing his face and hands. Kate stood over them with a worried look. Her famed beauty had been coarsened over the years, but she still maintained an innate metallic strength.

Wiggins was curled up on the bed—eyes closed—trembling.

"He's been in hidin' so long," Tessa said. "He barely sees the light of day. He avoids me, and all of you, for fear that any association will endanger us."

Kate put her hand on Tessa's shoulders and rubbed her neck. "He's home now. We'll take care of 'im. All for one."

With these words, Tessa wept. "I deserted him when he needed me most," Tessa confessed. "He left Dublin before the fighting began. I should have fought at his side."

"The Rising was doomed. You couldn't see that, blinded as you were by the cause," Kate said.

"The fight's not over for him. It will never be over."

"He must leave here—go to America or Australia."

Tessa wiped her brother's brow as his eyes fluttered. She put a glass of water to his lips. "He's very weak. He needs food and rest."

Dr. Watson stuck his head into the room. "I was wondering if I might be of some assistance?"

"The two women turned. Kate stepped back to let Watson approach. He bent over Wiggins and took his wrist as he retrieved his watch. "His pulse is weak, but regular."

Watson opened the lad's eyelids. His bloodshot eyes were sunken deep in his face. "He is undernourished and dehydrated. He needs considerable care—hospital I would say."

"He'll get all the care 'e needs 'ere, Doctor," Kate promised.

"Aye," Tessa agreed. "If he's found, he'll be imprisoned—or hung."

"I see," Watson replied. "That serious, is it? I had heard that he was caught up in the insurrection."

Tessa rose and grabbed Watson's hand. "I'm not certain as to where your sympathies lay, Doctor, but we are counting on the friendship that my brother has always shown to Mr. Holmes and you." Her lips trembled. "Please . . ."

Watson embraced her. "Now, now my dear. You can rely on me. But the only path for him lies far away from here."

"Aye," Kate echoed. "We don't need another martyr."

Holmes and Archie had found their way into the parlor. Archie sat down, slumping over to grasp his head in his hands.

"This is not the evening you had planned," Holmes remarked. "I want to be a friend to you, but I am struggling, given what I observed in the dining room."

"The money?"

"You avoided my question about ill-gotten gain."

Archie turned sharply. "I answered your question."

"You made a vague argument that it was not."

"I didn't steal the money! It was given to me for services rendered."

CHAPTER IX

LIKE BOOKENDS, HOLMES AND ARCHIE were poised on either side of a settee. Archie twisted toward Holmes. As he opened his mouth to speak, Holmes held up his hand in restraint.

"Archie, I am willing—eager even—to hear how you acquired what looks to be at least ten thousand pounds. However, please do not state your case as an excuse."

"Very well, this tale begins with Wiggins. He is in need of money. He came to me because he knew—I'm not certain how—of my current employment at Vickers."

"But it wasn't theft?" Holmes asked.

"It came by way of a man called Basil Zaharoff."

Holmes started. "The mystery man of Europe?"

"The very one, Mr. Holmes."

"I have a *dossier* on Mr. Zaharoff—quite a large one. He trades in war. He sells armaments to a country and, at the same time, to their enemy."

"I learned such things in the offices at Vickers. The war revealed that I had a natural ability with a rifle. As the war neared its end, I was hired to field test weapons at Vickers. Later, I took a job as an office messenger. Along the way, I discovered that the messages I bore made interesting reading. I became aware that there were managers at Vickers who had concerns about Basil Zaharoff. I assume your *dossier* revealed that he sits on the board of directors."

"Yes. The fellow has friends in lofty places, it seems."

"At Vickers, I befriended one of the managers, Mr. Killian—one of Zaharoff's detractors. He made no bones about it. I reasoned that, if I got on Killian's right side, it would be good for me. So, I followed Zaharoff. On several occasions I followed him to Whitehall—one time, to Downing Street."

"Really?" Holmes uttered, "I suppose that should not be shocking. However, it is disconcerting."

"At the same time, as if by some bizarre coincidence, I was contacted by Wiggins, who knew that I was employed at Vickers. He told me that he could help me obtain information about Zaharoff that he would pay to keep secret. I understood that Wiggins deserved the money, and such information, I calculated, would put me in favor with Mr. Killian."

"And so, you became a spy for Killian, and an instrument of Wiggins?"

"Yes. Although, at the time, I had no idea as to how much money might be involved."

"Did you ask Wiggins why he required this money?

"I assumed it was to book passage to America, and help him to make a new life."

"I see. How did Wiggins come upon this information about Zaharoff?"

"He never said—although, he once referred to a 'dark lady'."

"I should have guessed that a woman was involved."

"Yes, she passed on information to Wiggins—and Wiggins to me."

"And the nature of that information?"

"Basil Zaharoff's diary—a diary with damning information. To be honest, I only read the more scandalous bits of it."

"But you stole it?"

"I often fetched an' carried for the managers. On one occasion I was asked to stretch some drawings of a new airplane on the walls of the boardroom. As midday approached, the meeting was adjourned for a luncheon. Zaharoff went with the others and left his briefcase in the boardroom."

"Very tantalizing."

"Indeed, I closed the boardroom door, and sifted through his briefcase. I found the leather-bound diary, just as Wiggins had described it."

"And you say it made interesting reading."

A mischievous smile appeared on Archie's face. "Clandestine business affairs, to be sure, not to mention indiscretions—including a dalliance with the actress Sarah Bernhardt."

Holmes groaned.

"Wiggins helped me to orchestrate the ransom note, if you can call it that. Wiggins had suggested five thousand pounds would be an appropriate amount of ransom."

"But you thought better of it?"

"I doubled it, and received ten thousand."

Holmes shot to his feet and leaned over Archie. "I had hoped that you had left your foolishness behind in Spitalfields, but I see that it has only magnified."

Archie pulled back. "Mr. Holmes, I assure you that Zaharoff has no idea who lifted his papers. You see . . .

Holmes pointed a finger. "He knows. Trust me. He knows. He will soon find you. People with his power have vast resources at their disposal. For him, it isn't the money. He cannot let you live knowing what you do."

"I'll take that chance, Mr. Holmes."

"It's all very well to gamble with your own life, but what of the others—Kate, Tessa and the others? You involved everyone here tonight—including Dr. Watson and myself."

"No one is in danger," Archie said. He looked over to see Kate standing in the doorway. She stood stock-still, glaring at Archie. "Wiggins is asking for you."

She did not spare Archie a look as he swept by her. Holmes motioned for her to sit next to him. She sat down and put her hand in his.

Over the years, Holmes had learned how to administer comforting behaviors. But the path to his heart came through his head—feelings coming only after he had assessed a situation. Often times, in the midst of his analysis, the opportunity to express his feelings was lost. This gave the impression, to some, that Holmes had no emotions. This reputation may have served him in days past. Now his sluggish emotional clockworks merely separated him from the people whom he cared about.

Wiggins was sitting up in bed sipping from a cup that Tessa held to his lips. Archie approached. "Here," Archie said, "give me the cup."

Tessa handed the cup to Archie, and caressed the cheek of her brother. "I'll bring you some dinner."

The two men waited until Tessa was out of earshot. As Archie raised the cup, Wiggins pushed it away. "I may need to apologize to the uvvers , but not to you," Wiggins began. "We 'ad an understanding—an arrangement. I trusted you."

"You 'ave your five thousand. Your days of running are over, my friend."

"Fleeing was a wild fancy. You know that I can't abandon the cause—mi people," Wiggins rasped. "The money is abaht 'em."

"There're many ways to fight, but all ov them require that you live. The dead can do nothin'. One more martyr will not make a difference."

Wiggins wore a haggard look. "I fled—deserted my battalion. I told myself it was to save Tessa. Commander Ashe ordered 'at we should take a stand at Swords. There were sixty ov us. We 'ad scant word about what 'appened in Dublin that mornin', but we knew it was bad. Ashe told the women to leave. Tessa wouldn't go without me. She was pleading wiv me. The Commander told me to take 'em to safety. I was afraid for Tessa—but I was afraid for myself also." Wiggins closed his eyes and clenched his fists. "The Fingal Battalion didn't 'ave a prayer. Ashe was captured and hung. The others died in Frongoch before they could be tried."

"You followed orders. You saved those women—and Tessa."

Wiggins was in a dreadful trance as he, once again, saw the faces of the men in his battalion that he left behind.

Tessa bustled into the room with a tray of food. She stopped. "Am I—?"

"No," Archie replied. "I'll come back later. He needs his dinner."

Wiggins grabbed Archie's hand. Archie waited, and then slowly pulled his hand away. "You're safe now. No mawer running. And, don't worry—you'll 'ave all the money."

Holmes and Watson were waiting in the parlor when the rest of the party, seemingly in collusion, walked in. In the lead was the largest. He bore a grim expression, and a bruise on his cheek. His eyes locked on Holmes. "Mr. 'Olmes, can you help us settle a wager?"

Holmes was amused. "What is the wager, Snape?"

No sooner were the words out of Holmes's mouth when laughter and jeers arose.

Snape ran his hand through his shaggy red hair. "The wager—that you'd not be able to remember all of us by name."

Holmes stood and pointed at Snape. "That mop of red hair was a big clue. But, I must say, you almost fooled me, as there were no hammers strapped to your forearms. It appears you no longer dance in the square ring. However, that tiny bruise—let me venture a guess. You're married."

Cheers arose from his brothers and sister.

"Yes, but she's out of my weight class. All right, then," Snape said, spreading a hand toward the others. "The lady here you know well. No contest there. And the last three lads—," Snape said, pointing to a handsome young fellow with blue eyes and the chin of an actor.

"Hello, Benjie," Holmes said. "It appears you're no longer keeping your older brother out of trouble."

A hush fell over the room. Benjie put on a smile and walked over to the next fellow—a rail-thin young man with jug-ears. His suit was well cut, but was becoming a rag pickers' envy. He walked toward Holmes, who held out his hand in restraint. The lad pushed it aside and embraced him.

"Ugly," Holmes said. "Do they still call you Ugly?"

"I've taken to the name Drake. I'm told it means dragon."

"Well you've got the wings for it," Snape jested.

A howl came from the gang.

"Drake," Holmes said. "You've turned out well."

"Ugly to you, if you don't mind, sir."

"And, what of me, Mr. Detective?" a voice beckoned from the corner of the room.

The fellow had slicked-back red hair. Blue vapor rose from a cigar clenched in his lips. His eyes studied Holmes coolly. Holmes noticed the grim fellow's left shoulder hung lower than his right. He unconsciously flexed his right hand as if preparing to fight.

"Ruck, it appears your darker nature may have gotten the best of you," Holmes remarked.

"What does that mean, Mr. 'igh-an'-mighty?"

A hush came over the group.

"'Ere now! Ugly said.

Holmes steadied Ugly with a hand on his shoulder and stepped closer to Ruck. His face hardened.

"Ruck, you come among your friends carrying a pistol. What should we make of that?"

"Well," he drawled, pulling back his jacket to reveal a holstered pistol hanging from his left shoulder. "You still 'ave a sharp eye, I see. This 'ere pistol ensures that I get respect from uvvers, Mr. 'Olmes."

"You are mistaking fear for respect, Ruck."

Archie had been observing the reunion from afar, his arm around Kate. He shrugged off Kate's arm and walked into the gathering.

"I believe I owe all of you an apology," he said, in a near whisper. "With regard to the dessert served earlier . . ."

"Ah, the money," Holmes said. "I must decline your offer."

"Very well, Mr. Holmes," Archie replied. "And, I would like my share to go to Wiggins. He is the true source of the money. It's rightfully his."

"Yes," Ugly said. "Wiggins can have my share as well."

"And mine," Benjie joined in.

"Yes," Snape said, "But I'd like to run the gold through me fingers for a while."

Ruck laughed. "I believe that you over-rate my generosity, my friends. I have never refused a gift, and I won't start now."

"You're welcome to it then," Archie said.

"It's difficult to refuse a man with a gun, ain't it, Arch?"

"It isn't your pistol, Ruck. You need the money more than us—more than Wiggins—more than friendship."

The color rose to Rucks face. "This is goin' to be an interesting evenin'."

Wiggins was slow to eat at first, but he soon downed the entire plate of food. Tessa buttered his bread and chatted away. Her green eyes flashed with excitement as she saw her brother come to life.

"With God's help you will heal quickly. I pray that Jesus will put you, once again, on the right path," Tessa exclaimed.

"Our paths separated some time ago, Tessa. How you 'ave found your faith, I will never understand. You're a good women, my dear sister, but I fear I'm beyond your prayers."

A sharp knock came to the door. Tessa got up from the edge of the bed. When she saw all the irregulars, she removed the tray and stepped back. The entourage filed in silently. Archie and Kate came last carrying a bundle. They walked to the bed, and set the heavy tablecloth sack in Wiggins' lap. As Archie let go of the ends, the tablecloth fell open, and hundreds of sovereigns spilled out over the blanket, clattering and rolling across the floor.

"All for one, an' one for all," Kate said.

CHAPTER X

WATSON QUIETY OBSERVED HOLMES as they rode back to his flat on Sheen Lane. The detective's well-ordered mind was sorting fact from emotion, differentiating law from justice, and balancing integrity and loyalty. These inner examinations would eventually coalesce into a single assessment: right or wrong. From there, a clear choice could be made: to act or not. This distillation process, often stretching beyond two pipes—for days at times—had always worked for Sherlock Holmes. However, tonight, Watson had a premonition that his friend's meticulous methodology might fail him.

"I must say that this evening was one of the most bizarre I have ever experienced," Watson said.

There was no response. No movement.

"After a good night's sleep, it might make more sense. Do you agree, Holmes?"

The remainder of the ride home was made in silence.

The next morning, Watson walked into the kitchen with the hope that his previous evening's prediction would manifest. However, he was met with an empty chair where, most mornings, Holmes would have sat sipping from his cup.

Walking to the stove, Watson tested the kettle for heat. The cold touch indicated that Holmes had broken a long-standing pattern of rising early. While unexpected, Watson felt no alarm until a tour of the flat revealed that Holmes was nowhere to be found.

A more thorough search brought Watson to his desk, where he found a sheet of folded paper under a letter-weight. Unfolding it, he read:

Watson –

I'm off for a walk and a chat with my brother. Much to ponder. I shall return for lunch – my treat!

Holmes.

<••>

Holmes made his way along the thoroughfare that stretches from Trafalgar Square to the Houses of Parliament. The skies threatened rain, and fog swirled above like angry banshees.

Just ahead a five-story white stone edifice, the War Office, had been the hub of the Empire for the previous five years. This pale building stood on the corner of Whitehall and Whitehall Place, and was guarded by crowning turrets—rooks defending the corners of a global chessboard.

A frequent visitor during the war, Holmes was waved through by the guards. He climbed to the fourth floor, down a corridor, toward an ornately carved oak door with a sign above: "Intelligence."

He knocked and entered. The aroma of hot coffee permeated the air. Mycroft was ensconced at his desk below a large map of the world, lit with garish electric lighting. *The keeper of secrets*, Holmes thought as he approached.

Holmes had not completed his analysis of the previous night—too many pipes to count. The next step: more information.

His brother did not look up from his reading. "It must be a real poser, brother," Mycroft mumbled.

Holmes unbuttoned his coat, placed his hat upon the corner of Mycroft's desk, and sat down across from him.

Holmes had his brother's attention with one word: "Zaharoff."

His bulky sibling peered over the top of his reading glasses. "Meddling in state affairs again?"

"Sitting below a map of the world does not give you command over it. However, your admonishment tells me that Basil Zaharoff may fall under the protection of our government."

Mycroft closed his file and pushed it aside. "Not at all. The French have considerable affection for the man. Our relationship with him is purely pragmatic. Basil Zaharoff is a necessary ally. Admittedly, we are strange bed-fellows."

"As an arms-dealer, his usefulness during the war is understandable. But the war is over!" Holmes retorted.

"Is it? I wonder."

Holmes leaned back and thrust his thumbs into the pockets of his waistcoat. "The man seems to have a rather checkered history. Is he likely to be held to account for his ignoble activities?"

Mycroft laughed. "Ah, we are, once again, in Sherlock's court. You are seeking testimony *against* the defendant Basil Zaharoff. Well, I can offer none. His business has been under scrutiny for many years, Sherlock. However, he has amassed great wealth, and with it friends and allies in high places. If you tangle with him, you do so at your peril."

Mycroft rose, braced himself on the edge of his desk, and leaned toward his brother. "The checkered black and white world you have known has become one more casualty of the war. It is no longer white knight against black king. The game board is painted in shades of gray. Basil Zaharoff is not Moriarty *redux*—though he might be considered a blend of Moriarty and Sir Galahad." Mycroft returned to his seat. "How do you pass judgment on a man like that?"

"How? For me it comes down to a simple truth. It is natural for everyone to seek to better him or herself. However, if one does so at the expense of others, they are, to a greater or lesser degree, immoral. So, if you will remain in the witness box a while longer, I would ask: How many thousands of people in the world have been killed or hurt by Basil Zaharoff?"

"Even after all these years, you continue to amaze me with your *naïve* notions, Sherlock. This is not about good versus evil. It's about one good versus a lesser good, or one evil against a greater evil. The differences are sometimes a hair's breadth apart."

Holmes looked at his brother with appreciation. "That seems to describe the circumstance that brought me here."

"Basil Zaharoff is the harbinger of a new commerce catering to man's baser nature. He uncorks the bottle and releases the imp."

Holmes smiled. "Mycroft, your perspective may serve me well, today."

"Yes, of course. Putting thoughts into words provides clarity, and presents new pathways to action. I have often thought it strange that people do not see that speaking is an action—is it not?"

Simpson's in the Strand remained Watson's favorite restaurant, despite the death of Chef Davey. The Doctor referred to it as "the temple of food" because it offered all of his favorites. The war being over, meat, once again, abounded on the *menu*.

"I cannot tell you how special this beef Wellington is, Holmes. How is the lamb?"

"Satisfactory, I should say. I pecked at my dinner last night. I am famished."

"About last evening, Holmes, what do you make of it all?"

"I must say that it put me in a quandary for a time, but I am satisfied that lessons were learned, and that my intervention may not be required."

"I'm pleased to hear that. All that money—and Wiggins. It's all Greek to me."

"Ha! Greek indeed. Do you know the name Basil Zaharoff?

"The enigmatic munitions mogul?"

"The very same. He is the source of the sovereigns that were heaped upon our platters yesterday."

"It seems as if your irregulars have climbed a few rungs on the fiscal ladder."

"Actually not, Watson. Zaharoff's money was not given willingly."

Watson mouth gapped, and his eyes bobbled. "They stole from Basil Zaharoff?"

"Blackmail."

Watson put down his fork. "Good Lord!"

"Indeed, I fear for the former members of our urban army. While I should like to help them, they may have ventured too far over the line."

"You have danced on the edge of the law for most of your life, Holmes. Your employment of these hooligans has, I have always felt, taken you perilously close to teetering over that line."

Holmes pushed his plate away and signaled for the waiter. After the table was cleared, he lit a cigarette. As he exhaled, his shoulders relaxed. Holmes propped himself up in his chair.

"I am particularly concerned for Wiggins. He walks a precarious path."

"I understand that your sympathies may be divided, Holmes, but he is a traitor, and a fugitive from justice."

"He fought for his country. Something I would think you might appreciate. He is—was—a soldier."

"Then, you do not intend to act?"

"I have always felt that before passing sentence on another, one must be willing to look into his eyes and hear his words. I will refrain from judgment until I have done so."

The mist had thickened and a cold drizzle sprayed the streets. The taxicab's wheels splashed along the thoroughfare until it delivered them to the promised warmth of Watson's residence. As they disembarked, a young woman dashed across the street toward them. Her black dress rustled in the wind. She struggled to keep her bonnet in place with one hand—the other holding a newspaper overhead.

"Mr. Holmes, something terrible has happened."

CHAPTER XI

TESSA'S GREEN EYES were rimmed in red. Tears, mixed with rainwater, trickled from her face. Holmes hustled her into the parlor and stoked the coals in the hearth.

"I'll put the kettle on," Watson said, as Holmes settled Tessa down.

"Mr. Holmes, something has happened to Archie and the rest. Something horrible."

She swept the wet hair from her forehead. Holmes knelt down before the trembling woman. "Take it slowly," he said. "From the beginning."

"After you left last night, Archie and Benjie took my brother to the old neighborhood—to Benjie's old room. I went along to care for my brother. Archie offered him clean clothes, and Benjie promised he would be safe there."

"What time was this, Tessa?"

"Just after eleven—half-past, at the latest—after the servants had left. Archie said he would come back in the morning to bring whatever we might need. You saw him—my brother was drained. He needed rest. Well, it took but a few minutes and my brother nodded off. Benjie wanted to stay, but I told him to go back to Grosvenor Place where he could get a proper night's sleep.

Watson offered Tessa a cup of tea and put his hand on her forehead. "We'd better get you out of those damp clothes."

"No, no, you don't understand!" Tessa protested. "They're gone. They're all gone!"

Holmes saw the fear in her eyes. "Everyone at Grosvenor Place?"

"Yes. I stayed the night with my brother. When morning came, I was able to make a bachelor's breakfast with some canned salmon and biscuits, but we had little else. I waited for Archie or Benjie to come. As noon came and went, I decided to go to Archie and the others. My brother cannot be seen in the streets, you see."

"And—?" Holmes asked.

Tessa trembled. "When I got there—" she wiped her eyes. "When I got there, the door was ajar. It was quiet. I walked into the dining room. I called out for Benjie and Archie. I went to the parlor . . ." Long sobs punctuated her report: "The room was a shambles—chairs, furniture, scattered about—and then, behind the settee—Ruck. He—he was dead!"

Tessa's face lost all of its color.

"Watson, see to her."

The Doctor helped Tessa into the bedroom and sat her on the edge of the bed. She continued to weep and babble: "They're gone!—Ruck!—the blood!"

Holmes stood by as Watson removed Tessa's shoes, and helped her lie down. "I don't think she will be much use to you in this state, Holmes. I should give her a sedative."

"Very well, Watson, I have but one more question."

Tessa curled up in a tight knot on the bed. Holmes stood to one side.

"Tessa, did you go to anyone else—the police?"

"No. I came to you straight away."

"I will go, Tessa. Dr. Watson will stay with you. You're safe here."

Seven, Grosvenor Place had lost its allure in the grim gray light that seeped from the bleak clouds. Holmes exited the taxicab a block before, and casually walked past the address. Except for the occasional passer-by, there was little activity, and few people about. He circled the block, and then climbed the stairs to number seven. Bloody fingerprints were smeared on the edge of the white doorframe. Holmes touched them and found them to be dry.

He took out his handkerchief and twisted the knob, unlatching the door. It noiselessly swung open. There was a fetid smell in the air, *rancid food*, Holmes thought. He crept from room to room. Instinct drew him to the kitchen. The rear door was open. A neighborhood cat, feasting on the kitchen table, hissed as Holmes walked by.

Dirty streaks on the floor led Holmes outside. He noticed drops of blood on the porch steps. Twisted tracks, scratches, and footprints were scrawled along the ground. He followed the trail into the back alley, where it disappeared. *They departed in vehicles*, Holmes surmised. *Four men, maybe more—and, by necessity, two motorcars.*

As he turned toward the house, he noticed the lid of a dustbin was ajar. With handkerchief in hand, he raised the lid. There, on top, were a number of gray cotton gloves turned inside out—four pair of men's gloves—*professionals.*

He went back through the kitchen and into the parlor. A floor lamp, still lit, revealed a spray of blood on the shade and surrounding wall. *A shooting took place here.* He could see Ruck's feet in the distance, poking out from behind the settee.

The shots had been to Ruck's heart. The cause of death, two brass cartridges, glistening on the floor. He picked up one of the cartridges and placed it in his pocket. Just under the settee, Holmes found Ruck's pistol. The smell told him it had not been fired.

Ruck's body had been carefully arranged. His hands were folded over his chest, and two gold sovereigns lay upon his eyes—*a message from Basil Zaharoff.*

Holmes retraced the pathway from where Ruck was shot to where he was laid to rest. He found nothing of note until something glinted on the floor. He pinched a small patch of paper tape between his fingers. It was a perfect square, a little less than one inch across. It stuck to his fingers. He opened his wallet and stuck it to one of his cards. He returned to the body. *Rigor mortis* had set in, beyond the neck and jaw, into the arms and legs. He glanced at his watch and judged the time of death to be about midnight.

As Holmes rose to leave, he caught site of two well-dressed men—one standing at each of the two entrances to the parlor. Holmes relaxed himself, and slowly brought his hands to his sides.

"I think introductions are in order," Holmes said.

The older of the two men smiled. "Mr. Sherlock Holmes, I am detective Sean Bale. Detective Grantham and I are with Special Branch. I think you had better come with us."

The younger of the two detectives had a huge unkempt mustache, adding some years to his boyish face. He walked forward, retrieving handcuffs from his belt.

The older one, who had the face of a former pugilist, cautioned his partner. "I don't believe that will be necessary, Oliver. Right, Mr. Holmes?"

"Identification?"

Bale offered his identification, and Grantham did likewise.

"Did Mycroft send you?" Holmes asked.

"If Mycroft resides at the War Office—yes."

Holmes glanced back at Ruck's body.

"Don't worry, Mr. Holmes. We will see to that fellow there. Is he a friend of yours?"

"An acquaintance."

Knowing his brother's temperament, Mycroft dislodged himself from his oak-paneled loft in the War Office, and waited in the lobby. It would be an unsuccessful attempt to defuse his brother's ire.

It would trivialize the relationship of Mycroft and Sherlock to characterize theirs as mere competition among brothers. While there were certainly games of one-upmanship, Mycroft offered Holmes a mirror of sorts—a way for him to understand himself.

Holmes was, from an early age, aware that he lacked something most people possessed—the ability to connect with others at an emotional level. Mycroft shared this condition. Each encounter Holmes had with his brother, offered additional meager insight, and also provided a sense of relief. *It's not just me. I'm not alone.*

Holmes stalked into the lobby of the War Office building, flanked by the two soldier-like gentlemen in black. His brother stood inert, unmoving, until Holmes was within

231

KIM KRISCO

five feet of him. At that point, Mycroft waved off the two escorts.

Holmes stood toe-to-toe with his brother and waited—his eyes narrowing.

"I suggest we adjourn upstairs," Mycroft began.

"Of course," Holmes shot back. "A public apology would not serve your image as the unerring oracle of Whitehall."

"This will not serve you—or your aging urban tribe."

Mycroft turned and walked toward the lift.

Mycroft directed his brother to a sitting area tucked into the far corner of his cavernous office. A Tiffany lampshade with a dragonfly motif splashed radiant colors across the room. The crimson eyes of the carnivorous insect seemed intent on the siblings as they sat in comfortable leather chairs.

"Your interference in my affairs," said Sherlock, "while far from rare, is unwelcome. The war seems to have made you more arrogant than ever."

Mycroft chuckled. "I have always envied your ability to fashion verbal slights."

"It was not a slight, Mycroft. It was an insult."

Mycroft pulled a white kerchief from his pocket, and waved it in front of Holmes. Then his hand fell into his lap. He looked up sheepishly at Holmes. "Would you believe that I did it to protect you?"

Holmes cocked his head as if a new thought had just entered his brain.

"When have I ever needed protection?"

"From your point of view, never. Not since you were seven. However, you have never butted heads with the likes of Basil Zaharoff."

"Moriarty?"

"He frolicked on the streets of London. Zaharoff plays on the world stage. He has infinite resources at his disposal. And, more importantly, friends in high places."

Holmes's complexion paled. "Do you know what happened at Grosvenor Place?"

"Not precisely, but a call just before you arrived told me someone of your acquaintance was murdered. I will have a full report within the hour."

"You must let me pursue this matter. Lives are at stake."

"That's clear, Sherlock. I'm told that among those lives may be that of a wanted man." Mycroft retrieved a report from a nearby table and paged through it. "A Rory Wiggins— an Irish rebel."

CHAPTER XII

CHECK AND MATE, Mycroft thought as he revealed the name of the former leader of Holmes's irregulars.

"Are you harboring a fugitive from justice, Sherlock?"

Holmes took in a measured breath. "Your information is faulty, Mycroft. Your sense of justice is as well."

"I don't interpret the law," the bulky brother bellowed.

"You don't serve it, either. Your law is like cobwebs, catching only small flies. The hornets, like Basil Zaharoff, break through the snare and remain free."

"And you think you're going to change that, Sherlock? Aiding and abetting. I cannot allow that."

"Possibly you can turn the same blind eye toward me that you turn toward Zaharoff!"

Mycroft shrugged his shoulders. Seconds passed before he spoke again: "What may I do for you, Sherlock?"

"Admit that you are not always right. Barring that—" Holmes reached into his vest pocket to retrieve the cartridge that he picked up near Ruck's body, and placed it on the table.

"Anything you can tell me about the gun that killed my acquaintance would be helpful."

Then, opening his wallet, he handed the sticky patch of paper to Mycroft. "What do you make of this?"

Mycroft examined it under the lamp, smelled it, and handed it back to Holmes. "I believe it is a seal used to fasten the end of a roll of film."

Holmes nodded. "Of course. One more thing, I want you to disengage your people at the scene of the crime for one hour. I need one undisturbed hour."

Mycroft hoisted himself to his feet. "I will do this for you. But, please—act with caution. Zaharoff is beyond my reach—and he's beyond yours as well."

Before leaving the War Department, Holmes called Watson to allay any concerns, and to check on Tessa. "Is she able to speak with me?"

Watson assured Holmes that she was much improved and brought Tessa to the phone.

"Mr. Holmes?"

"Hello, Tessa. I am looking after things at Archie's residence. I need to know where your brother is at this moment. I need to see him."

"He is safe, Mr. Holmes. I don't recall the exact address, but the room is on Dray Walk."

Tessa gave a detailed description and paused. "And Ruck?"

"Yes, he is dead. There were no others in the house. They were taken away. I believe they are safe for now."

Tessa's began to cry again.

"Please may I speak to the Doctor again?"

There was a long pause before Watson returned to the telephone.

"Watson, I need your help."

Those words always made Watson smile.

"You are an amateur photographer, are you not?"

"Only in the broadest sense of the word, Holmes."

"I may, at some point, require some information regarding film. I need a list of places where one might go to make prints of film if the photographer needed to keep the content of his images confidential. Can you do that?"

"I will do my best. Where are you now?"

"I am returning to Grosvenor Place. I will be going from there to find Wiggins. I should be back before supper."

"Very good, Holmes." Watson said, with a slight snicker in his voice. "You know, Holmes, this is the first time I have heard your voice over the telephone. You sound much older."

"I've aged a decade in the last twenty-four hours."

When Holmes returned to Archie's residence, he found the mansion bordered by a number of official looking chaps with their hands in their pockets. Words did not pass as he walked through a gauntlet of detectives and agents. He passed the coroner's van at the curb, and glanced into the rear window. It was empty.

He made a direct line for the alley and the dustbin, which seemed undisturbed. The gray gloves were still there. He picked them out, one by one. As he did so, something clanged against the can and fell deeper into the rubbish. Wincing a little, he felt around until he found a small, empty glass vial. He was familiar with this type of container. He sniffed at it, and placed it in his pocket. Likewise, he gathered up the gloves.

Holmes swung around and examined the alleyway for tire tracks. The dirt was mostly dry and did not bear imprints. However, there was a considerable puddle of oil. He dabbed his finger in it. The viscosity told him that it came from a gearbox. Holding his finger to his nose, he detected a burnt smell that confirmed his assessment.

As he began to rise, he noticed the butt of a cigarette—no, two. He snatched them up and wrapped them in his handkerchief.

He stopped as he approached the rear porch, turning to circumnavigate the home. Fresh footprints in a flowerbed outside the dining room window revealed that the killers and abductors were careful people. A little further on, something caught his eye: a cut wire—the telephone line.

Holmes checked his watch. Ten minutes remained.

He walked around to the street and entered the house. He stood by Ruck's body as the coroner's stretcher arrived. Removing the two gold coins, he helped to place the dead man on the pallet. "His name is Ruck," Holmes said.

The power of a name is something Holmes had reflected upon—primarily with regard to his own. It seemed silly to suppose that a name could define, shape, or limit an individual. How could figures, scribbling on a page, and sounds uttered, change anything? Yet, something deep within him suggested otherwise. *When you label a thing, you change it.* As Holmes watched the stretcher disappear beyond the doorway, he appreciated how the man's name had embodied the hulking, coarse, individual who numbered as one of his rough-and-ready band more than twenty years ago. All that remained now was his name, and memories of those who knew him.

The ride to Dray Walk followed Victoria Embankment for a time, turning just before the crimson and cream-colored Black Friars Bridge. Not knowing the address, Holmes instructed the driver to slow to a crawl. Tessa had said that Benjie's third-floor flat was adjacent to a laundry. As soon as he spotted the laundry he stopped the driver, paid the fare, and took to foot.

Directly in front of Wiggins' flat was a shiny black car—a Bentley—very much out of place in this neighborhood. Two men were waiting in the front seat. The engine was running. Holmes took up a post in a mew twenty yards from the vehicle. He made note of the license plate—YB 1217.

The heads of the passengers snapped around as the door to the apartment house opened. Two men in black hustled down the stairs and leaned into the open window of the Bentley. A conversation ensued for several minutes before they jumped into the automobile. It drove off slowly down the street.

Holmes waited to ensure that they were well out of sight.

As the sun settled on the tops of the buildings, Holmes marched to 912, Dray Walk. His eye caught sight of a puddle of oil near the curb. He pushed the toe of his boot into the edge of the spill. As he turned to mount the stairs, a rotund, red-cheeked woman in a dirty apron called out: "Mister— mister. You're Mr. Holmes ain't you?"

"I am."

"Beg pardon, sir. Come along with me, if you please," the woman said, turning and walking away.

She waddled down the sidewalk toward the laundry, turned, and waited as Holmes approached. She stepped back to usher him inside the door. "You're quite alone, ain't you?"

Holmes nodded. She made several sidelong glances through the window, and in a gruff whisper said: "Here's a fellow who wishes to talk with you." She motioned with her hand inside the steamy laundry.

Holmes walked to a small counter adjacent to the front door. The woman stood guard at the door and pointed beyond the counter. Holmes made his way through a gauntlet of canvas bags hanging on hooks from the ceiling. His nose twitched in confusion—the mingling of soiled clothing and caustic soap. Just before he reached the rear wall a voice called out. "Mr. 'Olmes, over 'ere!"

The voice came from a dark corner next to a dirty window. The shadows made it impossible for Holmes to make out the figure, but he recognized the voice.

"Wiggins, are you well?"

The man walked into the light, silhouetting himself. A loose shirt hung open, reminiscent of the ragamuffin who, long ago, helped him to recruit the irregulars.

"I knew there was trouble when Tessa didn't return. I hoped she would go to you. Is she well?"

"She's safe—with Watson."

"The others?"

Holmes took in a deep breath. The Irishman clenched his fists in a vain hope. "Please—tell me they are well."

Holmes took Wiggins by the shoulders. He could feel the young man's boney body beneath his shirt. "Let us go to a safe place where we might talk."

"No, I need to know!"

"Tessa is well, as I said. The others—Archie and the rest—have been taken away." Holmes paused. "Ruck was killed."

Wiggins' body trembled. A low, groan came up from his belly and burst from his lips: "Ruck—the hot-headed jackass!"

"I'm on their trail—and they have left some clues. How did you escape?"

"I've learned a few tricks, and Maggie Moran here was another set of eyes."

"The money?" Holmes asked.

Wiggins grabbed a canvas laundry sack at his feet and held it high. "I have plans for it."

"They know you are here in London."

"They?"

"The government—my brother."

"Are they comin'?"

"No. But they are watching me."

"Then you ain't handin' me over to them?"

"No. It's my hope that you will put the money to good use, but I fear that may not be so."

"Your fears may be justified, Mr. Holmes. I don't expect you to understand. It might be best for all of us if you was to leave me alone."

"I might do that, but I must help the others."

"I'm responsible for what 'appened."

"Then you may come along, but you must leave the money behind for now."

"I'll leave it wiv Mrs. Moran."

"Hallo!" came a cry from the front of the store. Holmes and Wiggins turned to see the stout washerwoman batting the laundry sacks aside as she ran toward them.

"Maggie," Wiggins shouted. "What's happening?"

"They're back. Be gone with you now."

"Look after the laundry," Wiggins said, pointing to the bag of gold on the floor.

Maggie nodded and opened the rear door. She peeked her head just beyond the sill and waved them through. "God bless you now, lad. *Erin go bragh.*"

CHAPTER XIII

IT WAS NIGHTFALL before Holmes and Wiggins were able to make their way to Kilburn, where the home of Wiggins' friend was located. They were careful to evade pursuit, using omnibuses that eventually delivered them several blocks from their final destination. From there they could walk, and determine if they were being followed.

Wiggins sighed as he passed a bombed out shell. "That use ta be the Carlton Tavern. Had many a good night there."

"The work of Zeppelins," Holmes said.

"Mi mouth's waterin' for a pint of Guinness."

Passers-by seemed less than friendly to Holmes. Strangers hereabouts were rare, it seemed. As they turned onto Carlton Vale, Wiggins piped up: "There's Donnie's place just ahead."

Holmes hesitated. "I think it's best if you go in by yourself. My presence will cause unnecessary attention—and anyway, I have work to do."

"Very well, Mr. 'Olmes." The younger man looked dewy-eyed at him. "You 'ave gone above an' beyon' this time, sir. I don't know 'ow to thank you."

"You're welcome, Wiggins. You stay here. I'll send Tessa this way."

"No! Tessa's not safe wiv me. Don't tell 'er where I am. And promise me, when you find out where mi bruvvers an' sisters are, you'll call on me to 'elp."

"I have Watson, and others. It would be madness for you to jump into the fray."

"Mr. Holmes, it was me as put the idea in Archie's 'ead."

A deep regret showed in his face. "I was a feef. Picked pockets. It was wrong, but you never quit me."

Holmes nodded.

"You once said, 'The greatest good to the greatest number of people is the true measure ov right an' wrong.' I fought to free two million people. I was wrong, some say."

Holmes looked affectionately on the man who had transformed himself from a non-commissioned Baker Street irregular to an Irish Volunteer.

"Wiggins, I believe that it is not always a choice between right and wrong. A wise man once told me that it's often a battle between two different kinds of right."

"We can talk abaht that later, Mr. 'Olmes. But this is about Archie, Kate, an' the uvvers. I must make it right for 'em."

<•••>

Tessa was waiting at the door when Holmes returned to Watson's abode.

"My brother? Where's my brother?"

"Safe, Tessa. With a friend."

"I must go to him."

Holmes restrained her. "They are watching us."

Watson, who was standing nearby, stiffened.

"Tessa, we could lead others to his hiding place. He is with friends now."

Tessa relaxed. Watson offered the magic elixir: "I think a spot of tea is called for here."

Over tea, Holmes relayed recent events and, in so doing, laid on the table a dirty glass vial, a cigarette butt, and several pairs of soiled gloves—one with blood on it. He had left the shell casing with Mycroft.

Watson gawked at the items littering his mahogany teatable. "Holmes, I suggest that you set up your laboratory in the kitchen, if you don't mind."

"Of course. Have you discovered any popular places where film might be discretely developed and put onto paper?"

"Indeed, Holmes. I consulted our recent acquaintance at the R. P. S., Mr. Barrenger. I would add that Mr. Barrenger showed some wariness with regard to my inquiry."

"Really, why so?"

"Well, it appears that members of the society, at times, receive—shall we say, uncommon requests with regard to printing film." He made a furtive glance at Tessa.

"Uncommon?" Holmes queried.

"Such requests—you see—often involve prurient subject matter."

"Prurient?" Holmes blurted.

"Forgive me, Tessa." Watson leaned over the table and, in a forced whisper: "Blast it, Holmes, indecent subject matter." Then, in response to Holmes's continued vacant expression, Watson added: "Lewd photographs!"

Holmes's eyebrows lifted. Tessa blushed and chuckled.

Holmes joined her. "I fear we may have besmirched your reputation, Watson."

"Your reputation, Holmes. I explained that it was you who was seeking the information."

With that, Tessa snickered. "Mr. Holmes—really!"

"Jests aside, Watson, anything of substance?"

"Yes. The developing of the film is something anyone can do with a few chemicals, and a little knowledge. The printing requires some specialized equipment. Evidently, there are a number of businesses that have a reputation for discretely developing and printing film. I made a list of them for you."

"Thank you, Watson. We should hold that information in reserve, as we have several other clues that offer greater insight. With regard to the film, the question is: why would someone take pictures during an abduction?"

Watson settled back in his chair. "Blackmail, I should think."

"No, Watson. If it were blackmail, the photography would come later, after the victims were taken away."

Tessa tapped the table with her finger. "To show to someone else."

"Yes!" Holmes replied. "I believe you are correct, Tessa. They are intended for someone who wants to keep an arm's length from this dastardly business—Basil Zaharoff."

As Holmes's chemicals and laboratory apparatus were ensconced in dusty boxes far away in Sussex, his analysis of the artifacts from Grosvenor Place relied solely upon his powers of observation.

At least three different cases, in the past, had benefited from his study of the ashes of various tobaccos. A monograph on this subject was on a bookshelf in his cottage. However, one sniff of the Grosvenor Place cigarette butts told him that it was a foreign brand. Watson seated himself at the table and looked on.

"A foreign brand, you believe," the Doctor repeated.

"Yes, the distinctive spicy aroma puts it as Turkish, Greek, or Indian."

"Greek, eh?"

"Indeed, Watson. Greek. A Karelia Rex possibly."

"What do you make of the gloves, Watson?"

"Chauffeur's gloves. All the same." The Doctor turned one of them inside out. "Hand stitching. The tags were removed. Not much here."

"It does confirm that these men are professional criminals. And, together with the cigarettes, suggests foreign imports," Holmes explained.

"And the vial, you say, once held cocaine. Bad habit for a criminal, I should think."

"You would be wrong, Watson. Taken just before one goes into action, the drug unleashes energy and enhances the overall experience. I only found one vial, so I suspect only one of the gang has the practice. I will receive a report about the shell casing from Mycroft, soon. And, with that, we have the sum total of clues." Holmes paused, "Wait a moment, I forgot the license plate."

Holmes removed a small notebook: "YB 1217. Would you be up for a small trip to wherever one goes to license a motor vehicle? If I am not mistaken there is a letter scheme which will tell us where one of the vehicles in question was licensed."

"Certainly, Holmes. I believe Tessa is on level ground again. Let me make a note of the number." Holmes tore the page from his notebook and handed it to the other.

Holmes wandered through the flat until he came upon Tessa gazing out a window into the thoroughfare below.

"A penny for your thoughts."

Without turning, Tessa said, "My penny man, I fear I'm being an awful burden. I'll be on my way soon."

"Nonsense. Watson loves playing the host. You must stay here. I will soon meet with my brother Mycroft at his club. I will stay there this evening. There is more than enough room for you here, you see. You haven't met Norah, but I know she will enjoy having you about."

Tessa sighed. "Thank you. You are a Godsend. I'm most grateful for the help you've given my brother and me. But for my brother, I would be a fugitive also—or dead."

"He told me about you, and the other women. It was a gallant thing for him to do."

"You would say so, but he judges himself to be a deserter. The others in his battalion were killed or imprisoned. They hung Ashe."

Holmes approached and put a hand on her shoulder.

"Mr. Holmes, he has dreams, bad dreams of Ashe, Donnie, Brian and the others." She burst into tears, wiping her eyes with her sleeve.

"Survivors' guilt, they call it. It's been an epidemic since the war. Your brother needs a new start. The money could buy him passage and more. Time will heal him."

"You don't know Rory," Tessa said.

The Westminster chime of Watson's mantel clock brought Holmes and Tessa back to the present moment.

"Well now," Holmes said, as he stepped back and straightened his coat. "I think we could both do with a bite to eat. Then, I must be off to the Diogenes Club."

The Diogenes Club offered the soothing ambiance that appealed to Sherlock Holmes. It was a refuge for misanthropes, ascetics and closet geniuses. Fortunately, Holmes and Mycroft had, long ago, found the keys to their respective closets.

Well acquainted with the rules of the club, Holmes quietly circumnavigated the rooms until he found Mycroft buried in a worn leather wing-back. He was thumbing a newspaper.

Holmes approached to within three feet of his big brother and waited.

Mycroft's eyes imperceptibly crept over the top of the paper. Holmes walked off toward the Strangers' Room.

Curious eyes followed the brothers as they made their way to the one room where verbal discourse was allowed.

Face to face, Mycroft retrieved the brass cartridge from his vest pocket. "Thirty-two caliber. Most likely from a Beretta."

Holmes pinched the casing in his hand. "A decent pocket pistol."

"Yes, very popular during the war, as only officers were issued pistols. More commonly found in Italy, Greece, and Turkey because of the availability of ammunition."

"Thank you. For this and for everything else," Holmes said, handing the cartridge back. "Can you see if the markings are on file?"

"Sherlock, I can see your thoughts moving toward Zaharoff." Mycroft impulsively grasped the sleeve of his brother's jacket. "Caution." He then, self-consciously, removed his hand.

"Where is he at the moment?"

"Still in the country. As you may know, he is on the board of Vickers."

Holmes waited silently. The other continued: "They will soon be testing a new weapon, and the board of directors is gathering for the big show."

"Where?"

"At Vickers in Barrow-in-Furness."

CHAPTER XIV

WATSON WAS AGLOW when he returned to his flat. But, the glow noticeably dimmed when Tessa informed him that Holmes had gone to meet with Mycroft.

"I have some important information for him. Let's hope that he returns directly," Watson huffed, as he fell in a heap into his comfy chair by the hearth.

"I'm not certain he will return," Tessa countered. "It seems he intends to stay the night at the club."

"That won't do. I must ring up the Diogenes Club immediately."

Fortunately, Mycroft and Holmes were still in the Strangers' Room when Watson's call came in. Following the club's reclusive protocol, an attendant at the desk took the message and walked to the bulletin-board near the entrance to post it. However, as he made his way, he waved the note at Mycroft. This caught Holmes's attention as well.

Mycroft harrumphed. "There is a message for you, Holmes—it must be for you, as my office would not dare to encroach upon my private time."

The older brother waved the attendant in his direction. Holmes snatched the note from the attendant's hand and read it.

"Ha! Good old Watson! He has traced a motor-car license-plate associated with the kidnapping and murder."

"Let me guess," Mycroft said. "It is registered in Lancashire."

"Yes—Lancashire. The county that is home to . . . Barrow-in-Furness."

"Indeed," Mycroft huffed. "And, you believe they would transport your friends three hundred miles across country?"

"I may be pulling at threads, Mycroft. But Zaharoff is known to take a personal hand in managing his affairs. He has sailed halfway around the world to make a sale. He made a trans-Atlantic voyage to see Sarah Bernhardts' farewell performance of *Mort de Cleopatre* in New York—as a special guest of the actress. Time, money and distance are never limitations for that man." Holmes froze for a brief moment as if he were testing his assertion—then nodded to himself in approval.

"Mycroft, I have one last favor to ask."

"Only one?" replied the other.

A return phone call to Dr. Watson put travel plans into play. By the time Holmes returned to Sheen Lane, the good Doctor had booked accommodations on the train to Liverpool, and a connection to the last ferry going to Barrow-in-Furness.

Tessa was waiting in the hallway when Holmes crossed the threshold. "I'll not be left behind!" the plucky woman exclaimed. "My Benjie is in need, as well as the others. They're my family."

"Your brother made that abundantly clear, Tessa," Holmes replied. "I'm bound, as a gentleman, to honor your brother's request, and I suppose that you're part of the bundle."

Her left hand went to her hip and her right index finger wagged at Holmes. "I'm not a bundle. I love you, but I'll not be treated that way. I'm a formidable woman, Mr. Holmes!"

On the edge of retreat, Holmes had to admit to himself that Tessa was, every inch, a strong woman. Watson looked on in mild amusement.

"My apologies," Holmes said, with a deferential nod. "However, I would suggest you change your garments, as they may attract far too much attention. So, you have some shopping to do. Then you will fetch your brother. Take a cab. Stay alert, and stay in the shadows, going and coming, as you may be followed. We will meet the two of you at—Watson?"

"Euston Station, 6.45—I suggest at the statue of Robert Stephenson in the ticket hall."

"Thank you, Mr. Holmes. I'm sorry to trouble you."

"No apologies needed,' Holmes replied. "That's to be expected. You are one of the irregulars, after all. And—that was delightfully irregular."

Tessa and Watson chuckled.

Holmes retrieved the two gold sovereigns he had taken from Ruck's eyes and gave them to Tessa. As she dashed off, Watson looked his old comrade in the face, "The old dogs are in the hunt again."

"Are you up to it?"

"Wouldn't miss it for the world. I'll fetch my revolver. I believe it is clean, but it could probably use a drop of oil. I must arrange for two more tickets."

Holmes waited in the ticket hall at Euston while Watson finalized arrangements inside. Two tightly wrapped figures made their way toward the life-sized statue of the fellow who pioneered the railway across much of Britain, and other parts of Europe. Holmes was pleased that the misty weather had colluded to hide the face of Rory Wiggins.

Watson was waiting as they made their way to their compartment. "I bought first-class tickets to ensure our privacy," Watson explained, as they hustled down the platform.

As they settled into their seats, the train moved out. A collective exhalation emanated from the foursome.

"I should begin by telling you that I am not certain we are on the right trail," Holmes said.

Watson's brow wrinkled. "I don't follow you, Holmes."

"The truth is, there are but two converging clues that might lead us to the location of the others. The license plate is registered in a location where Basil Zaharoff will soon be—Barrow-in-Furness, and the Vickers Naval Yard. While my instincts tell me we should go there, I could be wrong."

A dull silence gave way to the click-clack of the wheels on the rails.

As Holmes and Watson took up their newspapers, Wiggins nudged Tessa. "What's all this I hear about Benjie?"

Tessa reddened.

"He's a feisty one, little sister!"

"And you're the one to know," Tessa kidded.

Wiggins brushed the hair from Tessa's forehead. His eyes grew wide and wet. "You know, I wasn't altogether pleased when you started walkin' the streets preachin' an' singin' hymns with the Sally Army. I thought they were takin' advantage of your good nature."

"I am blessed to be able to give my help to the people who need it."

"But it's not safe!"

"Rory, I can walk into any pub or low gambling-house in Spitalfields as a Salvationist knowing that I am completely safe. We care for them, and they care for us."

"You're a fine woman," Wiggins declared. "I suppose, you don't need the likes of me lookin' after you any more."

"I always want you looking after me—and me looking after you. You must promise me that you'll be an uncle to my children."

"Children, is it?" Wiggins said.

"Stop it. You know what I mean. Don't do anything foolish."

"Seems like that's all I've done most of mi life. I'm not sure I can stop."

"You'll stop, all right, Rory. I need you."

"Don't you worry, Tessa."

The screeching brakes signaled their arrival at Lime Street Station. The train-ride offered time for reflection. Holmes had used it to cobble together a plan. During the ferry-trip from Liverpool to Barrow, he sat in the familiar chair as commander of the irregulars—with his loyal lieutenant, Wiggins, once again, at his side.

As soon as the ferry took to the water, Wiggins made his way to the bow. The wind was brisk, and the salt spray splashed on his face and lips. Tessa watched him from the enclosed upper deck. Watson, with a cup of tea in each hand, drew near to the young woman. Looking over her shoulder he spied Wiggins. "He loves the sea, doesn't he?" Watson said, handing her the tea.

"He's thinking: just over there is home. He can smell the green grass and the foamy dark porter on the wind."

"I suppose he'd rather be going there than to Barrow."

"He would, but he cannot. There especially, they'd be looking for him. He's taken a chance just boarding this ferry."

"Archie said he might be going abroad—maybe America."

"That would be a nice dream. But I fear his memories will take him back to Ireland—to fight on." Tessa turned. "Does it bother you, Dr. Watson, when I say these things?"

"I understand about fighting for a cause—for freedom. I've fought for King and country. In the midst of battle, I would look across the field at my enemy, knowing that they were probably honorable men fighting for what they believed was right. Such thoughts were not good, because I knew that I would soon be asked to kill those men."

Holmes wrapped his scarf around his neck and pushed his hat down tightly upon his head. He walked along the rail until he came to Wiggins. For a long while, they held a respectful silence.

The wind suddenly buffeted, and Holmes made a quick grab for his hat. "Rory, my friend." Holmes waited.

His lieutenant smiled. "It doesn't sound proper comin' from you, Mr. 'Olmes."

"All these years and I never called you by your first name."

Wiggins continued to stare out over the water. "Friend. You never called me friend."

"You knew, though."

"I'm 'onored to be your friend."

Wiggins chortled. "It's getting' too treacly fer me."

Holmes laughed, "For me also. Wiggins, I have hope that you will be using that money in London to buy your freedom. You see, I cannot permit you to purchase arms for an insurrection."

Wiggins' gaze remained on the open waters that stretched out before the bow. "The decision you're askin' me to make is an impossible one. Desert mi people, or face the disapproval of one of mi oldest an' dearest friends."

"I think you can see that I am facing a similar dilemma."

"A man 'as to do what 'is conscience demands."

"Exactly so," Holmes said. "I know your heart is a good one, Wiggins. If you thought only of yourself, you would not be here. You would have fled, or stayed in London."

"You see, Mr. 'Olmes, the same heart that insists that I must help the uvvers, insists that I 'elp the people of mi homeland. How can mi heart be right in one case, an' wrong in anuvver? Your own words, sir: the greatest good, fer the greatest number of people, is the true measure of right an' wrong."

"And I still hold to that principle. The dilemma springs from the fact that you stand with your people on that shore across the water. I stand with my people on the shore we left behind. It seems fitting that we have this conversation here, in the waters that separate our two countries. For a while we will, once again, become allies. But, when this quest is done, we shall have to choose sides."

"And folla our 'arts."

"Come, let's go inside with the others. We have some planning to do."

"Wait, Mr. 'Olmes. I need to say somethin'—ask you somethin'."

Holmes nodded.

"I'm not sure as 'ow all this'll turn out. But, if somethin' 'appens to me, I want you to promise that you won't let me be buried on English soil."

Holmes's eyes softened and narrowed. "I believe we have a good chance . . ."

"Mister Holmes. Please. It's not abaht you, or your plans, or abaht Archie an' the rest. Please don't let me be buried on English soil."

Holmes's body slackened. "I imagine you've had more reason than most to think about death. Do you recall?—you must have been fourteen or fifteen. After Fanny died, Watson and I were debating about what, if anything, lay beyond this life. You came along, like a junior professor, and declared that the Vikings had it right. They didn't want to be buried in any soil."

"Funny—isn't it—the fings we recall. I remember dippin' in a gentleman's pocket an' pullin' up an old inkwell."

Holmes's head cocked in recollection. "An inkwell and a handkerchief."

"A 'andkerchief with an 'ole in it!"

They chuckled.

"Come, we have some planning to do—and I could use a cup of coffee," Holmes declared.

As they walked away, Wiggins turned back and pointed off the port bow. "Ireland is just over there."

"And, beyond it, America," Holmes added.

Watson motioned for Holmes and Wiggins to follow him to a secluded section of the dining room. Tessa was waiting in a dimly lit corner at a small round table. The other passengers were gathered nearer to the café.

"Why the secrecy?" Wiggins asked.

"It's possible that some of Zaharoff's associates are aboard," Holmes explained.

As they gathered, Watson piped up. "Tea? Coffee?"

"Later, Watson. When we arrive at Barrow, a telegram from Mycroft will be waiting for me telling us the location of Basil Zaharoff and his entourage. We must watch him. The hope is that those who contact Zaharoff will lead us to the others."

"You believe that they are still . . . I mean, that we can find them?" Watson asked, almost expressing the fears that all of them held.

"I believe so. He did not get his money back, and he is the kind of fellow who confronts his adversaries. He has a reputation as a fierce rival who not only needs to win, but likes to crush his opponents."

Tessa cringed.

Watson retrieved a scrap of paper from his pocket and placed it in the center of the table.

Holmes nodded. "Remember this number, YB 1217. I believe it is the license plaque of Zaharoff's henchmen. That car offers the best opportunity for us to find the others. If that car is there, it may lead us to where we want to go. It's a black touring car—a Bentley."

Wiggins picked up the paper and stuffed it in his pocket. "I'm the most likely to follow anyone. They don't know me."

"An excellent point," Watson agreed.

"Zaharoff's men may not know you, but the authorities do," Holmes added.

"I'll take mi chances!"

With the crux of the plan in place, details and assignments followed over a cup of coffee. The volunteers might have been irregular, but their planning and organization was impeccable, thanks to Sherlock Holmes.

The foursome waited near the gangplank as the ferry pulled to the dock.

"I'm off to the telegraph office," Holmes said, implementing the first part of the plan.

"And I'll secure transportation," Watson seconded.

"My brother and I will check the passengers disembarking," Tessa added, confirming their assignment.

Tessa and her brother were on the gangplank as it hit the wharf. They waited while a parade of hand-carts, bearing luggage, were hustled off the ferry. When the last trunk was wheeled down, Holmes and the others made for land.

Wiggins and Tessa took up their post a short distance from the ferry, where the luggage had been stacked. Two young porters stood near, their bright red caps with the insignia of the ferry line standing out in sharp contrast to their well-worn clothing.

Wiggins retrieved a cigarette and patted his pockets for matches. He leaned closer to one of the red-capped porters. "Hey, 'ave you got a match?"

The lad poked at his friend. "A match?"

The other nodded, and handed over a small box. Wiggins shook another cigarette from the pack and offered it to the two lads. The first waved it off, but the other pulled one out, twisted it in his fingers, and brought it to his nose, enjoying the aroma. He pointed at the red and white box in Wiggins' hand. "Irish, eh?"

Wiggins nodded, lit his cigarette, and handed the matches back.

The porters straightened up as a car pulled around between the ferry and the stack of luggage. It was a long black touring car. Wiggins' eyes widened as it swung around to reveal the license plaque YB 1217 in bold black letters.

Tessa's eyes were riveted on the string of passengers, and she didn't notice her brother as his brown eyes narrowed in thought. He nudged the older of the two porters, whispered in his ear, and put a shilling in his palm. The lad swept his red cap from his head and handed it to Wiggins.

The driver of the Bentley waited.

Two men approached the car—one in a black suit, the other with a large gray cape and matching wide-brimmed hat. The latter had a salt-and-pepper mustache and a pointy beard.

When the driver exited the vehicle, Wiggins dashed around and stood near him. Without speaking, the driver opened the rear door of the car, and the bearded gentleman entered. The escort in black walked around to where the bags and trunks were piled. Wiggins followed silently. The driver pointed to a suitcase, and then a second one. Wiggins tipped his cap, picked them up, and followed the driver to the rear of the car. A luggage platform hung off the back. Wiggins placed the two bags on the platform, and strapped them down. The escort popped a coin into Wiggins' open palm and joined the bearded man in the car.

Tessa watched wide-eyed—her mouth agape, as her brother crouched down onto the edge of the luggage platform. As the car swung toward the gates of the dock, Wiggins tossed the red cap away and winked at Tessa.

PART THREE

HOLMES AND THE IRREGULARS:
AN ADVENTURE.

CHAPTER XV

WIGGINS HELD ON FOR DEAR LIFE as the car made its way to the edge of town. It slowed as it came to the gates of a large estate. A gardener tipped his cap, swinging the gates open. Wiggins jumped off the platform and rolled into the bushes.

He scrambled along a ditch and hoisted himself up onto the wall surrounding the grounds. A sprawling brick edifice, in the Elizabethan style, loomed at the end of the driveway.

Wiggins dropped down, brushed himself off, and casually walked toward the entrance. The gardener was just closing the gates when he approached. "Oi! Do you know if they're lookin' for 'elp 'ere?"

"Who are you?"

"Rory's the name. Jack-of-all-trades."

"They might be needin' help this week as there's goin' to be a grand gathering. I'll ring up the house."

HOLMES returned to the wharf to find Watson consoling a tearful Tessa. "What's happened? Where's Wiggins?"

"He's ridden off on the back of the hooligans' motor-car," Watson explained.

Holmes shook his head in disbelief as the details were relayed to him.

"He knows where we are staying," Holmes said, consoling Tessa. "We will await word from him there. Mycroft came through," he added, unfolding a telegram. "Vickers owns a large estate on the edge of town. The board members, including Zaharoff, will be staying there while a demonstration at the Vickers facilities is being conducted. Mycroft is endeavoring to garner an invitation for him and me. Regardless, that is where we will reconnoiter, taking shifts—the three of us for now."

Watson led the way to a cab that took them to the Majestic Hotel in the heart of the city. They quickly acquired accommodations, reserving a room for a fourth guest who was yet to come.

WIGGINS stood to attention as the butler—a large man of jovial temper— quizzed him.

"So, you're a jack-of-all-trades. How are you with motorcars? Can you operate them?"

"Yes sir, Mr. Bates, operate 'em, wash 'em, an' repair 'em."

The old Butler's brows lifted. "Look here, are you saying you're a mechanic?"

"Yes, sir, that was mi job durin' the war."

"You were a soldier?"

"I fought under Kitchener."

"I see. Very well. You'll be a jack-of-all-trades this week. We have many guests arriving today. So, for now, you will help Mr. Meyers transport our guests from place to place. Mind you, while our need is great this week, I cannot promise anything beyond that."

"That's fine, sir," Wiggins said.

"Very well then, one of the lads will find a uniform for you. Clean yourself up, and report to Mr. Meyers in the carriage house."

"Thank ya so much, Mr. Bates," Wiggins replied, with all the deference he could muster.

HOLMES was recounting the contents of a telegram, recently arrived. "Mycroft was successful in ingratiating himself to a contingent of bureaucrats from the War Office who are coming to observe the testing of a new weapon. I am beginning to get the distinct impression that he wishes to limit our activities."

"Yes, I see," said Watson. "Rather a mixed blessing, what?"

Tessa was looking at the driveway leading to the Majestic's entrance. "I thought my brother would be here by now."

Holmes walked to the window. "He's a bright fellow, Tessa. He'll return soon. I tell you what—why don't you wait for him here? Dr. Watson and I will be among the chimneys of the Vickers plant. If you're hungry, order something for yourself downstairs."

"Ah, Holmes!" Watson called from the next room: "We might want a quick bite before we head out."

"Later, Watson."

The Doctor's shoulders slumped. His stomach growled as he went to the closet for their coats. He donned his wrap, and helped Holmes with his.

Steadfast at the window, Tessa waited. Within the hour her patience was rewarded. A familiar black touring car pulled up to the entrance of the hotel. A driver jumped out and disappeared under the portico.

Tessa immediately ran for the door, grabbing her sweater from the bed.

Racing down the stairs, she almost stumbled as she came to the expansive lobby. She calmed herself, then casually strolled through the lobby searching for the driver of the car.

Seeing no one, she went to the entrance and spied the empty vehicle. In a slow, carefree manner she walked out of the hotel. As she passed the car, she gasped when she saw the license number: YB 1217.

After several deep breaths, she walked along the side of the Bentley to the open window on the driver's side. She glanced about before she poked her head in the window.

"What's all this, now?" a gruff voice behind her growled.

With her heart in her throat, Tessa slowly pulled her head out of the window and turned.

She was greeted by the smiling face of her older brother.

"Rory! You beast," she said, stomping her foot. "You frightened the . . ." Tessa stopped as she took in the starched uniform her brother wore.

He gripped her shoulders. "I'm in, Tessa!"

Holmes and Watson watched people come and go from the fortified front gate at the expansive Vickers manufacturing facility. The sky darkened as Holmes approached the guardhouse.

The sentinel put up a hand when Holmes presented himself. "Excuse me, sir." Holmes said.

"Sergeant," the guard replied.

"Well, sergeant, I was wondering if you could tell me if my colleague, Mycroft Holmes, has arrived yet?"

"Does the gentleman work here?"

"No, no, my good man. He's with the War Office."

"Oh! Let me see."

The guard walked to his desk and ran his fingers over a long row of badges with blue ribbons attached. Holmes looked over his shoulder.

The tin badges were stamped: V.S. & M. Ltd., and the ribbon below said "VISITOR." Small scraps of paper, with names, were pinned to the ribbons.

"Here we are, sir!" the sergeant exclaimed, pointing to one of the badges. "Mycroft Holmes, is that right, sir?"

"Yes, sergeant."

"Well, sir, as his badge is here, it's safe to assume that he has not yet arrived."

"Thank you so much, sergeant. I'll await his arrival, if you don't mind."

"All right, sir—but outside, if you please."

Holmes made his way to Watson, who nervously flapped his arms to keep warm.

"There's bad weather coming, Holmes. What did you find?"

Holmes reached into his pocket and pulled out two badges with ribbons attached.

"Right-o, Holmes!"

"I believe we will wait until the guard is changed."

WIGGINS gave Tessa the address of the mansion in Barrow, and headed off to complete the errand for which he had been dispatched—three cases of champagne for the evening's reception.

His sister tugged at his sleeve as he turned to go.

"Remember your promise, Rory. Nothing foolish."

"I promise," he said, with a mischievous smile. "Tell Mr. 'Olmes abaht what I learned the moment 'e returns. I may not be able to come 'ere again, but I'll send more information when I can.

As Wiggins carried the last case of champagne into the kitchen, the butler, Bates, requested that he come to his office.

"Rory, you and Stanley will be picking up our guests at the station this afternoon. When everyone has arrived, wash and polish the motorcars—including those of our guests. You may have the evening off, but be ready to go early tomorrow. Our guests will be leaving for Vickers at eight."

"Right-o, Mr. Bates."

As he turned to leave the butler called out: "Wait—wait a moment." He reached into his desk drawer and took out two tin badges. "You and Stanley will need these tomorrow to get into the factory. You should pin it on the breast pocket of your uniform."

Wiggins smiled and gave a friendly salute. Bates frowned.

"Beg pardon, sir. A habit."

"The war's over, Rory. A simple 'Yes, sir,' will suffice."

Returning to the garage, Wiggins relayed Mr. Bates' instructions, and gave a badge to Stanley.

"So we both have the night off?"

Wiggins shrugged. "I suppose so—as soon as we get the guests 'ere, and then clean and polish these cars."

The phone rang. Stanley answered it.

"Well, we're off to the station. The London train arrives in thirty minutes." Stanley straightened Wiggins' tie. "You're to pick up Mr. Zaharoff at the guest house on the way out, as he wishes to greet the guests as they arrive. You'll follow the lane just west of the big house. Stanley will show you the way."

A few minutes later, Wiggins pulled the motor-car up to the front door of the cottage. In full evening dress, Zaharoff was waiting at the door smoking a cigar. He looked at Wiggins, cocking his head to fully take in the stranger in.

A maid came to the door with a cape and assisted him in putting it over his shoulders. As she buttoned the collar of the cape and adjusted it on his shoulders, he asked: "Who is that driver? I've not seen him before."

"New man, sir."

"His name?"

"Rory."

As Zaharoff walked to the car, Wiggins opened the door.

Zaharoff paused.

"Where are you from, Rory?"

271

"The Isle of Man, sir."

Zaharoff smiled. "One wouldn't think so from your accent."

CHAPTER XVI

HOLMES NUDGED WATSON as a new guard took his place in the gatehouse at the entrance to the Vickers plant.

They made their way to the gate, waited for the guard to poke his head out, and pointed to the badges on the lapels of their coats.

"Do you require directions, sir?"

"Do you, perchance, have a diagram or map of the plant?" Holmes asked.

The private was accommodating, pulling out a printed plan of the facilities. "You're with the Whitechapel group, are you?"

"Yes." Watson said.

The guard pointed to the map. "This area over here is where the gathering will be tomorrow morning. It will be a great day for the trial—if the weather holds."

"Yes," Holmes agreed. "So where does the trial take place, exactly?"

"It will be off the wharf to the west."

They thanked the helpful soldier and walked on.

The Vickers plant was spread over 14,000 acres, and included a steel mill, jute works, airplane and munitions factories, and, of course, a massive shipyard. During the war, over 82,000 workers, including 8,000 women, worked and boarded here. Of course, that number had been greatly reduced since the war ended, but it was still a populous place.

Holmes and Watson were awed by the size of the plant. Hundreds of brick buildings, and scores of tall chimneys, cluttered the horizon. Railway tracks crisscrossed the ground that, due to the inclement weather, was as muddy as the soggiest moors in Scotland. They slowly made their way along the edge of a roadway toward the western wharf. A light drizzle began to fall.

"Holmes, my shoes are completely soaked. Judging from the scale of your map, we're a mile or more from our destination."

"An old soldier should be used to slogging in mud."

"The operative word here is *old*. Most old soldiers are wise enough to forego slogging in the muck."

"And, to what do you attribute the fact that you are not so wise?"

"I attribute it to you," Watson exclaimed. "Dry-footed old soldiers do not have you as a companion."

Holmes chuckled. Watson never failed to amuse. It seems that men never grow too old for juvenile taunts. He recalled the squabbles that Mycroft and he had when they were young. It never came to fisticuffs, largely because his brother had seven years and two stone on him. Now, Holmes could see that genuine affection lay behind Mycroft's frequent boyish banter.

At the sound of a motor-car coming up quickly behind them, Holmes and Watson turned to see a sedan bearing down. "Here we go!" Watson shouted. "Help is on the way."

274

The car went by without slowing, splashing mud in every direction.

"The blighter!" Watson cried.

"I second that, Watson. Did you notice it was a Bentley?"

<•••>

WIGGINS stood outside his vehicle parked at the entrance to the Barrow-in-Furness railway station. The grand glass-roofed edifice looked more like a gigantic conservatory than a railroad depot.

Basil Zaharoff exited the car with but two words: "Wait here."

Wiggins was 'bearding the lion' in his den by chauffeuring Zaharoff. He might have considered this a piece of good fortune, except for the feeling that the millionaire arms-dealer seemed to have formed suspicions about him.

Basil Zaharoff emerged from the station with a well-kept middle-aged woman on his arm. Her hair was pulled back from her face, fastened tightly behind her head with a red scarf. She carried a portfolio. A porter followed with her bags. The two seemed to be engaged in a serious conversation. As they approached, Wiggins stared in amazement. *It's Miss Murtagh!*

The woman shared Wiggins' look of surprise as he opened the door and waited. Entering the car, she winked at him, and put her finger to her lips. The porter helped Wiggins secure her luggage on the rack.

During the ride back to the manor house the conversation in the rear seat was light and inconsequential. Then, the woman opened her portfolio and laid it in Zaharoff's lap, showing him what appeared to be papers of some kind.

Zaharoff shuffled through them silently. "Are our friends managed?"

The woman nodded. "They are no longer a concern."

Zaharoff stroked his beard. "Why all of them?"

"The nature of this group is such that, if you deal with one, you deal with all. And, they have refused to return the funds."

The woman pointed to Wiggins. Zaharoff caught Wiggins' eyes in the mirror.

"Keep your eyes on the road, Rory," the Greek said, closing the portfolio and handing it back to Maeve Murtagh.

"Do you wish to keep it a while longer?" she inquired.

Zaharoff shook his head in the negative. "Burn it. Tomorrow we're off to the plant at eight. A briefing, a little breakfast, and then the demonstration."

"I understand this is a trial for your 'Jumping-Jack'," she said.

Zaharoff glanced at the mirror before answering. "Suffice it to say, Maeve, that you will witness something beyond traditional bombs, shells and torpedoes."

"Fireworks—jolly good! I like fireworks."

"The car pulled up to the steps of the Vickers house.

Zaharoff turned to Wiggins. "I will find my way. Take Miss Murtagh's bags to her room, then bring the car around to the cottage. I have an errand for you."

HOLMES and Watson were prompted to make a change in course after the Bentley sped by. The license plate had been covered with mud, but the fact that the windows were draped led Holmes to believe that it might be one of the two motor-cars they were seeking.

Holmes bent down on one knee and examined the tire tracks in the mud. "I have to admit that I was grasping at straws when we came here, but the appearance of that vehicle confirms my instincts, Watson. These tracks look familiar."

"You have the cunning of a fox, Holmes."

"Reassuring, I'm sure. However, we both know that the most cunning creature on earth is man. And the man whose trail we are on is a consummate predator."

The drizzle turned to a light rain as they followed the roadway that the Bentley had taken. When they came to a fork, Holmes bent down.

"There are tire tracks in both lanes. The ones on the right are more recent."

Suddenly, Holmes ran forward and picked up something small and white from the edge of the road.

"Here, Watson—a discarded cigarette." He held it under his nose. "A familiar aroma."

"Like those at Grosvenor Place?"

Holmes nodded.

"Let me see the map," Watson said. "This road will take us either to a barge terminal, or to the wharf to the west—but not before we are thoroughly soaked."

"Hark! Do I hear the grousing of the Tommy in the trenches again?"

"Making light of it will not make us dry."

As if guided by Watson's wishes, a Rolls Royce pulled up. "Are you lost, gentlemen?" the driver asked.

"Yes, yes," Watson said.

Holmes intervened: "We're with the War Office. But the weather is getting the best of us. Would it be possible to catch a ride to the western wharf?"

"Here for the demonstration, eh? Well, that's where I'm headed, so I'd be pleased to take you."

When Watson's grumbling subsided, Holmes quizzed their benefactor: "Are you involved with the demonstration tomorrow?"

The man grimaced. "You may be from the War Office, but I know better than to divulge confidential information at a time of heightened security."

"I understand—?"

"Arthur."

"I understand, Arthur," Holmes conceded. "Do you know if the viewing area will be covered? I just wish to know how to dress."

"Yes sir, the pavilion is already in place. We've been preparing for a week now. If this weather doesn't clear, though, they may not get the plane up. Ah-h . . . are you looking forward to the festivities?" Arthur asked, changing the subject.

WIGGINS carted the luggage into the mansion and found his way to the east wing, where the newest guest, Maeve Murtagh, was staying. He knocked.

The door swung wide, revealing a buxom, raven-haired woman with a broad grin on her face.

"Your bags, miss," Wiggins began.

"No need for formalities, Mr. Wiggins."

"This is a shocker!" Wiggins began, quickly lowering his voice. "You forgot to mention that you an' Zaharoff are mates."

"Does it matter, really? You will get your rifles and weapons when I have the money."

"You know I 'ave the money! What I can't understand is why you suggested I steal it from your colleague—or partner—whatever he is."

"Former employer," Maeve answered. "My motivations are none of your concern. Ours is a simple transaction—money for guns. Don't complicate it."

"The transaction is far from simple. You can't blame me if I doubt you."

"Look here. With one call I can have you put away. I have the guns. When will I receive the money?"

"Our deal's on 'old until I can find mi friends. Zaharoff's taken 'em. You never warned me abaht 'im."

"I thought you were a smart boy," Maeve said. "I guess I was wrong. You had better wise up. I suggest you go back to London before you muck it up. You will lose the guns—and maybe more."

"As you say, a person's motivations shouldn't matter. Just you 'ave the guns ready."

"You have no idea who you are dealing with, do you, Rory?"

"You may be right," Wiggins replied, tipping his cap. As he was leaving, he noticed the portfolio on the bed. "Good evenin', Miss Murtagh."

Wiggins leaned against the Bentley he had parked in front of Zaharoff's cottage. Two men in tight black suits emerged, followed by Zaharoff. The larger one was darker skinned and had deep-set brown eyes. The shorter one was unshaven with a put-on grin. They took up places on either side of Wiggins.

Zaharoff stood in the doorway. "I just had an interesting phone call." The Greek strolled toward the car, retrieving a cigarette from his pocket. The small man on Wiggins' right lit it.

"Aidan," Zaharoff said to the larger of the two, "This is Rory—Rory, Aidan."

Aidan leaned toward Wiggins, uttering the enigmatic words: "*Loayr Gaelg rhym, my sailt.*"

Wiggins was silent.

"Nothing to say, Rory?" Zaharoff asked. "Aidan is speaking in your mother tongue."

Wiggins' eyes flashed back and forth as if searching for an escape. "Left Man when I was young."

Zaharoff smiled. "That's a shame. Open the rear door, Rory," he ordered.

Wiggins did as he was told.

"Now get in."

The bigger man grinned and pushed Wiggins into the back seat, quickly getting in next to him. The shorter man took his place behind the wheel.

"Look 'ere!" Wiggins shouted.

"No, you look!" the brute said, poking a Beretta in Wiggins' side. "Be good or I'll let some daylight in ta ya."

The car started.

Zaharoff thrust his head through the open window. "I'm not certain who you are, Rory, but I know who you are not."

CHAPTER XVII

HOLMES OBSERVED A BEEHIVE OF ACTIVITY as he and Watson approached the Vickers wharf.

"Will this do, gentleman?" their driver asked, pulling to a stop.

"Thank you, Arthur," Watson said. "It looks as though the rain has let up."

"Yes. It bodes well for tomorrow."

Watson stretched and stomped his feet, flapping his arms as the car drove off.

"You look like a fish out of water, Watson."

"A man out of water, I should say—and glad of it."

It seemed that most of the activity on the wharf was directed toward beautification. Trolleys, piled high with crates, were being hauled into nearby warehouses, broom and bucket brigades were aplenty, and tugboats pulled barges away from the water's edge. Nearby, a white tent, like Camelot's castle, stood high and tall.

Holmes made for the tent and Watson followed.

Men setting up tables and chairs only gave the duo a passing glance as they entered the pavilion. Boxes of bunting waited in the corner.

Holmes stopped in the middle, and turned in a slow arc toward a platform set between bollards at the edge of the wharf. The only other object in his view was a rusty, derelict ship anchored in the distance.

"What do you make of all this, Watson?"

"I doubt that there is anything to see at the moment, Holmes. It's clear, from the loose-lipped Arthur, that the demonstration tomorrow is aerial in nature."

"Yes. No doubt this aircraft will swoop out over the water to the collective *ooh*'s and *aah*'s of inebriated guests."

"Disconcerting, to say the least, Holmes. To think that, after the war, anyone could treat weapons as an entertainment."

"If any of these guests had spent one day on a battlefield, they would shrink from any such display."

"Amen to that, Holmes."

WIGGINS turned in his seat to ascertain his surroundings. "Where ar' we goin'?" he asked.

"You were looking lonely, so we thought you'd like some company."

The motor-car made its way through the Vickers gates unimpeded, and on toward a warehouse that sat adjacent to the water's edge. The sign above the door simply read—W42. A twin of their car sat outside the building. The larger man, holding the pistol, spoke to the driver: "Up ahead, Jake, the door. We need to go inside."

The car braked and turned to face a large pair of doors at the end of a metal-clad building. The driver pressed the horn—two sharp blasts. The tall doors parted, and a head poked through the gap. The driver waved.

Two men exited the building, each taking one of the doors in hand. The doors were rusty, and opening them proved difficult for the well-dressed men. One of them cursed as his door jammed.

The driver laughed. "Bert 'asn't lifted anything heavier than a bottle of gin in the last ten years."

The larger man chortled. "Give 'im a 'and, Jake." The driver stepped out.

Wiggins was aware that his captor was fully engaged in the goings-on outside. The barrel of the pistol, which had been pushed tightly against his ribs, began to relax.

In one quick move, Wiggins grabbed the barrel of the pistol with both hands, and slid away, turning the barrel down.

The pistol fired—the bullet shattering the floorboards. Wiggins wrenched the weapon away and opened the door. As he emerged, the driver parried and pulled a pistol from his jacket. Wiggins aimed and fired. The brute's right leg buckled, and he fell to the ground. The man in the back seat reached through the open door. Wiggins turned the pistol in his direction, halting him, motioning with the gun for him to get out. His former captor stepped out of the car.

The two men standing by the partially open warehouse doors slowly walked toward Wiggins. He fired two shots at their feet, opened the driver's door, and jumped into the car. He tossed the pistol aside, and slammed the vehicle into reverse. His right hand was bleeding and burning, making it difficult for him to manage the wheel. A shot rang out. Searing pain erupted in Wiggins' shoulder. He stepped on the gas-pedal and raced away with the echo of gunshots reverberating in his ears.

<•••>

HOLMES and Watson made their way along the wharf, toward what the map indicated was a barge terminal. Suddenly, they heard a loud crack in the distance.

"Was that a gunshot?" Watson asked, echoing Holmes's thoughts.

Then more reports came, confirming Watson's suspicion. They looked about to see if others had heard the gunfire, but no one was in the immediate area. Those preparing the viewing stand were now a mile away.

As Holmes quickened his pace, Watson spoke: "We're unarmed, Holmes. My revolver is at the hotel."

"That old relic!" Holmes jested.

"Relic? I keep it in tip-top condition, I'll have you know," Watson harrumphed. Shrugging his shoulders he added: "Maybe it was someone shooting rats, or some kind of machinery."

"What is the cause of your sudden timidity?"

"Not timidity—common sense, as we are at a considerable disadvantage—trespassing, as it were."

"Yes, but the lives of many people are at stake here. We know Zaharoff's scoundrels may be about, and that they carry weapons."

"And, they know how to use them!"

"Agreed—but I feel bound to pursue our quarry."

Their pace had slowed, but they continued to move in the direction of the gunshots.

Moments later, a new sound reverberated from the far end of the wharf. They saw a motor-launch in the distance pushing off from a pier, and arcing out to sea. A sizable crew was aboard. Holmes and Watson moved on, watching all the while.

The boat went in the direction of the rusty cruiser.

"Do you suppose they're headed for that derelict, Watson?"

"Who knows? They're probably going to tow it away—it may be spoiling the view, as it were."

Holmes hastened his pace. Watson felt the weight of his sixty-six years as he struggled to keep up. "Holmes, I fear I must hang back a little. I'll be close behind."

Holmes continued on, watching the boats in the distance. He glanced back at Watson, who now walked at a slow, steady pace, breathing deeply.

Minutes later, Holmes reached the pier and scanned the horizon. The boat had disappeared beyond the rusty derelict.

Holmes anxiously waited for Watson. They paused briefly, before resuming their search for the source of the gunshots.

They came to a building, situated not twenty yards from the pier. White letters were stenciled over the door—W13.

Watson yanked on the door handle. It was locked. Holmes circled around in an effort to find entry. He peered into a dirty window. There were no signs of life.

As he rounded the corner of the building, he saw a familiar vehicle—the draped Bentley that had passed Watson and him earlier. Next to it was a small lorry pulled up near the warehouse.

"Ha! What have we here, Watson?"

Holmes approached the car cautiously. He silently signaled for Watson to go to the lorry. A quick peek through the rear window told Holmes that no one was inside. He opened the driver's door and searched about. Watson followed suit with the lorry.

Watson called out: "Holmes, there's some blood here."

〈●●●〉

WIGGINS slowed down as soon as he left the warehouse area. He stopped and tore a bandage from his shirt-tail, and wrapped it around his hand. The role of fugitive was hardly new, but now he had two adversaries hunting him. One possible refuge was the Majestic Hotel. However, getting there would prove an issue. The vehicle would make him too easy to find.

He drove until he found a deserted alley, pulled in and parked. As he walked away from the Bentley, Wiggins was momentarily disoriented and confused. It was many miles back to Barrow. His shoulder was bleeding and would attract unwanted attention from the local constabulary, as well as from Zaharoff's thugs. He decided to wait until it was dark before he making his way to the hotel. It would be another two hours before the sun would set. He felt weak and nauseous.

Slowly and cautiously, he weaved his way through the complex of buildings, ducking into shadows with every passing person or lorry. As he rounded a corner, he noticed what appeared to be an empty building. A sign above the door read *East Garage*. Making his way across the road, he pressed himself against the side of the building, and worked his way to a windowed door. Noticing a sink in the far corner of the garage, he turned the door handle. Locked. He could neither hear or see anyone inside.

He knocked. "Hallo!"

He looked about, and then gave a forceful kick to the door. The jamb split, and the door swung open.

The garage itself was vacant, but there was a room off to the side. A quick look showed it was an office—more importantly, an office with a telephone.

Wiggins entered, picked up the earpiece, and rattled the cradle.

"Operator."

A toneless voice responded.

He was short of breath. "Majestic 'otel, Barrow."

One ring and the hotel was on the line.

"I wanna to speak to Mr. Sherlock Holmes."

"One moment."

Nearly a minute passed before the voice returned. "Yes, he is registered here, but his key is on the hook. He is out."

"Take a message, please," Wiggins ordered. "It's important."

"Very good, sir. You may proceed."

"Zaharoff is on to me. . . ."

"Zaharoff, sir? Can you spell that please."

"Z-A-R . . ." He was confused. "Z-A-H-A-R-O-F—I believe."

"Zaharoff is on to me. Proceed, sir."

"Zaharoff is on to me. Important documents at mansion with woman guest—Murtagh. I'll come after dark." A sharp pain shot though his arm. "Do you have that?"

"Yes, sir. And, the name?"

"Wiggins."

"Very well, sir."

"He must get this message the moment he arrives."

HOLMES and Watson stood amidst a large number of broken wooden crates, scattered about, inside W-13.

Holmes examined one of the crates. "No dust. Recently opened. See if you can find anything about the former contents, Watson."

"Is this going to put us on the trail of the irregulars, Holmes?"

"The Bentley outside indicates that there is some relationship between these crates and Zaharoff's people. We know that this gang is responsible for abducting the irregulars. Sooner or later, they will lead us where we need to go. Look over there! What is written on that one?"

Watson turned a wooden carton around to get a better look. It was one-yard square. "It's an address: one-one-seven Hermitage Road, London."

"In Harringay—a warehouse, no doubt. Here we are again," Holmes said, lifting the cover from another box. "Here's something . . ."

"What is it?"

"There's writing—RCP-212B receiver."

"A radio?"

"I believe so. And, over here, Duro LP-37."

"Yes, and over here, the other half, I venture—not as yet opened," Watson exclaimed. "RCP-212 transmitter. Equipment for tomorrow's demonstration?"

"Doubtful, Watson. If it were, it would already be in place."

Holmes became still and closed his eyes.

"I feel we have some of the pieces, but the puzzle still has gaping holes in it."

"You believe, then, that the kidnapped irregulars are connected to tomorrow's demonstration, Holmes?"

"Zaharoff is attending the demonstration. And, while he is careful not to dirty his hands, the devil likes to keep a tight hold on the strings of his puppets. If we continue to tug on these strings, we'll find our way to him and the irregulars."

Holmes consulted his watch. "Mycroft will be arriving soon. We must meet him at the station. He is our eyes and ears at the Vickers estate. We must hurry."

Holmes and Watson walked out, only to face the barrel of a Webley automatic. When they realized a British soldier held the pistol, their momentary alarm dissipated.

"Stop right there!" the man said.

Holmes decoded the brevet on the man's uniform. "We are pleased to see you, Lieutenant. We heard gunshots and investigated."

"Indeed," the officer replied. "So did we."

Holmes held his arms wide with his hands open. "As you can see, we have no weapons, Lieutenant . . .?"

"Lieutenant Watling."

Behind the officer was another soldier in an olive-green staff car. He wore a red beret. His pistol was drawn as well.

"Well, Lieutenant Watling, I am Sherlock Holmes. My friend Dr. Watson and I are guests of the War Office—my brother Mycroft Holmes, specifically," he said, flashing his tin badge. "You may wish to examine the contents of this building, which are most unusual."

"That will be done. Thank you, sir. However, you are well away from the viewing area, and the curfew is approaching. I think it best if we give you a ride back to the gate."

"Yes, of course."

As they walked out of the building, Holmes pointed out over the water. "I noticed several launches making their way out to sea. Would you know what that's about?"

"I have no idea, sir, really. Perhaps they are securing the target."

CHAPTER XVIII

HOLMES AND WATSON had no sooner stepped out of the cab at the Majestic Hotel, than Tessa accosted them. "Where have you been? My brother is in danger. I know it!"

Holmes stepped back as Watson instinctively comforted Tessa. Holmes valued Watson's ministrations—clearing the "emotional fog," as Holmes put it.

"Tessa, Tessa, slow down," Watson began. "What's upset you so?

"Rory's found employment at the Vickers mansion."

Holmes's ears pricked up at this news, and he ventured closer.

"Employment?" Watson said, incredulously.

"As a chauffeur. Oh, and there is a message for you at the desk, but they will not give it to me. I know it's from Rory."

Holmes stepped in. "How do you know there's a message?"

"It hangs on your key-hook."

"Watson, see to the message." Holmes said, guiding the frightened woman back into the lobby. "Tessa, the situation may not be as desperate as it seems. Your brother is unknown to these people. He has done a singularly astute thing. My brother will soon be at the Vickers compound. I suggest that you . . ."

Watson shuffled toward them, holding high a piece of paper. "Holmes, Holmes, this is for you."

Watson's brow furrowed as he handed over the message.

"What does it say? It's from Rory isn't it?" Tessa's voice trembled.

Holmes silently read the missive written on a yellow piece of paper. As he turned a concerned face to Watson, Tessa snatched it from his hand and read it aloud:

Zaharof is onto me. Important documents at Vickers mansion with female guest— Murtagh. I will come after dark. —

Wiggins.

"He's all right, isn't he?" Tessa said, trying to convince herself.

Holmes and Watson looked far from convinced. Holmes's solemn nod to Watson so much as said: *She's back.*

It had been over five years since Maeve Murtagh had crossed their paths. It was in Africa, before the war—the adventure Watson called: "The Kongo Nkisi Spirit Train." The wayward daughter of Professor Moriarty had nearly succeeded in killing Holmes. Zaharoff was lurking in the background there as well.

Holmes and Watson concealed the alarm that they shared.

"Watson, I don't believe we need to change, do you? We're a little behind our time, and we don't wish to keep Mycroft waiting. If you will, please take Tessa back to her room, and let the desk know that she may retrieve any messages for us."

"Thank you, Mr. Holmes."

"Now Tessa, we may not be back for dinner. It's best you await your brother," Holmes said, awkwardly patting her shoulder. "Watson, I will secure transportation. I suggest you retrieve your . . . that old army relic."

WIGGINS struggled to cleanse his shoulder and hand. His arm was black and blue, and the pain was subsiding, but his hand ached and burned. The recoil of the pistol had lacerated his fingers, and blistered the skin on his right palm. He donned a soiled jacket he found in the garage to cover his bloody shirt. He saw a tool chest in the corner, and dug through it looking for a weapon, finding nothing better than an awl.

The clouds were returning, and a mist was in the air. He bundled up and waited just outside the garage. If someone were to return, he would have to beat a hasty retreat. His heart was pumping, and the beat pulsed in his head and ears. His thoughts drifted as he reflected upon how he came to this.

He had always taken care of others, but the burdens became heavier as he grew older. *This situation is too familiar*, he thought—feeling the complete weight of responsibility for the lives of the irregulars. For, even after Archie had taken the mantle of leadership for the irregulars, Wiggins had always maintained a paternal responsibility for the band. Up until the time he went to Ireland, he often encountered his friends on the streets. These meetings inevitably sent him catapulting back in time to a dank clubhouse, under the lumberyard, in Spitalfields.

Then the war came—wars, really—the great one on the continent, and the little one in Ireland. The two wars mingled in the Easter Rising, with arms unsuccessfully being sent to Ireland via a German submarine. Wiggins had always felt that was wrong. "Collaborating with the enemy" did not help their cause, and put an indelible stain on their souls.

A gust of wind splashed mist on Wiggins' face, momentarily startling him.

The gray sky was dimming. The cloak of darkness would be upon him soon. He had planned to make his way to the Majestic Hotel, to Tessa, Holmes, and Watson. But, something in his recollection gave him pause: *We thought you'd like some company,* one of the thugs had said.

Wiggins pulled the collar of his jacket up around his neck, patted the awl in his pocket, and set out back toward the warehouse where they had attempted to take him.

HOLMES was sorting ideas and options on the way to Lime Street Station. Watson was well acquainted with his companion's trance-like demeanor, and knew better than to engage him in conversation. As they arrived at the train station, Holmes turned to Watson.

"You've been very quiet," he said.

Watson chuckled. "Yes, indeed. Wiggins' news puts a rather new twist on the situation."

"Yes, Watson. I expect that my brother will have a few more tit-bits for us, and he should be here soon."

Watson thought it strange that Holmes chose not to wait in the station for his brother, or outside the cab that idled at the curb. *Was it simply so as not to attract attention*, he wondered?

Mycroft, for his part, did not seem to expect a demonstrative greeting. When he came into view, Holmes waved from the cab window. Mycroft approached, carrying his own luggage. The cabby took his bag and opened the door. Mycroft settled into the cab next to Holmes, and only after the cab began to move were words spoken.

Mycroft retrieved the thirty-two-caliber shell casing from his vest pocket and dropped it into the hat sitting on Holmes's lap. "As I told you earlier, it is from a Beretta, the markings do not match any on file."

"Unfortunate," Holmes answered, "but irrelevant at this point. What would you think if I told you that my irregulars were being held captive somewhere in Barrow-in-Furness?"

Mycroft wrinkled his face skeptically. "Why bring them here?

"For Zaharoff's pleasure."

"Come now, Sherlock. You paint the man as a monster, dragging his prey back to his lair."

"Your words, not mine. But yes, Mycroft. And what is more, I believe his *protégée*, Mavae Murtagh, is there to serve up my friends."

Mycroft's eyes flashed briefly at the mention of Holmes's newest arch-enemy. "She learned her lessons well from her father. You escaped her clutches in Africa, but just barely."

"The possibility of another encounter with Miss Murtagh sweetens the pot for me," Holmes said.

"And, if Mavae knows of your involvement, it sweetens the pot for her as well," Watson added.

<***>

WIGGINS found the alley where he had left the Bentley. The car was gone. He was perspiring profusely. He struggled to retrace his route back to the warehouse from which he had fled two hours earlier. The surrounding buildings all looked the same.

Fifteen minutes later, Wiggins came upon large metal-clad doors that looked familiar. As he approached, several brass shells near the entry confirmed this was where his confrontation and escape had taken place.

The lack of windows made it difficult to reconnoiter, but he was able to find an entry door on the far side of the warehouse. It was locked. Forced entry would raise alarm, so he took a page from Sherlock Holmes's book of tricks, placed the awl in the lock and, with one powerful rap, drove it home. He rattled the handle, and the lock gave way.

Upon entering, he listened. There was no sound, bar the skittering of a rat. He felt his way toward the front of the warehouse, where the double doors were located. Skylights, which might have been helpful during the day, were almost useless now. He thought it unwise to turn on the lights.

His eyes adjusted to the darkness as he went along. It seemed the building was one large room. A faint sliver of light in the distance told him the double doors were ahead. When he got to the doors he found them locked with a large bolt. Throwing back the bolt with his one good hand, he pushed one of the doors aside. A sharp pain erupted in his left arm, and his knees buckled.

A dim light sliced down the center of the room, providing enough illumination for him to see his surroundings. He saw what looked like tool benches lining one wall. A heavy chain stretched along the floor toward the base of a wood-burning stove. An open padlock lay next to it. Dust and dirt was thick on the floor. He could see that a number of persons had recently been scuffling along the grimy floor. In one place he noticed a crude drawing in the dust. It looked like a bowl with the letters H—E—L under it.

They were here, he thought.

Before Wiggins could grasp the full import of his discovery, a voice echoed from behind him: "Wiggins!"

He turned to see a familiar face—one with jug-ears, broad lips, and bushy brows.

"Ugly, is 'at you?"

CHAPTER XIX

HOLMES AND WATSON took the cab to the Majestic Hotel, having left Mycroft at the Vickers estate. They had a plan.

"Holmes, before we go up, I believe a stiff libation is in order."

Holmes concurred and followed Watson into the dining room.

When their drinks arrived, Watson raised his glass: "May good prevail, and our enemies fail."

"Most appropriate, my friend."

The whiskey went down quickly and easily. As Watson rose to go to the bar again, he nudged Holmes. "Tessa's here."

Tessa stood at the door of the dining room looking none too pleased. Watson signaled for her to come to the table.

Tessa stalked across the room as Holmes pulled back a chair. She sat, and folded her arms.

"Has your brother called or come?"

"No."

"I am pleased to see you," Holmes said.

"Really?" the other querulously replied, throwing a glance at the empty whiskey glass on the table. In contrast to her delicate features, her mouth was clenched in rigid resolve. Holmes's expression shifted from amusement to admiration as he took in the strong middle-aged woman, who still possessed an innocent waif-like quality.

Holmes fumbled in his coat and produced a penny. He took her hand and placed the coin in it. "We will find your brother and the others," Holmes promised. "As I have so many times before, I require your help."

Tessa stiffened, and her eyes flashed as if fireworks were exploding in the distance.

"It will require your best acting, the greatest stealth, and your brave heart."

Watson returned with three glasses of whiskey. "I wasn't sure . . ." he began.

Tessa grabbed one of the glasses, raised it high, and waited. Holmes and Watson, somewhat surprised, followed suit.

"Alcohol leaves you senseless, death leaves you lifeless," she began. Watson and Holmes wore perplexed expressions. "—but, God won't leave you, regardless." She offered a reproving look, and set her glass back down on the table.

Holmes and Watson followed suit.

"I believe you're right," said Holmes, "with regard to keeping a clear head. It would not be good for a secretary from the War Office to be inebriated. Watson, please learn when the next train from London will arrive."

Watson retrieved his glass, and left the table.

"So, what's my part?" Tessa asked.

"You are now in the employ of Mycroft Holmes. You will arrive at the Vickers mansion with information for my brother. He has already alerted the staff to your advent."

Tessa's eyes lit up. "Is Rory still there, do you think?"

"If he is, he'll likely have duties elsewhere. But, your efforts will help him—and the others."

"What am I to do, exactly?"

"You will arrive just before, or during, dinner. The staff and guests, who will have arrived by then, will be engaged. This will allow you to search the rooms of Mr. Zaharoff and Miss Maeve Murtagh. Their rooms may be locked, but . . ."

"Mr. Holmes, at the risk of alarming you, I can say that there is nary a lock that I cannot manage."

Holmes nodded. "Nothing like a good childhood education."

Tessa smiled.

Watson arrived holding his open watch in his hand. "Seven-twenty, Holmes. That leaves almost two hours."

"Excellent," Holmes replied. "Just enough time to see to your wardrobe, Tessa. Watson, Tessa will need a portfolio or case—filled with newspapers."

WIGGINS groaned as Ugly seized him in a deep embrace. Ugly stepped back in surprise.

"My shoulder—it's hurtin'. It's so good to see yur magnificent face!"

"It is a beauty," Ugly replied.

"The uvvers?"

"Gone. I broke away during an argy-bargy outside—thanks to a bad link on the chain. They were carted off—to a boat or ship of some kind."

"Boat!" *That's what the bowl scratched in the dirt was trying to tell me.*

"The talk was of a large boat."

"Can you recall more?"

Ugly tilted his head back, and closed his eyes momentarily. "No. Not about the boat. There were complaints from a couple of the men about a daft woman . . . and a radio. I didn't get it all."

"How's our crew?"

Ugly swallowed. "They killed Ruck."

"I know—back in London."

"Snape got himself beat up proper. The others were walking, but weak. They didn't give us much food or water."

"Is there anythin' else you can recall?"

"No, but something is going to happen soon. They were preparing to cart us off when gunfire . . ." Ugly grinned. "That was you, was it Wiggins?"

Wiggins nodded and pointed to his shoulder with a bandaged hand.

HOLMES stood behind Tessa as she appraised herself in the mirror.

"Blimey, this is grand, Mr. Holmes," Tessa remarked, running her hands over the high-waisted velveteen dress. It offered a stark contrast to the dull black uniform that she wore in the London slums.

"Can't have my brother's amanuensis looking shabby." Holmes turned to Watson who was putting newspapers into a black leather portfolio on the bed. "Give it some weight, Watson. Bureaucracy at its best, you see."

Watson completed his packing and put the portfolio under Tessa's arm. "That completes the picture."

Tessa straightened up and took on the look of a proper Whitehall bureaucrat. Holmes admired his Galatea. He had a classic British respect for feminine weaknesses, and a cautious regard for female strengths.

"Tessa, you are a beautiful lady," Holmes acknowledged. "More importantly, you have a sharp mind and a stout heart."

As Tessa peered into the looking glass, she caught a soft expression on Holmes's face over her shoulder. Watson looked on in wonder at Holmes's accolade. He had never thought of Holmes as having a paternal nature. Caring yes—fatherly, no. This is what the irregulars had offered him: an outlet for his kinder nature. The irregulars were the perfect children for Holmes: They demanded little of his time and attention, were helpful, self-sufficient, and self-nurturing. And somehow, what had begun as a simple business transaction twenty-five years ago, had metamorphosed into something else. "Fondness" is as far as Holmes would go in describing it.

Holmes became self-conscious. "Tessa, as you take on your mission at the Vickers mansion, there are important instructions I wish to share with you."

Tessa was put into a cab at 7.15 to coincide with the arrival of the next train from London. Holmes and Watson watched her cab leave, and took the next one to Applegarth

Tavern on Abby Road, a scant quarter mile from the Vickers estate.

Promptly received at the door, Tessa was guided into the library while Mycroft was summoned. She admired the hundreds of books that lined the three walls of this room. She reflected that she had but one book on her shelf—*The Rosary*. Her brother had given it to her for her sixteenth birthday. It was a love story in the truest sense of the word. She understood that a motion picture of the novel had been made in America. It was doubtful she would ever have the opportunity to see this film. She consoled herself with the thought that there was no actor alive who could play Gareth Dalmain to her satisfaction.

Mycroft was shown to the library. He shut the door, and guided Tessa to a chair with a wave of his hand.

"Mycroft Holmes, pleased to meet you," he began.

"Tessa Wiggins," she replied. "Mr. Holmes is your brother?" she asked incredulously.

"My younger brother," he said. "The guests will soon be at dinner. I will tell the staff that you are weary from your trip and wish to go to your room. I am not sure where they will put you, but I have made a crude map of the rooms upstairs. My room is here, Miss Murtagh's here, and Basil Zaharoff is in the guest cottage on the perimeter of the grounds, over here."

"Murtagh and Zaharoff will be at dinner, then?"

"They are at the reception now, and will be going into dinner shortly. However, Miss Murtagh may return to her room immediately after dinner, so see to her room first. You have an hour, I would suspect."

"Yes, sir. When do we again meet with your brother?"

"I will find your room after dinner. Wait there for me. Having dinner with the brother of Sherlock Holmes may make

Zaharoff and Murtagh wary. We will sneak out later, as the other guests are retiring."

A maid showed Tessa to her room and offered tea, which she declined. Waiting five minutes, with map and portfolio in hand, she strolled into the long hallway that led to Maeve Murtagh's room. The door was locked. As Holmes had suggested, she carefully inspected the door and jamb. She did not find a matchstick, or a piece of paper, but she did spy a long strand of black hair stuck in place, as if to seal the door. She pulled it away, wet her finger, and stuck the strand of hair to the wall next to the door.

A slight turn of the knob revealed the door was unlocked.

Upon entering, her nose picked up a dark scent reminiscent of cloves or spiced plums. She stood in the center of the room and turned slowly. There were only so many places in which one could hide a portfolio—if it were here.

She began the search: wardrobe, suitcase, bed, mattress, drawers, and under cushions. Nothing.

Poking her head out of the door first, she entered the hall, replaced the hair on the door jam, and went down the stairs and out the front door. She followed the drive until she came to the small stone cottage, where a faint light glowed from the windows. She knocked on the front door and waited, then tried the door and found it locked. Removing a pin from her hair, she worked it into the keyhole. The door swung open, revealing three rooms. She swept through the parlor and dining room, and went straight to the bedroom.

She opened a large wardrobe. There was a high shelf with three suits hanging beneath it. She felt along the edge. "Ha!"

Tessa retrieved the portfolio, which was smaller than she had expected. It was tied with a thick red ribbon.

She placed her portfolio next to the smaller one on the bed. A noise outside caused her to stop. She let out a deep breath when all was quiet, and returned to the file.

Yanking on the red ribbon, the file popped open—photographs slid out on the bed. Tessa smothered a cry.

There, sitting atop a number of photographs, was a picture of Ruck sprawled on the floor. She became dizzy, and had to steady herself on the bedpost. *The grisly bastard,* she thought.

She could see that there were at least a dozen more images under the top one. She closed her eyes, hoping that when she opened them again, she would be somewhere else.

She took one finger and slid the top photograph to one side, revealing a picture of Kate cringing in Archie's arms, as a large man pointed a gun at them. More photos showed her friends lined up under threat. There was one of Benjie, who looked as though he was in shock. Tessa touched the face of her lover. *Will I ever see you again?*

Remembering where she was, Tessa examined the remainder of the photos. Her brother's picture wasn't among them. But the last one set off an alarm. It was Mr. Holmes, climbing the steps to number seven, Grosvenor Place.

CHAPTER XX

HOLMES SAW THE INNKEEPER moving to their table yet again. Watson, being ever the good soldier, had dutifully consumed two pints of ale. He eyed the third wearily as it was set before him.

"Your friend has a good thirst," the innkeeper declared.

"Some people improve with age—Watson here improves with ale!"

The man chuckled and pointed a finger at Watson. "This must be the last one, sir. We're closing soon."

"No time for that one, Watson. Our rendezvous with Mycroft is nearly at hand."

Promptly at ten, the innkeeper rousted the Applegarth's last two patrons, followed them out, and locked the door.

The clouds had cleared away. The night sky was glimmering with stars. The moon was full. Here, on the edge of the Irish Sea, the firmament cast a colossal shroud over the world. The glittering belts of the galaxy reigned over the night, smothering egos, and swallowing a man's troubles like a great goblin.

Holmes and Watson made their way down Abbey Road toward the Vickers mansion in the distance. Every window was alight. Inside were two of Holmes's dearest people, and two of his deadliest enemies.

"Must we walk so quickly, Holmes?"

Before Holmes could respond, two headlights appeared in the distance, followed by the sound of a motor. Holmes tugged on Watson's coat sleeve, pulling him into the brush by the side of the road.

The vehicle was one of the notorious black Bentleys. It turned into the driveway not fifty yards away.

"You remain here, Watson."

Holmes cut through the shadows as he dashed after the Bentley. He stopped and watched as it passed the portico of the great house, disappearing into a grove of trees behind the mansion.

Holmes looked back toward Abbey Road. Watson was shuffling along the edge of the driveway. He waved. Holmes returned the greeting and waited.

Watson arrived and paused to replenish his breath. "Was that our motor-car?"

"I believe so. It did not go to the house, but somewhere beyond."

"Look there, Holmes," Watson said, pointing toward the Vickers mansion.

There, silhouetted in the doorway was the corpulent form of Holmes's brother.

"Wait here, Watson—off the lane."

Holmes kept to the shadows as he made his way to the mansion. When Mycroft saw him, he descended the stairs and walked into the trees at the edge of the lawn.

Homes saw the red glow from his brother's cigar, and noticed he was holding something at his side.

"Quickly, what have you found?" Holmes asked.

Mycroft handed his brother Tessa's portfolio. "She's quite a clever woman," Mycroft began. "She found the papers you mentioned in Zaharoff's cottage—actually, photos of your irregulars taken on the evening of the abduction. This explains the tape from the roll-film you found. What do you suppose is the motivation?"

"Not blackmail, as there have been no demands. I believe these were taken solely for Zaharoff's gratification. He is careful never to dirty his hands, and savors terror and pain like a vile voyeur."

"I would agree that his malice runs deep, but you make him out to be a cannibal who keeps his victims locked away so that he can have his feast whenever he desires it."

"He is all that—and clever. However, keeping photographs in his room was not clever at all."

"Indeed. Tessa was smart enough to leave most of the photographs, but took the two most important ones—one of the fellow who was murdered . . .

"Ruck," Holmes noted.

"Yes, Ruck. And, one of *you* on the stairs at Grosvenor Place."

Holmes sighed. "So, they know that I am involved."

"Definitely," Mycroft replied. "It would seem that Zaharoff's retribution may have as much to do with you as your irregulars."

His brother's statement put the lives of the irregulars squarely into Holmes's reticent hands. He drew a deep breath.

"Sherlock, I suggest you take these photographs. They are evidence. This might well be the sum total of my contribution to your quest. Guilt by association, you see. Zaharoff is guarded and secretive while I am about. "

"Very well. Before we part—two more tidbits of information: Do you know the nature of the demonstration?"

"An explosive device. It will be delivered by air. Our host has, on several occasions, expressed concern about the weather. I was admonished to dress warmly in the morning as we will be at the seashore."

"I've seen the pavilion at the wharf," Holmes interjected.

Mycroft chuckled. "Of course you have. This brings up a small point," Mycroft said, folding his hands in a tidy manner before his vest. "I wish you wouldn't bandy my name about when you are trespassing on private property."

"Mycroft, you have my permission to disown me at any time."

"Ah-h-h-h, would that this were possible. But, if I did so, you might find yourself writing your memoir from a prison cell. I will leave word at the gate tomorrow morning so that you, and Dr. Watson, might obtain *proper* badges."

"When do the festivities begin?"

"Early. We depart at eight. We return here for a luncheon. There is your opportunity."

Holmes looked over Mycroft's shoulder toward the house. "One more thing: did you notice the black motor-car earlier?"

"Yes. I asked Tessa to investigate."

As if summoned by those words, they saw Tessa rushing up the lane. As she drew close, Holmes let out a low whistle. Hearing it, she joined them among the trees.

"Quickly, Tessa!" Holmes said, as she approached.

"The motor-car went to a garden building. Two men carried a large box inside."

"Describe it," Holmes said.

"It was twice the size of a breadbox, and light reflected on it—maybe metal or glass."

"That could be one of many things," Mycroft muttered, puffing on his cigar.

"Oh," Tessa exclaimed. "There was something else too. One of the men retrieved some poles that were tied together with rope or wire. It looked like a clothes-line."

"A radio," Holmes and Mycroft said simultaneously.

WIGGINS' plan was not well received by Ugly, who continued to insist that they both go to Holmes with their news.

Ugly noticed the pale face of his friend. "Your shoulder, Wiggins—you must get it seen to. You're losing blood."

"There'll be time enough for that. Time is running out for our friends. I must go on to find that ship or boat. You go to the Majestic. It's on the main road into Barrow. Mr. "Olmes, Dr. Watson, an' Tessa are there. Tell them what we know. I'll send you more news if I can."

Ugly set off toward town.

Wiggins pulled his jacket down over his shoulders. With his other hand, and his teeth clenched, he tightened the bandage around his arm to stem the trickle of blood that was soaking his shirt. He looked for blood on the jacket. Seeing none, he carefully put his arm through the sleeve and buttoned it up. The night sky had cleared, and there was a chill in the air.

He knew he had to find his way to the wharf that undoubtedly stretched for miles. Finding "the boat" seemed an impossible task. He needed more information. He had only gone a quarter mile when, he heard music—a jig.

He followed the music to a tavern, where a brilliant amber light spilled through windows fogged with vapor. He examined his jacket again for blood, took the bandage from his hand, and entered. Thankfully, no one turned to notice.

There was something fine about the place, he thought. The smell of good ale, cheap tobacco, and the sweat from a hard day of labor. There was laughter, music, and the friendly clink of glasses.

Wiggins slowly walked to the far end of the bar, and placed a handful of coins on the polished oak. "A pint of your best," he said, when the barkeeper approached.

As the schooner was set in front of him, a curious fellow nearby slid his mug down the bar and joined him.

"And who would you be?"

Wiggins was momentarily flummoxed. "Me? Ah— Kelly's the name. Sean Kelly."

"Ah, so you're from the Emerald Isle, are you?"

"Yes, but I've been too long away now—what with the war an' all."

"Connor," the fellow said, in introduction. Noticing Wiggins' pallid complexion he added, "You don't look well, mi lad."

"I've taken a wee chill." Wiggins raised his glass. "This 'ill soon set me right."

Wiggins noticed the Vickers badge on the man's lapel. He reached into his pants pocket and fingered the badge that the butler, Bates, had given him earlier in the day.

"What brings you to Barrow?" Connor inquired.

"Work. I thought I might find a place at Vickers."

"Just a year ago there was over twenty thousand. Now, less than half that."

"But, you work there?"

"Aye, but for how much longer, I cannot say. I count my blessings, and don't dwell on tomorrow."

"I see," Wiggins said, taking a long draw from his pint. "I served in the navy. Thought there might be need of seamen."

"Well, you might ask to talk with Jenkins—Mr. Jenkins, at the shipyard. Of course, we don't sail 'em, we build 'em. The moment they slide from the dock, they belong to the Navy."

"So, there's no vessels abaht?"

"Not now—except for salvage. The Collingwood is anchored off the wharf now—got somethin' to do with tomorrow's spectacle."

Wiggins could barely contain his composure. "Where's that now?"

The man turned to him and gave a careful look. "You ask a lot of questions, Sean. Are you some kind of spy?"

Wiggins grimaced. He was woozy. His vision blurred.

The man laughed, and slapped him on the back. Wiggins gasped.

"There's a big show tomorrow morning on the western wharf. We're to stay clear of the high muckamucks from London, here to see what the next war will look like." The man feigned a chuckle.

313

Wiggins took hold of his pint and turned to watch the fiddler. "A grand jig for a céilí there."

His companion turned. "Murphy is a true son of Erin. He fought in the Fingal Battalion."

"Did he now?" Wiggins enquired, rhetorically. He set down his glass and walked over to the fiddler as he finished his tune. Wiggins offered his good hand and whispered in his ear. The two men locked eyes, and Murphy grew solemn.

As Wiggins returned to the bar, the fiddler struck up a new tune. A hush fell over the tavern. Men swept their caps from their heads. The dulcet strains of *A Nation Once Again* lilted in the air. It seemed as though the entire saloon was transported across the Irish Sea. Certainly their thoughts were, as patrons recalled family living there, and friends buried there. Such recollections inevitably lead to thoughts of what might have been, and what was left to do.

When the last note quivered on the fiddler's strings, Wiggins left the tavern and walked into the night.

CHAPTER XXI

HOLMES, WATSON AND TESSA waited for the cab that Mycroft called for them from the Vickers mansion. Fortunately, it was but a short walk back to the Applegarth Tavern, as a chilling sea breeze arose suddenly. The covered entryway of the pub offered little protection. Watson and Tessa huddled closer in a vain attempt to avoid the smoke from Holmes's pipe.

"I am anxious to learn if Rory made it to the hotel," Tessa said, breaking the silence. "I saw nothing of him at the big house."

"I hope that he may be waiting for us," Watson answered; and, taking his turn at capturing Holmes's attention, added, "So, we're off early tomorrow, are we?"

Holmes took his pipe from his lips and shook the dottle into the palm of his hand. "You and I shall be at Vickers before dawn. We may bide a while at the Majestic, enough for a brief nap and a change of clothes."

"I am certainly in favor of warmer clothing!" Watson replied.

<•••>

WIGGINS pinned the Vickers badge to his jacket and walked toward one of the many gates into the sprawling facility. His entire body was aching, though his shoulder remained numb.

The gate was closed, but he could make out a man inside the lighted gatehouse. He heard music: Harry Lauder singing, "I Love a Lassie."

Wiggins approached. "I wish I 'ad a penny for every time 'at song was played," he said.

The guard started in alarm. "You caught me dreaming."

"I 'ave to admit, bonnie Harry sings sweetly."

The guard pointed a finger. "It's to be Sir Harry, do you know."

"Sir Harry, you say," Wiggins echoed. He flashed his badge with his good hand.

"This late?" the guard inquired. "I've not heard of any doings after curfew."

"You'll have to talk to Jenkins abaht that. They just called me in. Something's up—to do with tomorra's show."

"All right, then," the guard said, waving him in.

Wiggins walked a little way in and stopped to get his bearings. He was disoriented. The sea breeze, with its promise of home, felt good on his face.

A thousand lights flickered in all directions. Vickers was a metropolis of its own, and somewhere within were his cherished comrades. While he could hear a few faint sounds in the distance, Vickers was fast asleep. He walked for nearly a mile before he saw a fellow coming. He wore a red band on his sleeve, and a pistol on his hip—*a watchman*.

The streets had taught Wiggins that an amenable, preemptive approach worked best when one was not where one should be. "They 'ave you on extra duty too, eh?"

The man looked quizzically at Wiggins. "Do I know you?"

"I don't think so. I'm on the day shift. Jenkins called me in for extra duty. 'Ave you seen him? I'm to meet up with him on the west wharf."

"I've just come from there, and he's nowhere about."

"Stay warm," Wiggins replied, as he continued down the road from which the watchman had come.

HOLMES, Watson and Tessa stepped from the cab at the hotel. They very nearly stumbled over a man sitting, hunched over, on the steps of the portico. The chap startled from a mild slumber and gazed up at the trio. A broad smile spread across his singular face. "Mr. Holmes!"

"Ugly, is that you?" Tessa cried.

Holmes grabbed Ugly's hand and lifted him up. His haggard brown eyes told the tale of fear and desperate fatigue.

"What of the others?" Holmes inquired.

"Gone. Taken away," Ugly replied. "Wiggins is on their trail."

At the mention of her brother's name, Tessa's gasped, in both relief and alarm. Watson looked about to see if anyone was near. "Come, come, let us retreat to some place more suitable."

Holmes steadied Ugly. "Tessa, we will see to Ugly. Please remain in the lobby and await any further word from your brother." Holmes instructed.

They made their way to their room with only a casual glance from the night clerk at the desk.

Ugly's story corroborated Holmes's suppositions, and provided another critical piece of the puzzle.

"You say Zaharoff's thugs took the others to a boat?"

"That was their plan, Mr. Holmes."

Watson sat up in his chair. "Those two motor launches we saw earlier today!"

"Yes, exactly," Holmes said, "but where are they taking them? If radios are involved, it could be some distance."

"Wiggins is inside Vickers now, I'm sure," Ugly said. "He's wounded, and we must help him."

"Indeed, the best-laid plans gang aft agley," Holmes quoted. "We've no time to change clothes now, Watson, nor wait on Mycroft. Tessa must remain here out of harms way. Watson, fetch your pistol, and meet me in the lobby. I'll leave a message for Mycroft and arrange our transportation."

WIGGINS walked briskly along the wharf. Every step sent pain through his body. His shoulder was throbbing now. Despite the cool breeze, he was perspiring. The bullet was doing its best to bring him down. A pint of ale was the only food he'd had in the last twelve hours. He wanted to rest, but he dared not. Wild thoughts and surreal notions flashed through his mind. He looked toward Ireland. Though it was a hundred miles away, he fancied he could see the rocky shoreline glimmering in the moonlight.

He stumbled on. Then, something caught his eye that sent a bolt of energy through his body. It was the twin black

Bentleys sitting outside a warehouse at the edge of the wharf—W-13. In his delirium, he imagined a ghost rising up from behind the sign, pointing a boney finger: "*Judas!*" he heard it say.

A new resolve filled his being, and he walked resolutely toward the two cars. The light above the door enabled him to see that no one was in either vehicle. He slid along the side of the building to the door. He listened—praying he might hear the voices of his friends. Hearing nothing, Wiggins decided to try the door. As he turned the knob, he heard an engine racing in the distance.

The sound was coming from the wharf—beyond the pier—out at sea. He could see moonlight illuminating the tops of the waves, as and they splashed across the prow of a boat racing toward shore. He pulled back from the door and into the shadows.

As the boat came closer, Wiggins could see that it was headed for a pier that jutted out from the wharf. It was a motor launch, twenty-five feet or more, traveling at high speed. Just short of the pier, the motor cut to an idle and the craft drifted in. One of the crew jumped onto the pier, secured the launch, and waited as two more jumped out. The three men made their way toward the warehouse.

When it became apparent that these men were heading toward the motor-cars, Wiggins slid between two large crates. The trio chatted in hushed tones. Two of the men got into the first Bentley. The other paused as he opened the door of the second vehicle. "What was that channel again?" he asked.

"One-two-two-point-two-five. Get that number to her and come back for Jake."

The motors started, and Wiggins watched as the two vehicles drove off. He paused for a scant few seconds, then he walked to the door of the warehouse and opened it.

He called out: "Archie! Kate! Anyone here?" His words reverberated. His mind was foggy. He shook himself awake.

Exiting the warehouse, something on the horizon caught his eye. The setting moon cast the silhouette of a ship on the horizon. *The boat!*

HOLMES, Watson and Ugly made straight for Vickers. Watson was glowering and grumbling in the back seat. "I can't believe you simply absconded with a motor-car."

"The robbed that smiles, steals something from the theft," Holmes murmured.

"That may play well at Drury Lane, Holmes, but not at the Old Bailey."

Ugly could not contain his laughter. "And to think, you once scolded me for nickin' an apple."

"Enough!" You should know that only the deepest concern could cause me to break the law. Many lives hang in the balance. Their fate is linked to the demonstration that commences in less than five hours."

"What of Wiggins?" Ugly asked.

"From what you tell me," Watson replied, "his life is in jeopardy. If a bullet is in his shoulder, sepsis might set in."

As their car approached the main gate, Holmes hoped that his stolen Vickers badge would be enough to grant them passage.

They turned into the Vickers entrance. The headlights illuminated the guard who was standing in front of the gate. He waved them forward.

Holmes got out and walked to the gatehouse. As he chatted with the guard, his gestures became more animated.

"Something is wrong," Watson said.

Holmes came back to the motor-car. "We are being asked to wait here for an escort."

"How long?" Watson asked.

Holmes pointed to a red light high atop a pole attached to the gatehouse. "That red lamp is how the guard signals for security personnel on patrol. However, we cannot wait."

WIGGINS moved to the end of the pier. He tottered on the edge, and looked down on the empty motor launch bobbing in the waves below. He sank to his knees and muttered a prayer. Crossing himself, he cast off the hitch, and threw the rope into the craft.

Noticing two figures running toward him, he leaped into the motor-launch, and searched for a starter. A voice shouted from the shore: "Halt!"

He stood up to find two silhouetted figures standing on the pier. One held a torch that shone in his face—the other a pistol. The one holding the torch dangled a ring of keys in front of the light. "You'll be needing one of these, I would suppose."

CHAPTER XXII

SHERLOCK HOLMES had a well-deserved reputation for coolness in the face of calamity. This assessment was borne out by his outwardly calm demeanor. But in truth, Holmes could become exceedingly anxious, although this was only apparent to Watson, who had the advantage having catalogued thirty-eight years of Holmesian behavior. The telltale signs of Holmes's anxiety could be found in the frequency of puffs emanating from his pipe, and the involuntary tapping of his right index finger. Aside from these miniscule indicators, he seemed as calm as a cat lying in the sunshine. However, at this moment, Watson could discern that a more accurate metaphor would be that of a tiger crouching in the bush.

The guard had returned to the gatehouse and picked up a telephone. As he spoke on the phone, he turned sharply toward Holmes and his *entourage*.

Holmes stamped on the accelerator and hurled the vehicle headlong into the gate. It buckled and broke, shattering the headlights. As they sped away, a lone gunshot echoed into the night.

Watson and Ugly were frozen in their seats—mouths agape, and eyes bulging.

"Where are we headed?" Watson asked.

"W-13."

The eastern sky was beginning to glow as the sun resumed its mythological pursuit of the moon that shined on the opposite horizon.

As the car pulled up to W-13, three figures could be seen standing under the lighted doorway—one was holding a single hand in the air.

"Wiggins!" Ugly cried, as their vehicle pulled closer.

One of the guards, holding a torch, shone his light at their vehicle. The other stepped back and angled himself so as to see both Wiggins and the approaching motor-car.

"He is in trouble," Watson said, noticing the pistol pointed at their friend.

The car stopped just short of the threesome.

"You two stay here until I signal for you," Holmes said. "Keep your pistol handy, but out of sight."

Holmes exited the vehicle, and held out his arms to show he had no weapon. "My name is Sherlock Holmes. The weapons demonstration is in jeopardy, as are the lives of many individuals."

"Halt! Stay where you are," commanded the guard wielding the pistol. "Is this fellow with you?"

"Yes, he is endeavoring to find the very same people whom . . ."

"We caught him attempting to steal a boat."

Wiggins shrugged.

"This man is wounded, as you can see."

One guard approached Wiggins, and the other shone his torch in his direction. With his one hand, Wiggins opened his jacket to reveal a blood-soaked shirt. He wobbled and fell toward the guard, wrapping his arms around the man.

Watson dashed out of the motor-car and took Wiggins in his care, laying him on the ground.

"Mr. 'Olmes—Mr. 'Olmes!" Wiggins croaked.

Watson beckoned, and Holmes knelt down at Wiggins' side. Wiggins winked and poked his right hand into Holmes's leg. Seeing the glimmer of keys in Wiggins' hand, Holmes nodded.

"It is imperative that we get this fellow to hospital immediately," Holmes barked.

"What now?" The guard with the torch said, as he spied a new set of headlights racing toward them.

As a lorry screeched to a halt, armed soldiers jumped out of the back and quickly surrounded them.

"I'm afraid we're not going to talk our way out of this one," Watson murmured, raising his hands in the air.

Watson and Ugly soon found themselves sitting with four well-armed men in the back of the lorry. Their combined pleas had only yielded one concession: Holmes was allowed to care for Wiggins until an ambulance arrived.

The lorry sped off with but one guard to watch over Holmes and Wiggins.

"My good man," Holmes began. "Can you help me sit this fellow up? We need to get his head above his heart."

The guard moved closer. Tucking his pistol in his belt, he bent lower. Holmes swung around, grabbing the pistol from the guard's waistband. Wiggins scrambled to his feet. "You keep this fellow 'ere. I'm takin' the boat out to that ship in the distance."

"No," Holmes shouted. "You're in no condition . . ."

"Mr. 'Olmes, it's my fault . . . my duty!"

As Wiggins ran down the pier, Holmes called out—but to no avail.

"You're in a heap of trouble now," the guard said.

Wiggins quickly found the ignition and inserted the key. Bracing himself on the wheel, he twisted the key and yanked on the throttle. The engine thundered to life.

The powerful craft sliced through the water. Wiggins followed the reflection of the moon on the black surface. Within minutes he was circling the large vessel. The only way aboard was a steel gangplank hanging five feet above the water. He pulled alongside and looked up at the edge of the steps that appeared, at the moment, to be too far away. He waited for the waves to lift him closer and, leaping upward, took hold of the gangway. He screamed, and slowly pulled himself onboard, cursing a blue streak.

When he made it to the deck, he paused. His head throbbed, and his tortured body cried out for relief. Looking back toward the shore, the warehouse now appeared as a small speck of light in the haze.

He steadied himself at the rail and called out: "Archie! Archie! Kate!"

Nothing.

Then, a distant clanking sound—metal on metal.

Wiggins began walking in the direction of the sound. Coming to a hatchway, he entered, but immediately stopped. It was too dark to navigate. As he walked back to the deck, he felt a gun-barrel jam into his ribs.

"Ah, we meet again," a voice said. It was Jake, the driver whom Wiggins had wounded at the warehouse. "I thought it was my mates. You are a surprise—a pleasant one."

"Where are they?" Wiggins rasped.

"You are anxious for companionship. I understand."

Wiggins felt for the awl in his jacket. The gunman forced the pistol in Wiggins' ribs. "Here, take this," he said, handing him a torch. "Get going."

Wiggins stumbled and fell to one knee. Jake grabbed the collar of Wiggins' jacket. As he rose, Wiggins dropped the torch, jammed the spike under Jakes ribs, and thrust upward.

The gunman shrieked, dropped his pistol, and fell. He lay upon his back—quivering. Then, his body became still.

HOLMES and Wiggins weighed on Watson's mind as he and Ugly sat in an office adjacent to the Vickers main gate. A baby-faced Corporal stood nearby with his rifle pulled tightly across his chest.

Watson muttered: "This is humiliating."

Heads turned as a large, grizzled officer came into the room. "This had better be damn good," he began. He turned his eye upon the prisoners. "Who is the one who claims to be Sherlock Holmes?"

"He's at the warehouse awaiting an ambulance," the guard reported.

"I'm Dr. John Watson, his colleague."

"Ah!" the officer's eyes widened as he studied the man before him with an eager eye. "Dr. Watson! You authored those stories in the Strand, and the Union Jack—marvelous, really! That explains the service revolver, doesn't it?"

This conversation went on in a similar vein until a soldier marched into the office and presented a note to the Captain, who took it in hand.

The color rose in the officer's face, and he grimaced. "It appears that you have friends at the War Office. Someone is apparently on their way to verify your story."

"Captain!" Watson shouted. We cannot wait! Many lives are in . . . "

"Patience, Dr. Watson. Please. This will all be sorted out shortly. I really would appreciate it if you could sign . . ."

"You bally idiot!" Watson shouted, shooting up from his seat. Four persons, recently abducted, are prisoners on a rusty warship anchored just offshore!"

The Captain turned. "Do you mean the target ship?"

CHAPTER XXIII

RORY WIGGINS WORKED HIS WAY into the belly of the ship as the sun's gilded halo rose behind the shore in the distance. "Archie—Kate!"

Chains began to rattle, and a number of muted voices sang out. He followed the sounds to a stairway that led below. His last step put him in a foot of water. The sounds lured him deeper into the bowels of the ship. The water was at his knees now. He shivered.

Drowning rats—that was his first thought when he saw the remnants of the irregulars manacled to a pipe, standing in waist-deep water. A fecal odor permeated the damp air.

Kate was nearest to him, followed by Archie, Snape, and Benjie. All but Snape looked his way. Snape was unresponsive, his bloodied head hung down upon his chest.

"Tessa?" Kate asked, "Is Tessa all right?"

Wiggins looked at Benjie's expectant face. "Yes, she's safe. She's with Mr. 'Olmes."

Benjie's brows lifted. "Mr. Holmes is here?"

The chains rattled as the others harkened to the news.

"He's close—he's . . ." Wiggins' voice trailed off.

"He's coming—right?" Archie asked.

"Yes, but we're getting out now."

Wiggins' heart was racing in his chest. His body trembled as he worked the awl in the last padlock.

A loud burst of static echoed in the hull.

"It's that bloody radio," Kate cried.

"Good morning," a honeyed voice began. "It's me again. In the midst of the *mêlée* at Grosvenor Place you were frightened," the female voice said. "You found it difficult to answer the questions about the money—I understand."

Wiggins' eyes narrowed in recognition.

"I hear that your white knight as arrived," the voice continued.

"Can she hear us?" Wiggins asked.

"Yes, my friend," Maeve replied. "I can hear you. I had hoped that your friends would be able to tell me where the money is, but they continue to refuse."

"That is because they don't know!" Wiggins screamed.

"But, you do."

"Yes, Wiggins replied. "I do. I don't care abaht the money. You can 'ave it. Let us go free. That's all we ask."

"I'm afraid this situation has become more complicated that I had intended. As you say, Mr. Wiggins, the money has become a secondary matter. Time has run out for all of us.

"It is after eight. In a short while you will hear an aircraft overhead. That sound will be a Vickers Vimy flying above. This bomber aircraft will be carrying a black sphere approximately one yard in diameter—an experimental weapon called Jumping Jack.

"Count the passes of the aircraft overhead. You will hear one pass—then two. As you hear the aircraft make its third pass, you will know that it is releasing Jumping Jack.

"The bouncing bomb will skip across the water toward your vessel. When it hits, it will make a very, very loud noise. That will be the last sound that you hear—other than the screams belching from your burning lungs."

WATSON brushed aside a continuous barrage of apologies from the Captain who sat next to him in the staff car. The driver asked: "Where are we going, sir?"

"W-13. And, hurry!"

Who are these people in danger?" the Captain inquired of Watson. "And, that Ugly fellow back at the office—how is he involved with all this?"

"There's time enough for all of your questions, Captain. They were brought here by Basil Zaharoff."

"Impossible," the Captain exclaimed. "I know Mr. Zaharoff. He is . . ."

"He is a fiend!" Watson shot back.

The sun had just climbed over the skyline. Nearby warehouses cast huge shadows across the quay.

"We'll be there in a ten minutes, sir," the driver reported.

Watson checked his watch. "Captain, at what time does the demonstration commence?"

"Eight-thirty hours precisely. The aircraft will make two passes over the pavilion and, on the third pass, release Jumping Jack at the H.M.S. Collingwood."

"Jumping Jack?" Watson queried.

"An incendiary device designed to destroy ships."

<‹••›>

WIGGINS was swaying, struggling to keep his balance as he followed the others up the stairway to the deck. Archie and Benjie were carrying Snape, who, although conscious, was delirious and unstable.

Wiggins directed the troop toward the stern, where the launch awaited. As they stepped over the dead gunman, Archie turned to Wiggins. "You got one of the bastards!"

Kate shrank away from the body. Archie grabbed her arm and kept her moving.

"Just ahead," Wiggins said, pointing.

Kate looked over the rail. "Where? There's nothing here."

Wiggins leaned over the side of the ship. "It was 'ere. I tied . . ."

Archie and Benjie propped Snape up against one of the gun turrets and raced around the deck, looking in all directions.

Wiggins collapsed to his knees and shook his head.

"There!" Benjie shouted. Kate and Archie ran to the rail next to Benjie. More than one hundred yards from the ship, the rising sun silhouetted an empty launch bobbing on the waves, moving toward the shore.

Benjie tore his shirt off, kicked off his shoes, and leaped over the side.

"Can he swim?" Kate asked in amazement.

"Like a fish," his brother Archie replied. "He used to help Gordi sweep the barges. Remember?"

<‹••›>

HOLMES was waiting with gun in hand, as Watson jumped out of the staff car the moment it came to a full stop.

"Over there!" Holmes said, pointing to a launch drifting offshore.

"Corporal, please retrieve the weapon from Mr. Holmes," the Captain ordered.

Holmes gazed out beyond the launch to the ship. The Captain retrieved his field-glasses from the staff car and peered out beyond the wharf. "There are people on board— and one in the water!"

The Captain handed the field-glasses to Holmes, and grabbed the Corporal by his sleeve. "See if there is another launch at the pier."

"It's them," Holmes exclaimed. "I'm not sure who is in the water, but he's swimming for the launch."

The Corporal ran back and saluted. "There are no boats at the pier, sir."

Watson took the glasses from Holmes and focused them. "That chap's a good swimmer. I think he might just get to the launch!"

Just as it looked as though Benjie would be able to reach the craft, a strong current pushed the boat farther away.

"He's tiring, Holmes," Watson reported.

"There must be another motor-boat nearby, Captain," Holmes said.

"They've been put away for the demonstration, Mr. Holmes."

"I'm not certain that fellow will make it," Watson sighed."

<悦●●>

WIGGINS and the others watched as Benjie pulled, stroke by stroke, closer to the drifting motor-launch.

"He's going to make it. Not to worry," Archie said. "Snape, how are you faring?"

A raspy voice replied: "Well enough."

Kate turned to find Wiggins wavering. Before she could reach out, he collapsed on the deck. Archie swung around. Kate gasped as she saw Wiggins' blood-soaked shirt.

"He'll be all right, Kate," Archie assured. "We'll be on shore soon."

Archie returned his attention to his brother, still fighting the strong current. "Come on, little brother!" he shouted.

A loud droning sound burst overhead. Archie and Kate looked up at a large yellow bi-plane flying low, over the wharf.

HOLMES twisted his neck as the Vickers Vimy roared overhead.

"Holmes, that's the bomber," Watson shouted.

Holmes turned to the Captain.

"Yes, I'm afraid it is," the Captain confirmed.

Cheers could be heard in the distance.

"Radio the plane," Holmes ordered.

"There's no radio in our car," the Corporal replied.

"Corporal," the Captain ordered, "drive to the command center and call the tower. Wave the plane off!"

The Corporal saluted and ran toward the staff car.

"Watson, go with him," Holmes said.

Holmes took the field-glasses from Watson and swung them toward the sea. "He's at the launch!"

Holmes watched as the swimmer dragged himself into the boat.

Benjie turned the key in the ignition, and the engine sputtered to life. He headed toward the ship and circled behind it.

The Captain and Holmes watched the Vimy make a sweeping turn in front of the pavilion and come back in their direction. As it passed over, a large black sphere could be seen, attached to the underside of the Vimy.

"This is the second pass," the Captain said. "It will be going into a bombing run after this."

The broad-winged bi-plane made another sweeping turn and circled behind the wharf.

"Word should have reached the tower by now," the Captain said. "It will be . . ."

The airplane suddenly roared above, flying low over the water and straight toward the ship.

WIGGINS regained consciousness as Snape lowered him into stern of the launch, laying his head in Kate's lap. Wiggins looked up into Kate's tear-filled eyes. She stroked his forehead. "You're going to be fine," she said.

Archie threw off the line and signaled Benjie. The engine thundered, and the launch steered away from the ship. As it cleared the stern of the ship, they could see the aircraft flying low over the water straight toward them.

"Oh my God!" Archie cried.

Kate, Snape, and Benjie turned to see a large black ball bouncing on the water toward the ship. Benjie pushed on the throttle and steered the launch sharply out to sea. Seconds later a gigantic explosion lifted the launch out of the water, and slammed it down again. A massive fireball shot upward. Debris rained down into the water all around them.

PART FOUR

AN IRREGULAR FAREWELL.

CHAPTER XXIV

WIGGINS CRIED OUT as the motor-launch bounced on the waves toward shore. Kate held him. Benjie was at the wheel. Archie and Snape stood at the bow.

As the wharf came into sight, Archie could see a squad of soldiers running onto the pier. The Captain trailed behind, shouting orders: "Get them in hand! On the double!"

Holmes waited at the head of the pier. Other vehicles were converging upon the scene. One of the staff cars carried Holmes's brother and Ugly.

Mycroft squeezed out of the car and stomped toward Holmes, bending close to his brother's ear. "What, in God's name, have you done now?"

"Mycroft, restrain yourself until you have heard the facts."

Their heated conversation was drowned by a cacophony of lorries and other vehicles converging around the pier. A screaming ambulance plowed its way through the thickening throng. Two attendants got out and opened the back doors in preparation for receiving the wounded. Fire engines converged near the edge of the wharf, and pump hoses dropped into the water.

The launch made a long sweeping turn in front of the pier.

Ugly held the palms of his hands out as a signal to stop. Then, as Archie and the others came into view, Ugly made a slicing manner across this neck signaling danger.

The Captain pointed to Ugly. "What's he doing there? Take him into custody now."

Seeing the soldiers running toward him, Ugly swiveled and plunged into the throng on the pier, eluding his pursuers.

A collective groan came from the crowd as they saw the launch reverse course and head out to sea. Mycroft and Holmes looked on.

"Looks like your band of thieves is at it again," Mycroft exclaimed.

"The real thieves are over there!" Holmes said, pointing toward the pavilion in the distance. "Zaharoff and Murtagh. Come, let us get this sorted out properly."

Watson sat quietly in the corner of the office as Holmes related his story to an unbelieving Captain.

"Zaharoff is behind all of this. I have photos taken by his henchmen. If you search his cottage quickly, you will find the rest."

"This is all too bizarre, Mr. Holmes," the Captain replied. "We will need permission to conduct a search on the Vickers property."

"I suggest you do that immediately," Mycroft said. "I have every confidence that my brother is mostly correct."

"Mostly?" Holmes retorted.

Zaharoff stood at the door of his cottage. "This is most irregular." His chested puffed up—reminiscent of a pompous rooster.

Mycroft stood, immobile, in the parlor of Zaharoff's cottage. Soldiers began to search the premises. Holmes was already heading for the bedroom.

"You're trespassing," the Greek said, struggling to make himself pleasant.

"We have permission from your host to look over the cottage," replied Mycroft.

"Look over? What exactly are you looking for?" the Greek asked, with a savage sharpness.

Holmes walked into the parlor with the portfolio in hand.

Zaharoff's face turned ashen. "What are you saying?"

Mycroft cleared his throat. "Mr. Zaharoff, I am sure you heard about the commotion at the demonstration today."

"Something about stowaways on the target ship, I believe."

"Stowaways? Hostages chained in that vessel!" Holmes barked.

"What has that to do with me?"

"It seems that it has to do with some dealings you had with those 'stowaways'."

"I doubt that."

"Do you doubt these?" Mycroft asked, opening the portfolio and pointing to the photographs.

Zaharoff could not contain his shock. "The little bitch!"

"You're speaking of Miss Murtagh, I assume," Holmes said.

As the questioning continued, it became clear that, while not innocent by any means, Zaharoff had become a pawn in Maeve Murtagh's deadly game.

<•••>

Holmes and Watson were returned to the Majestic Hotel under guard. Once again, Mycroft intervened on his brother's behalf. Now, he and the Captain waited for the Vickers management group at the gatehouse offices.

They recounted the morning's events: "That is one devil of a woman," Watson remarked. "She was angling to put a noose around her boss's neck and take over his business."

"Yes," Holmes replied. "It appears that she sold the arms to Wiggins without Zaharoff's knowledge, and imparted the information that allowed Wiggins to blackmail him."

"And she was behind the kidnapping and murder," Watson added.

"I don't believe kidnapping was in her original plan. The murder was intended to incriminate Zaharoff."

"And strike back at you, Holmes."

"Yes. I was to be the icing on the cake. She used irregulars as bait. And the blackmail money would put a cherry on top of it all."

"And, when she did not . . ."

Watson paused as he saw Tessa come into the room. "Go on, Doctor. I think it's grand that you both have solved another mystery, but I would remind you that my brother has paid a price for your success."

"Yes, Tessa," Holmes answered. "Your brother and the others as well. Maeve thought that the others would lead her to the money, but the only three people who knew the whereabouts of the ten thousand pounds were not ensnared."

342

"Three people?" asked Watson.

"Wiggins and I," Holmes admitted, "and a patriotic laundress."

"Who cares!" Tessa cried. "Who cares about the money! Where is my brother?"

Tessa sat down and put her face in her hands. Watson approached. "He is badly wounded, but the others are caring for him. I am certain we will receive word soon."

As if in reply, a knock came to their door. Holmes opened it to find a worried Ugly.

"Mr. Holmes—is Tessa here?"

"What is it?" Tessa cried, as she ran to the door. "Where's my brother?"

"He's on his way home. I'm to get you to the Isle of Man as soon as possible."

Holmes pulled Ugly into the room and closed the door.

"How are Wiggins and the others faring?" Watson asked.

"He's weak, sir," Ugly said. "Kate said he's cold and sweaty. He seems nervous—anxious."

Watson shook his head. "That could be shock."

"We must hurry," Ugly exclaimed. "We're to meet them at the docks in Douglas."

Wiggins' eyes flickered open. Kate smiled. "You're going home, Rory. We're going home."

The lights from Barrow dimmed, and slid down into the sea. The drone of the engine grew quieter as they made their way to open water.

"How many miles to Douglas?" Archie asked.

"Fifty or so," Benjie replied.

"We will have to stop there and wait for Tessa." Archie said. "Benjie, have we enough petrol to make it?"

"There's more in the stern," Snape interjected.

Kate wiped Wiggins' brow. "Rory, tomorrow morning you'll be home. A good meal, and a pint of Guinness, will get you well again."

Snape gave Archie a worried glance. Kate began to sing:

> *Sure I've roamed this wide world over,*
> *But of all the lands I've seen,*
> *There's no spot I'd rather dwell in*
> *Than my little isle of Green!*

The song echoed in the night, and in the hearts of those aboard.

Kate wiped her tears with her sleeve, and Archie put his arm around her. Snape, like a great sphinx, stared off into the night.

> *Oh, how good and how real it did seem*
> *I could hear me mother singin',*
> *sweet Shannon bells ringin'*
> *But 'twas only an Irishman's dream.*

"Bonnie song, Kate," Benjie offered.

Kate looked down and let out a low moan: "Oh-o-o, he's gone."

CHAPTER XXV

STANDING AT THE BOW OF THE FERRY, Tessa was overcome with the feeling that something had gone amiss. She hurried to the gangplank as the ferry pulled into Douglas. Snape was waiting at the edge of the dock. Holmes and Watson hung back as Tessa ran to Snape. He lowered his head and shook it as he spoke. Tessa swooned. Snape caught her up in his arms.

"He's gone then?" Watson confirmed, as he and Holmes approached.

"We must hurry," Snape said. "The authorities are growing suspicious. The tides won't wait."

Nairbyl Bay was deserted, as they were told it would be. Benjie idled the engine at the opening of a small inlet near the mouth of the bay. "What do you think?"

"I think this will do," Snape said.

Watson was sitting next to Holmes, arms folded. "This is mad, Holmes. Not sensible."

"There was a time I would have agreed with you. However, I am finding some of my older notions have changed," Holmes replied.

Holmes and Watson observed the sad tableau at the stern, where Archie and Kate were helping Tessa cradle Wiggins' body. Heads were bowed as if in prayer, and a tempest of memories whirled around them all.

Snape and Ugly manned the bow, gazing toward the shore in readiness. Snape's swollen and bruised face was vacant. Ugly steadied himself on the other's shoulder. *The rock*, Ugly thought. But then, the rock began to crumble as tears flowed down the bruiser's cheeks. No one had ever seen Snape shed a tear.

Snape had always felt that he lived outside the world of ordinary people. His size had always set him apart. The scars on his face sent an unintended message—*stay away*. And there, next to him, sharing the same thoughts, was his physical antithesis—a diminutive fellow who bore a derisive appellation for his entire life. They had both risen above their hardships, in large part because of their mutual love.

The launch shuttered to a halt as it rode up on the rocky shore. Snape and Ugly jumped out with a line. Holmes and Watson climbed over the seats toward the bow. Snape offered a hand that Watson gladly accepted. Holmes followed. The foursome waited.

As Archie and Kate reached for Wiggins' body, Tessa slapped their hands away. "No, no, Rory's resting."

Archie retreated. Kate rested her hand on Tessa's shoulder. "Tessa, if we're going to do this, we must do it now."

Tessa relaxed and sobbed. She cradled her brother's head in her hands briefly, and then held them up in surrender. Kate turned and waved to Snape and Ugly. They clambered into the boat and, together with Archie, lifted Wiggins from of Tessa's lap and carried him to shore.

Snape and Archie laid Wiggins on a broad flat rock and wrapped blankets tightly around him. The wind blew toward the sea, caressing the hair on Wiggins' forehead.

Holmes and Watson looked on as wood was gathered and piled in the launch.

"Holmes, this mythology does not offer a pragmatic means of burial. The temperatures will not . . ."

"Watson, your protestations are inappropriate. It is for us, who mourn, to say what is right and proper. Putting a body in a box and burying it does not seem any less barbaric than burning it on a boat. We promised Wiggins that he would not be buried on British soil."

"But this Viking funeral custom is only a fictional notion."

"No doubt, but who is to say that such notions are any the less reasonable than our own."

"You surprise me, that's all. I could always count on you for reason and rationality. Now you're going in for neo-pagan mythology!"

When the launch could hold no more wood, Snape poured petrol over the logs, and then walked toward the others who were gathered around Wiggins' corpse. Tessa had composed herself. She stood at the head of her brother and looked around at the gathering.

"All those who are dearest to Rory are here. You know this. He was going home when he died. It falls to us to help him to his journey's end. I would welcome a few words from you."

Snape straightened up. "When I came to the city as a boy, it was Wiggins who took me in off the street. I ran from a smithy's life in Basildon, with a few clothes and a hammer. When I first laid eyes on the city, I was afraid. I forgot why I'd run away. Wiggins understood. He said, *you're allowed to make your own life.* He did that. He made his life about 'is land, and 'is people."

Ugly wiped a tear from his eye. "I recall the day Mr. Holmes struck his first deal with Wiggins. I knew something was wrong. My Da had gone missing. I was frightened. As we walked away, Wiggins put his arm around me and said, 'I understand. You don't want to be here." Ugly choked up. "For the first time, I felt as though someone really saw me—saw beyond my face. Because of him, I never see an ugly face when I look in the mirror."

Kate's face was clear and bright. The tears had vanished. "I once thought I had to crop my hair and wear men's clothes to be safe. I didn't understand that doing this made me feel more helpless and ashamed—but Wiggins—somehow—knew this. One day, he swept the cap from my head and told me it was time I started dressing like a girl." Her face reddened and she chuckled. "Of course, I promptly fell in love with him." Tessa smiled and patted Kate's hand. "He understood that bravery was acknowledging your fear—then acting in the face of it. If that is so, then Rory Wiggins is the bravest man I have ever known. I will miss him forever."

After a long silence, Benjie spoke: "I never had much use for teachers. But, listening to all of you, I realize Wiggins was a teacher—and he taught us that there is only one lesson we need learn—that is, to learn what you're supposed to do with your life."

Archie nodded at Benjie. "Amen to that. When Wiggins left the city more than twenty years ago, he took me aside and told me it was up to me to look after all of you." Archie paused and pursed his lips in deep reflection. "I don't know if I should say this. The idea that he left his battalion behind in Ireland ate at 'im. All this business about the money—Zaharoff and the rest—it wasn't about that. It was about being true to those he'd left behind. He was true to us. I think he rests well, knowing that he was true to 'is comrades."

Watson had now settled into a peaceful mood. He lifted his head and looked about. "I feel I must begin with an apology. I was being a humbug about all of this, but I was wrong. I did not know Wiggins as well as all of you, but he was a soldier. As such, the measure of a soldier is best taken in the heat of battle, and in that regard, he more than measured up. It is an honor to have known him."

Holmes glanced at Tessa who had fallen into ruins. It took more than a moment for him to gather up his thoughts. "As I listened to your words, I could not help but recall that, long ago, Wiggins told me he wanted to go out bellowin' and blazin'. In the intervening years, it appears that civilization was unable to tame him. He did what he thought he must. In the end, that may be the only measure of a life well spent."

Tessa was smiling as Holmes finished his thought. "My brother often referred to himself as a 'dip'—a pickpocket. I suppose because that's how he began his life. But he was the most honest man I have known. Not because he never told a lie, or stole, but because he never lied to himself." She dropped into silence—and then looked up again. "Rory danced with death in a strange way I'll never understand. He told me, just last week, that his years of running had prepared him for death. I think he knew, somehow, that his end was at hand."

Tessa bent low to kiss her brother's face. The others filed slowly by.

Archie and Snape took the blanket, and with help from Ugly and Benjie, they lifted Wiggins onto their shoulders, and carried him to the launch.

Holmes and Watson followed and stood with Tessa and Kate as Wiggins was prepared for his voyage. When all was ready, Snape and Archie took their places behind the stern. Ugly lit a stick and stuck it in the timbers, igniting the pyre.

One great push and the boat headed into the receiving tide. It rocked and tipped for a few moments, before the current caught it, swept it beyond the mouth of the inlet, and out to sea.

The wind howled a dreadful dirge that fanned the flames.

The setting sun pierced the clouds, scattering shards of golden light in a halo around the fiery boat. It was impossible to take one's eyes away from the celestial arraignment that seemed to welcome Wiggins into a mightier presence.

The enigmatic fusion of grief and love clutched at the hearts of the irregulars, and their comrade Sherlock Holmes, as the blazing boat moved toward the horizon.

EPILOGUE

DR. WATSON HAD MADE BUT A FEEBLE EFFORT to read Holmes's tome, *A Practical Handbook of Bee Culture with Some Observations upon Segregation of the Queen.* The volume lay open upon his lap as he dozed in Holmes's Morris chair. He did not see the cyclist pumping his way along the Eastbourne to Brighton Road toward Holmes's cottage.

A knock upon the door startled Watson, who jolted awake, casting the heavy volume onto the floor. As the knocks continued, Watson rose, and made his way toward the door. "All right then, coming—coming!"

As he opened the door, the muted afternoon light illuminated the face of a heavy-shouldered man clutching an envelope.

"You're not Mr. Holmes."

Watson nodded. "On that we can agree. What can I do for you?"

"It's what I can do for you, sir. A message," the cyclist said, proffering an envelope.

Watson plumbed the depths of his pockets to produce fourpence, and placed it into the hand of the messenger as he took the missive. "Thank you, my good man," Watson said.

"Not at all, sir. Then, Mr. Holmes is not about?"

"He is working in the back garden."

"Of course, sir. You'll tell him Wiley came by then?"

"I will," Watson promised.

"And sir," the messenger continued, pointing to his trouser legs, "tell him Wiley's got 'is bicycle clips."

"Very well."

After an awkward pause, Wiley tipped his cap and turned away from the door.

The familiar-looking envelope was addressed to Mr. S. Holmes and Dr. J. Watson. But, as he was a guest, he thought it best that Holmes open it. He set it on a brass tray on the mantel, and retrieved the book from the floor. "I suppose I must finish it," he murmured, hefting the book in his hand, "maybe later."

Taking refuge in the kitchen, Watson set about making tea. This activity must have caught Holmes's attention because, just as the water was on the boil, Holmes found his way to kitchen table.

"Enjoying your afternoon, Watson?"

This was not idle conversation. Holmes was seeking a book report.

"I've made good headway on your book."

"Really? What stands out for you?"

"I am amazed that a creature that only lives five or six weeks demands such sophisticated observation and research."

"You're speaking of the workers, of course. A queen can live for up to five years—the drones but a few days. They die shortly after their mating flight."

"So, are there bachelor drones then?"

"I'm afraid that bachelorhood is rare among bees. If a drone is unsuccessful at mating, he is ejected from the hive to fend for himself. When the flowers are gone, he is as well."

"That gives me one more reason to be happy that I am not a bee."

Holmes watched as Watson prepared the tea. He wondered how many tea-times had they shared over the last thirty-eight years: *How many cups—how many adventures?*

Watson pushed one of the cups toward Holmes. "Then you're quite recovered from our irregular adventure?" Watson inquired.

"Recovered? Does one ever recover from the death of a loved one?"

"No. I can say that one does not. I was speaking more of balancing physical and mental processes—getting back on a firm footing, so to speak."

"I am on a firm footing, Watson, but I will continue to walk cautiously as long as Maeve Murtagh is about in the world."

"I suspect Zaharoff will soon put his hands on her—given his capacity for vengeance."

"I pray you may be correct in your prognostication, Watson."

Watson stirred the sugar in his tea. "You never told me about the money. Surely Zaharoff, and others, have some interest in the money—a sizeable sum."

"Not to Zaharoff. But he could hardly lay claim to the money without opening Pandora's box. Selling arms to Irish insurrectionists would do more than put him in great disfavor with our government."

"Of course. What are the plans for the money then?"

"I suspect the message that came a moment ago answered your question, Watson."

"I didn't open it."

"Let's do so now, shall we?"

They carried their cups into the parlor. Holmes set his tea down on the mantle, and retrieved the envelope. "Looks familiar, does it not?"

"From our friend S. P. Fields," Watson replied. He cocked his head in a novel thought: "S. P. Fields— Spitalfields!"

"Exactly so," Holmes said, pulling the flap, and retrieving the invitation and note. As he pulled the card from the envelope, a penny fell onto the floor. Holmes read the invitation aloud:

YOU ARE INVITED
TO THE DEDICATION OF
THE NEST

2.00
SATURDAY, MAY 10, 1919.
10, SPRINGFIELD,
UPPER CLAPTON, LONDON.

"So, can I assume that the money has been invested in this—orphanage is it?" Watson inquired.

"The Nest is an orphanage of a kind, Watson. It is a home for girls who have been sexually abused—a mission close to Tessa's heart."

"Most admirable. It is sad to think that this home is necessary, but heartening to learn that it is here to serve these unfortunate children."

As Holmes read the enclosed note, Watson carefully picked the penny up from the floor and handed it to Holmes with a quizzical look. "The penny?"

Holmes took the coin in hand and passed the note to the other, who read it aloud:

You used to give me pennies. But, it wasn't the pennies that made a difference in my life. It was the hope they represented. The simple coin said: someone cares. That is what you gave to all the irregulars.

I am blessed to be able to pass on the hope, given me, to these sweet girls. I believe it is a fitting memorial to Rory, who lived in hope, and loved us both so well.

—Tessa

Watson placed the note on the mantle. "You know . . . you've had a rather miraculous effect on your irregulars."

"Any miracles are of their own making, Watson. I simply strived to be useful. Of course, I was usually compensated for my efforts . . . which diminished my gratification."

Holmes twisted the penny in his fingers. "Knowing the irregulars could never repay me, my efforts on their behalf offered me a sense of fulfillment I have never experience before."

He placed the coin on top of the note.

"Now that's a miracle.

Watson patted his friend on the shoulder and picked up his cup. "I best get back to those bees."

"And me to their hives."

Holmes went to the kitchen, set his cup in the dry-sink, and walked out into his disheveled garden.

Watson sat down next to the massive volume resting on the arm of his chair. As he cracked the book open, he glanced through the kitchen window at Holmes who was wrapped in the soft amber glow of the setting sun.

ABOUT THE AUTHOR

KIM KRISCO, author of *Sherlock Holmes—The Golden Years,* and three non-fiction books on leadership, continues in the footsteps of the master storyteller, Sir Arthur Conan Doyle, by adding another, Sherlock Holmes novel to the canon.

In *Irregular Lives*, Kim tells the untold story of Sherlock Holmes's adventures, and his amazing relationship, with the Baker-street irregulars. Holmes employed this tribe of street urchins in some of his better-known cases—and also, in some unpublished cases contained in this new novel.

Meticulously researched, Krisco's stories read as historical novels. His attention to detail adds a welcome richness to his exciting tales.

Prior to writing full-time, Kim served as a consultant, trainer, and coach for business and non-profit organizations, and their leaders. You can find out more about Kim and his current activities at: www. kimkrisco.com.

He and his partner, Sara Rose, live in south-central Colorado (USA) in a home that they built themselves on the North Fork of the Purgatory River.

Also from Kim Krisco and MX Publishing

Sherlock Holmes – The Golden Years

The first in the Sherlock Holmes post-retirement series: A five-part saga begins with *The Bonnie Bag of Bones* that leads the infamous duo on a not-so-merry chase into the mythical mountains of Scotland, and ultimately to the "the woman" who haunted Holmes for a quarter century.

In *Curse of the Black Feather* Holmes teams up with the irregulars, and a gypsy matriarch, to expose a diabolical "baby-farming" enterprise that pits him against the diabolical Ciarán Malastier.

Maestro of Mysteries opens with a summons to Mycroft's office, and ends in a deadly chase in London's Undertown.

The Cure that Kills sees Holmes and Watson continuing in hot pursuit of Ciarán Malastier. They race across America, steps ahead of the largest detective agency in the world.

In *The Kongo Nkis Spirit Train*, Holmes and Watson travel to the Dark Continent to derail a "spirit train" that ensnares people's spirit, and enslaves their bodies.

In the end, this historically accurate chronicle sheds new light on greatest mystery of all, Sherlock Holmes himself.

www.mxpublishing.com

Also from MX Publishing

MX Publishing is the world's largest specialist Sherlock Holmes publisher, with over two hundred titles and one hundred authors creating the latest in Sherlock Holmes fiction and non-fiction.

From traditional short stories and novels to travel guides and quiz books, MX Publishing cater for all Holmes fans.

The collection includes leading titles such as Benedict Cumberbatch In Transition and The Norwood Author which won the 2011 Howlett Award (Sherlock Holmes Book of the Year).

MX Publishing also has one of the largest communities of Holmes fans on Facebook with regular contributions from dozens of authors.

www.mxpublishing.com

Also from MX Publishing

The Missing Authors Series

Sherlock Holmes and The Adventure of The Grinning Cat
Sherlock Holmes and The Nautilus Adventure
Sherlock Holmes and The Round Table Adventure

"Joseph Svec, III is brilliant in entwining two endearing
and enduring classics of literature, blending the factual with
the fantastical; the playful with the pensive; and the
mischievous with the mysterious. We shall, all of us young
and old, benefit with a cup of tea, a tranquil afternoon, and
a copy of Sherlock Holmes, The Adventure of the Grinning
Cat."
Amador County Holmes Hounds Sherlockian Society

www.mxpublishing.com

Also from MX Publishing

The American Literati Series

 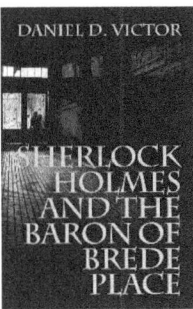 

The Final Page of Baker Street
The Baron of Brede Place
Seventeen Minutes To Baker Street

"The really amazing thing about this book is the author's ability to call up the 'essence' of both the Baker Street 'digs' of Holmes and Watson as well as that of the 'mean streets' of Marlowe's Los Angeles. Although none of the action takes place in either place, Holmes and Watson share a sense of camaraderie and self-confidence in facing threats and problems that also pervades many of the later tales in the Canon. Following their conversations and banter is a return to Edwardian England and its certainties and hope for the future. This is definitely the world before The Great War."
Philip K Jones

www.mxpublishing.com

Also from MX Publishing

The Detective and The Woman Series

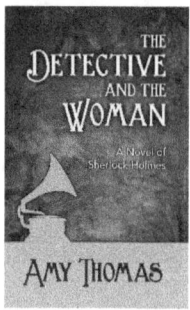  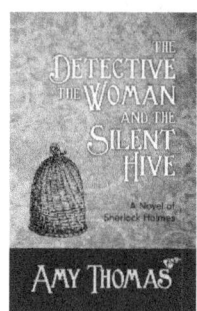

The Detective and The Woman
The Detective, The Woman and The Winking Tree
The Detective, The Woman and The Silent Hive

"The book is entertaining, puzzling and a lot of fun. I believe the author has hit on the only type of long-term relationship possible for Sherlock Holmes and Irene Adler. The details of the narrative only add force to the romantic defects we expect in both of them and their growth and development are truly marvelous to watch. This is not a love story. Instead, it is a coming-of-age tale starring two of our favorite characters."
Philip K Jones

www.ingramcontent.com/pod-product-compliance
Lightning Source LLC
Chambersburg PA
CBHW072307020726
47501CB00002B/430